The Flight of Birds

ANIMAL PUBLICS

Melissa Boyde & Fiona Probyn-Rapsey, Series Editors

The Animal Publics series publishes new interdisciplinary research in animal studies. Taking inspiration from the varied and changing ways that humans and non-human animals interact, it investigates how animal life becomes public: attended to, listened to, made visible, included and transformed.

The Flight of Birds

A Novel in Twelve Stories

Joshua Lobb

SYDNEY UNIVERSITY PRESS

First published by Sydney University Press
© Joshua Lobb 2019
© Sydney University Press 2019

Sydney University Press
Fisher Library F03
University of Sydney NSW 2006
AUSTRALIA
sup.info@sydney.edu.au
sydney.edu.au/sup

 A catalogue record for this book is available
from the National Library of Australia
NATIONAL
LIBRARY
OF AUSTRALIA

ISBN 9781743325834 paperback
ISBN 9781743325926 epub
ISBN 9781743322659 mobi

Cover image and internal illustrations by Amy Kersey
(kerseyink.com)
Cover design by Miguel Yamin and Alexandra Guzmán
Internal design by Alexandra Guzmán

For Jenny Gales

Contents

What He Heard

Maybe I heard a poem, seeping from its cracks. So I stood and listened, just for a minute, like a hungry robin listening for worms.

Or two minutes, or three.

David Mitchell, *Black Swan Green*

He was walking with his dog in the bush. It was the middle of nowhere. They were following a sort of track along a ridge: made by wombats, probably, or by the man and the dog the last time they'd walked this way. The rise of the ridge was clear of trees. A bony bit of scrub; a quartzy boulder unearthing itself from the hill. He stopped and took in the view. In the fuzzy winter light, the hills across the gorge blended into the charcoal sky. The air shivered. He trudged on.

The dog was tracing a line of scent with his nose. The thread would wriggle off the track for a moment, then veer back, tighten around an ossified rock, or thicken at a clump of grass. The scent was leading the dog—well, the man and the dog—to the eucalypts at the top of the hill. The dog reached the threshold of the trees, looked back insistently, and disappeared into the bush. The man followed.

He was staying in a friend's cabin; he'd been there a month. It was after what people called 'his breakdown', or what those closer to him called 'one of his breakdowns'. He just thought of it as 'normality'. It was a feeling he always had, hovering, just out of reach. Every few years it would swoop down, grab him by the shoulders and carry him away.

Broken leaves crunched underfoot. He was careful to sidestep the knuckles of eucalypt roots. He could hear the dog, sniffing, in the semi-darkness. He wasn't sure if the dog was still following the wombat track, or the line of scent, or charting his own way between the thin trees. Their bark was smooth, mostly: lavender-grey with purpling bruises. Every now and then his hand would brush against the rougher, splintery skin of a turpentine. The treetops creaked in the rasping breeze.

Then he heard it. An oozing, matted sound. Plods of noise like snoring; like sobbing. The sound was too incoherent to be nearby and yet it felt close, like a heartbeat, thumping. The dog lifted his nose, as if the scent had become airborne. Man and dog stood in the gloom: listening, sniffing. The sobs coagulated the air. Then the sound changed: from sobbing to wailing. One long wail. Shrill and jangling, it slapped against the man's skin. His instinct was to flee, to scamper over the dirt and to leap out into the light of the open hill. It was only the dog's growl and poised upraised paw that made him stay. He listened to the shriek more carefully. He knew now what it was. The wail was coming from a child.

He stumbled forward, following the call. It was difficult to work out its trajectory. Even the dog seemed uncertain, darting first over a termite mound, then scrabbling under a thorny bush. The man clambered after, ripping his hand on ironbark. The howl persisted. It was always too far away, just beyond the next clutch of trees. It was definitely a child's voice. A boy? A girl, maybe? Was the child lost? Had he tripped in the darkness and broken a bone? Where had the child come from? There were no houses nearby. The nearest neighbours were on the ridge across the gorge. The only other building was the old schoolhouse, a goldrush structure, just over the ridge. But that had been abandoned years ago and it was now just a half-collapsed shell of pockmarked stone. The wail intensified: a long siren of agony. The man tumbled over a protruding rock; the thump of his knee in the dirt scattered the dry leaves. He lay on the earth, trying to catch his breath. The dog trotted back and licked his dusty face. He listened to the bawling cry in the distance. Yes, it was definitely coming from the schoolhouse.

He made his way through the talon-scratched trees, listening to the lament of the child. It was difficult to know what he was calling for. Sometimes it sounded like the child was pleading, begging for something, or for something to stop. Sometimes it was the sound of deep sadness, the clamour of loneliness, the ache of fear. The wail was as abandoned as the land around him, as beaten as the fallen stones.

And there it was. The ruined schoolhouse. On the edge of the copse of trees, looking out over the ridge into the expansive gorge. The wail was definitely coming from inside: sharp and urgent, yearning and terrified. He was compelled to step through the hungry space where a door used to be. But the dog hung back, trembling.

Inside, it was cramped, shadowy. Most of the rusty corrugated roof was still there, but there was a large gap above the doorway through which he could see the blackening sky. The floorboards had either rotted away or been carted off for firewood. The ground was gravelly.

Behind him, in the doorway, the dog gave a few furtive sniffs but did not come in.

The man peered into the dark. There was nothing there. Even the wail had stopped.

Then, just as he was about to turn, the sound began again, sharp and stinging. It was coming from one of the dingy corners of the abandoned schoolhouse. The man froze, unable to move towards it. He wanted to call out to it, but his throat had seized and his saliva had curdled.

Then he saw something stepping out of the darkness.

It was beautiful. The arc of downy back was cinnamon and silver, with a streak of charcoal following the line of the wing. It was a lyrebird. The tail was down, coiled under a round torso, but as the bird poked forward, the feathers fanned upwards, forming a halo of grey and stripy brown. The lyrebird's beak opened, and the wailing noise streamed out. The bird paused, a lidless eye staring at the intruder. He, the man, did not look away. The lyrebird's beak opened again and the peep of a whipbird syruped the air. The man knew that lyrebirds could mimic almost anything—from kookaburras to cameras and chainsaws—but he'd never heard the sounds with his own ears, never been so close to a lyrebird to be able to see the beak open and close, each time producing a different sound. The bird seemed eager to perform, producing the sound of another whipbird, then the child-like wail, then the murmur of a currawong. After that, the lyrebird returned to the murky, sobbing sound he'd first heard through the trees. Three short sobs. Then another three. Then the wail again. The sound now seemed melodious: a warm line of music resonating in the stone room.

The man watched and listened for a few minutes, mesmerised by the tiny beak opening and shutting, the quiver of the bird's throat. Then he tiptoed out of the ruined building followed by the dog, tail down. The man offered his hand to the dog. The dog licked his palm and wagged a furtive tail.

They found their way through the bush. They could still hear the wail in the distance, fading away. It was almost comforting. They stepped out of the bushland on his side of the ridge. A few stars were surfacing from the blue-black sky. He took in the night, still thinking of the beauty of the bird and the melody of the wail.

Then he realised. Lyrebirds are mimickers. They hear the shriek of a chainsaw in the bush, or the buzz of a tourist's camera, and repeat it. But there has to be a logger or a tourist. The noise must be made by someone: a figure calling in the bush. As he made his way down the ridge, he pondered on this. There must have been a child in pain, once. Someone, at some time, had made that coagulating wail. But when? And how long ago?

There's an epilogue to this story, one that has nothing to do with the man or the dog. The lyrebird is scratching the dirt in the gravelly corner. He lifts his head. His larynx vibrates. Out of his beak come three short notes. The second is microtonally higher than the first and third. This is followed by a long high trill. The noise he is making is not full of sadness or pain. The lyrebird is not thinking about lost or abandoned children. His head pivots. The dwindling light points out a speck in the dirt. The lyrebird pecks and then he sings his song again.

Six Stories About Birds,
with Seven Questions

The first [question] is, is it important for us, for our own well-being or the realization of our human potential, that we live in intimate commensal relations with animals? The second is, is it important for the environment that we live in such relations? Does the world need us to continue to live in our ancestral communalism with animals?

Freya Mathews, 'Living with Animals'

Between the kitchen and the laundry is a small alcove with a door leading to the back garden. We call it the vestibule. We use it to store bits and pieces—muddy shoes, the broom, a stumpy torch that doesn't work, a bread-maker we tried once which is now quietly rusting. A low bookcase in the vestibule holds recipe books people have given us for Christmas, dog biscuits and other animal paraphernalia. On top of the bookcase there is a cage, and in the cage—among the water trough, the swing, the bell and a hunk of millet—lives (or, more accurately, lived) Charlotte.

Charlotte is a budgie. I didn't choose the name. I think I wanted to draw attention to the black and yellow stripes on the side of her face—call her 'Tiger' or 'Zebra' or something like that—but my daughter vetoed these. 'She's a *bird*, Daddy,' she said, and Charlotte ruffled her tail feathers as if to demonstrate this fact. My wife was more focused on the bird's out-of-proportion rib cage, lime-green and fluffy, which made her look, my wife said, like a plump schoolgirl in an Enid Blyton novel. 'What about "Bunty",' she suggested. 'Bunty the Budgie.' But my daughter persisted with Charlotte.

And, after all, she is my daughter's bird. My daughter hangs around in the vestibule, mesmerised by Charlotte's hops and the way she twitches her head; she laughs when Charlotte picks at the chunky millet or scratches the sandpaper floor. Charlotte skips over to the tinkly bell and nudges it: my daughter believes she has trained the bird to do this on cue, though I think the timing of the head-bangs is completely random. My daughter is teaching Charlotte to talk. Most of the time the bird just squeaks, clucking and beeping like an automatic teller machine, but the squeaks are sometimes punctuated with the words 'Charlotte', 'hello', 'beautiful' and, inexplicably, 'breakfast'. My daughter chirps along with Charlotte, shifting her voice up several tones so she sounds like a demented Disney character. 'Beautiful, breakfast, beautiful.' Charlotte's round eyes stare back at my enraptured daughter.

I'm less devoted to the bird. If we forget to slip the cover over her cage, she can bleep on all night. We sometimes neglect to change her water, which then reeks. When I do remember to change it—my fingers peeking in through the cage door—I'm mindful of Charlotte's pointed claws and enthusiastic beak. Charlotte flaps up to the high beam of the cage, squeezing her feathers close to her ribs.

One Sunday morning, Charlotte and my fingers are keeping their distance from each other. It's a sprightly day. A triangle of sunlight is shafting though the open door. The cheerful sounds of lawnmowers and whipper snippers warble in from the garden. My fingers draw out the water trough and retreat through the cage door. I scrabble through the junk on the bookshelf below, searching for a rectangle of sandpaper to re-line the cage floor. The dog ambles in, hoping for a secret biscuit. He sniffs the crook of my arm. I scratch his head. I almost don't hear a rattle and feel only a whiff of movement as something skims the top of my hair. I look up in time to see the yellow tail feathers flying through the open vestibule door. A chance moment. And Charlotte is gone.

That night, and for the weeks that follow, my daughter asks questions about what happened to Charlotte. I try to answer them the best way I can. I tell her stories. I tell stories to myself.

The First Story: Cinderella

After the wailing is over—after the frantic searches in the garden and the neighbour's garden and in the park down the street, after the flurry of accusations and flailing rage at my carelessness and the penances promised forevermore, after the sulky refusals to eat and the careful, staged dinner conversation between my wife and me about animals' adaptability and resilience, after the discussion about all the trees in the surrounding suburb that Charlotte could nest in, after the sobbing has lulled into sniffs and moony sighs, after the hugs and the piggy-back ride to bed—after all of that, I read my daughter the story of Cinderella. Not the best choice. I'd forgotten about the turtledoves and pigeons: Cinderella's faithful companions. They whirr in through the kitchen window to pluck the lentils out of the ashes. Later, they perch on the branch Cinderella has planted for her dead mother. At the end of the story, the birds peck out the stepsisters' eyes.

There are a lot of birds in my daughter's fairy tale book. I've read the stories to her many times. We have little rituals of narration: synchronised gestures and sound effects. In one story, bluebirds keep a princess company when the evil queen locks her in the tower. ('Clang!' my daughter cries as the metal bars swing shut.) In another, a girl's brother is taken by a witch, and a gaggle of flying geese guide the girl through the marsh. (My daughter's hands, clasped together, swoop past the lampshade and the birds soar across the bedroom walls.) Like

Cinderella's turtledoves, my daughter sings out when Prince Charming nearly marries the wrong sister. When an orphan shows kindness to a sparrow, breaking off crumbs from his last hunk of stale bread, my daughter's hand becomes the bird's beak, jabbing at the eiderdown. In that story, the grateful bird gives the boy the gift of all the animal languages of the world. The only language the sparrow can't teach the boy is Latin. When the story takes an unexpected turn, and the orphan finds that he has been anointed pope, two pigeons fly into St Peter's Basilica and, stationed on his shoulders, translate the litany for him. My daughter and I learn that in fairy tales birds can often be the ultimate treasure: the golden bird the youngest son seeks to make his fortune; the bird of truth who can tell the girl where her mother has been taken; the sun bird the serving maid spies in Kublai Khan's garden, whose plumage dazzles, and whose song is marvellous and unfathomable. I like to watch my daughter's furrowed face as she tries to imagine the unfathomable melody.

Then again, the birds in fairy tales sometimes turn against the children. Hansel and Gretel's breadcrumbs get eaten by greedy birds, leaving them lost and crying in the woods. In another story, ravens claw the high branches in a midnight forest, waiting for the heroine to trip and scratch her knee. Even at a wedding, the doves can draw blood. I skim over these sections of the stories.

In Cinderella—after the stepsisters have been bandaged and carted away, after the blood has been mopped up—the birds sing marvellously to the bride and groom, then fly off to other adventures. The illustration in my daughter's book shows the open-winged birds gliding over an etched background, a white void in a jet-black landscape. I skip past this picture, too, in the hope that the sobbing won't start up again.

My daughter's question:

Her red eyes look at me. She asks me to turn back the pages to the picture of the birds pecking in the ashes. I comply.

'Charlotte liked to do tricks for us,' my daughter says. 'She always whistled when I'd say good night to her. Do you think she'll whistle tonight?'

We scrutinise the air, but all we see is the loneliness of the night and all we hear is our own breathing.

The Second Story: New Caledonian Crows

A colleague sends me a YouTube clip about crows in a Japanese city. It's from a David Attenborough documentary, and Attenborough's affable, pleasantly amazed narration wafts over the scratchy images. The birds steal walnuts—from where, Attenborough doesn't say—and try to figure out a way of opening them. They soar sleekly above the busy streets and, ingeniously, drop the walnuts onto the asphalt. If the hard surface doesn't break the shell, the crows have learned that the weight of passing cars will. 'The problem now,' Attenborough muses, 'is collecting the bits without getting run over.' A reverse shot of thundering buses; the majestic black bird suddenly shrunk in size, hopping nervously from foot to foot. To avoid the rush of traffic, the crows drop the walnuts at intersections. When the green man pops up and the traffic abates, the crow flies down and retrieves the exposed food, poking at the broken shell before flitting away when the motorbikes and cars rev.

It's a slow day at the office, so I trawl deeper into YouTube, learning more about the ingenuity of crows. In another Attenborough clip, a crow lands on a log in a forest, her feathers splendid in the sunlight like wet tar. She holds a long twig in her beak. She's listening. The camera, confidingly, provides a close-up of a white grub, nibbling the inside of the log. The crow's eyes glisten. She threads the twig into a knot in the log. She stabs. The twig is thrust in deeper. The skewer is raised. Harpooned on the end of the stick is a fat witchetty grub. It looks like a jelly bean or a lolly snake. A nice, juicy close-up: a satisfied gleam in the crow's red-reflective eyes.

I bookmark several clips and file them carefully away. I can't help myself: I like collecting; making connections. I don't really know why. Under the bed at home, I have a shoebox of 'interesting things'—several shoeboxes, actually. Bits of newspaper, academic essays, snippets of poems. My wife calls me a bowerbird, and sometimes threatens to chuck out the boxes when the next council clean-up swings around.

I wander on to other online resources. In the journal *Science* I read further about the New Caledonian crow and what I discover is called their 'tool-related cognitive capability'. The journal recounts an experiment in which a crow had to use a hook and a bucket in combination to reach a reward. The experiment was run a few times before the hook was taken away. In the next experiment the crow fashioned her own, fixing one end of the wire to gaffer tape to create the bend, and then levering the wire into place. The researchers comment that the crow had never seen wire being bent before, and, to their knowledge, the crow had 'no opportunity for hook-making to emerge by chance shaping or reinforcement of randomly generated behaviour'. There was no instruction manual lying about the laboratory, no YouTube tutorial to watch. The researchers note that this activity is remarkable in 'a species so distantly related to humans and lacking symbolic language'. I ruminate on the crows in Japan, slicing through a city overstimulated with symbols, light and noise. I wonder what the crows think of the electronic red man flashing at the pedestrian crossing, and the incessant warning beeps.

Back in David Attenborough's forest, a young crow watches her experienced parent stabbing at a witchetty grub. The fledgling squawks inquisitively; the parent, possibly irritated, flaps away. The fledgling picks up her parent's twig, tries to insert it in the log, but the twig slips into the grass. 'She hasn't got all the details exactly right,' Attenborough comments, wryly. 'It will be about a year before she masters the skill.'

My daughter's question:

She's tracing ski tracks in her mashed potato. 'What will Charlotte eat?' she asks.

'Birds are very resourceful,' I say. 'Finish your peas.'

The Third Story: Birds of Paradise

I flick through the weekend magazine, stopping at a feature article about birds of paradise. It is one of those history-of-the-topic-in-one-fell-swoop articles and quotes the nineteenth-century natural historian Alfred Russel Wallace describing the bird of paradise as 'the most extraordinary and the most beautiful of the feathered inhabitants of the earth'.

One of the glossy photographs accompanying the story captures a bird of paradise mid-air, leaping for a bug. The bird has a yellow cowl, purply-brown wings and a grandiloquent fanning tail, which is gleaming white and wispy. His tail looks ridiculously long: double the length of the bird's torso. According to the article, the white plumage was shorn from the birds, to be worn ostentatiously by sophisticated European ladies and also as part of the ceremonial garments of the Yonggom tribe in upper New Guinea. The French miniature painter Jean Baptiste Audebert created a new pigment, with a golden iridescence, to more accurately capture the feathers' sheen.

The Latin name for birds of paradise is *Paradisaea apoda*. Apoda means 'without feet'. When explorers to the Pacific first encountered birds of paradise and needed to send them to Europe, they stuffed them and cut off their legs for easier transportation. When the ornithologists of the Royal Society examined the specimens they didn't realise the legs had been removed. They developed an elaborate theory about a species of bird that was always in flight: feeding, sleeping and copulating in an elegant dance above the ocean. In his 1774 work *A History of the Earth, and Animated Nature*, Oliver Goldsmith writes: 'the extraordinary splendour of its plumage assisted this deception; and as it had heavenly beauty, so it was asserted to have a heavenly residence.' When Alfred Russel Wallace explored the Malay Archipelago in 1854, he encountered another mutation of the bird's body. He observed a local process for preserving the plumage of birds of paradise, writing:

The native mode of preserving them … is to cut off the wings and feet, and then skin the body up to the beak, taking out the skull. A stout stick is then run up through the specimen coming out at the mouth. Round this some leaves are stuffed, and the whole is wrapped up in a palm spathe and dried in the smoky hut. By this plan the head, which is really large, is shrunk up almost to nothing, the body is much reduced and shortened, and the greatest prominence is given to the flowing plumage … [this produces] a most erroneous idea of the proportions of the living bird.

The article ends its exotic story-weaving with an account of the illegal bird of paradise skin trade throughout Indonesia. Interestingly, because hunters have always sought out the most outlandish plumage, in many generations only the alpha males are slaughtered, and the surviving lesser males can continue the species. Birds of paradise, the article notes, are polygynous, so one male can impregnate multiple females. The journalist takes as much delight in calling the birds Casanovas as he does in retelling the tales of severed feet and ceremonial dancing. As much delight as I have when I cut out the article and stick it into a box under my bed.

My daughter's question:

We're out walking the dog, ostensibly looking for Charlotte, even though it's been a week since her disappearance. There are spits of rain, but my daughter is—wilfully, resolutely—ignoring them. Each tree we pass is a site of possibility. 'Beautiful,' my daughter offers to the branches. There's nothing there. 'Breakfast,' she whispers, half-hopefully.

Our steps fall into a rhythm as the dog lollops ahead, sniffing out clues. We're quiet for a minute or two. Sadness hovers, so I tentatively return to my refrain about natural resilience: that animals have genetic instincts and will know where to peck in the earth for worms, will know which twigs are best to line a nest. There are plenty of wild birds in the neighbourhood, I tell her. Maybe there's another budgie out there for her, and she's settled down with her own family.

'And what if bad men catch her?' my daughter asks.

I can't answer that question. I think of feathered hats and the illegal skin trade and wonder what constitutes a bad man. I think of an open vestibule door.

The Fourth Story: St Kevin and the Blackbird

My wife and I go to a wedding. The reading is Seamus Heaney's poem 'St Kevin and the Blackbird'. I don't know the poem, but I'll find it later in the local library. St Kevin was a hermit, living in a hut, or maybe a cave, or even just under an awning to keep out of the rain. He's often associated with the natural world: his loneliness, they say, was eased when the bushes and the creepers round the cave used to sing sweet tunes to him.

St Kevin prays with his arms in crucifix position so he can experience the authentic suffering of faith. A blackbird lands on St Kevin's outstretched arm. The bird has twigs in her mouth and is making a nest. St Kevin watches. He lets the bird lay her egg and waits for it to hatch. Weeks pass, rain and sunshine pelt down, and St Kevin's arm remains outstretched. He finds himself, as Heaney puts it, 'linked / into the network of eternal life'. The poem is about patience and endurance, about selfless or even thankless love. As he waits, Heaney's St Kevin prays 'to labour and not to seek reward'. In the end, the bird, the man, the rain and the landscape are all absorbed into one limitless prayer.

At the reception there's a lot of bemused chuckling about what an odd choice the poem was for a reading, and the best man makes an off-colour joke about honeymoons and smashing eggs for omelettes.

My daughter's question:

She peers out the back window into a bedraggled garden. It's been raining all week. She turns to look at me. She doesn't articulate the question, but I can read it in her eyes. Doesn't she need me any more?

The Fifth Story: The Siege of Acre

I watch a documentary on the History Channel about the Crusades and falconry. My daughter has clambered into my lap. Her arms are shoelaced round my neck. It's latish at night: my wife has an early start and has taken herself off to bed. The last thing she does after brushing her teeth is to remind me to put our daughter to bed at a decent hour. I promise, but the television takes hold, and the girl's curled body is so warm, and I don't want to disturb her sleep.

In the twelfth century, the TV tells me and my snoring daughter, falcons were popular animals both in Europe and in the East. The secrets and skills of bird-training were even offered as diplomatic gestures: the knowledge was a symbol, if not of peace then of chivalry. It's well known that the leather hawk hood was an invention of the Orient, and some historians claim that the falcon hunt on horseback was introduced to the East by the Christians. Falcons were also used by chroniclers of the Crusades to make sense of the world. Richard the Lionheart's passion is often described through analogies with birds. The late nineteenth-century historian T.A. Archer recounts an event that took place on Richard's journey to the Holy Land in September 1190. The king is riding through Salerno in south-west Italy to join the rest of the Crusaders in the port of Messina. Passing through a village he hears the cry of a hawk in one of the cottages. As king, Richard decrees that the bird should fall into his possession. Archer tells the story like this:

This house he entered and took the bird; but the rustics, who were unwilling to let it go, came running up from every side and attacked him with stones and staves. One of them even drew his knife upon the king. Upon this the king smote him with the side of his sword and broke it.

In contrast, Saladin is generally represented more favourably. The documentary includes an interview with the historian and writer Helen Macdonald, who has written widely on hawks and falcons. In the later stages of the siege of Acre, she says, when the Crusaders' water supply became contaminated and the soldiers suffered fever and dysentery, 'A besieged Richard I sent an envoy to Saladin to request food for his starving falcons; Saladin immediately delivered baskets of his best poultry for the falcons alone.' Macdonald also relates a more famous moment earlier in the siege when:

a prized gyrfalcon belonging to King Philip I broke its leash and flew straight to the top of the city walls. Philip was horrified. An envoy requesting that the falcon be returned was refused.

I imagine a conference taking place under the frayed off-white canvas of a Crusader's tent. Richard clanks about, sweating in his armour, slashing out a scheme to launch another foolhardy assault. Philip of France, flush-cheeked, the baby of the royal group, pouts and weeps over the loss of his plaything, clutching at the bird's blanket and her pale leather hood. A preening advisor, rancid with dirt and hunger, having suffered months of royal whims, suggests tentatively that perhaps it might be better if we didn't show the enemy our passions, that perhaps the best show of strength is the one that dismisses moments of grief as matters of no importance. It's only a bird, after all.

His pleas are unheard: Macdonald tells us that a second envoy was dispatched by the Europeans 'accompanied by trumpets, ensigns and heralds, offering a thousand gold crowns to Saladin in exchange for the errant falcon'. I think of Saladin, strutting atop the city walls, surveying the approaching heraldry. Noble and exotic, he's played by Omar Sharif, or Laurence Olivier with a fake tan. In his outstretched hand the falcon plumes: his prize, his pawn. The falcon's claws are curled around the sultan's finger, or perhaps her talon is chained to the monarch's elegant wrist. The falcon sniffs the air. Her blank eyes stare at the ocean shimmering in the distance. Saladin sniffs, too. Majestically, triumphantly, he holds the power of the world in his hands.

I wonder why I am imagining this, with the dog flopped at my feet and my daughter curled around my torso.

My daughter's question:

On Saturday morning, we're dodging the clanking trolley through the crowds in the shopping centre. My daughter stops and lingers by the window of the pet shop. She'd normally be coveting the kittens, giggling as they roll around on top of each other or snuggle together in the far corner of the glass cabinet. But today she's looking at the bird cages beyond. I let her go in. The cages are full: brown and striped finches, with flecks of red on their beaks, snap in the air. Tufty-faced cockatiels, their cheeks flushed with orange, flirt with a captivated family. My daughter, of course, has her eye on the budgies. She fancies one in the corner who is squeezing his wings against the cage. The bird is bigger than Charlotte was, puffier around the head, his beak almost buried in the swollen yellow feathers.

'Do you think Charlotte would mind?' my daughter asks.

The Sixth Story: The Swan and the Goose

That night, the cover safely over Charlotte II's cage in the vestibule, we read Aesop's fables together. My daughter is reading them aloud to me: a new trick she's learned. She falters over some words, but, for the most part, the sentences flow.

She tells me the story of the swan and the goose:

A farmer goes to market and buys two birds—a swan for her beauty and a goose to eat. When he goes at night to kill the goose, he mistakenly catches the swan. But, just as he is about to kill her, the swan sings a beautiful song and the man realises his mistake. The moral is 'sweet words deliver us from peril, when harsh words would fail'.

My daughter stumbles over the word 'peril'. She doesn't ask what it means, but I can hear her mind fluttering.

I've read the fable before in other books. Sometimes the moral is different. In one, it's simply 'gentle speech does no harm'. There's a history of the tale being used by scholars—Latin orators, medieval clerics—as a parable about the necessity of eloquent persuasion. I imagine Cicero and Mark Antony, pontificating in the Senate or on the white steps of the Forum. I remember the envoy of Philip I threading together words for the release of the falcon. I conjure up Machiavelli. Or maybe not Machiavelli. I think of the thumbscrews of the Medicis, and wince.

There's another version of the fable which adds an extra scene. After the farmer discovers his mistake, he asks the swan why her song was so beautiful when she was in danger of being killed. The swan replies that 'death is a gift, a release of the misery of life'.

I'm glad this isn't the moral included in my daughter's book.

There's also another, more ambiguous moral sung by the swan in a different version. The swan is lying upside-down on the chopping block, her long neck pinned down by the farmer's gnarled hand. In his other hand, the cleaver is poised. The swan opens her beak to sing and the farmer feels the reverberation through his rough palm. The song glistens in the air. It haunts the evening, drifts out over the man's shack, the outhouses, the fields, the roads and the creek. The wild birds hear it as they slumber in the reeds. The man, cleaver still in hand, listens: marble-stilled, hushed. The swan sings, 'Music can delay death.'

My daughter's question:

She's allowing the word 'peril' to shape and re-shape her lips. She moves on to other interesting words. 'Swan,' she says. 'Swan song.'

She thinks.

'Charlotte can sing,' she says.

Then, after a few moments of word-shaping, she asks:

'What happened to the goose?'

My question:

I imagine Charlotte, the first Charlotte. I know the stories I've spun about animal resilience are just fantasies, stories in the air. They're cuttings of ideas, severed, like a bird of paradise's feet.

I think of Charlotte's first night of freedom in the trees in the park. No millet to nibble at, the bark hard and dry. The wind trembles her feathers. In the pet shop next to the gaudy parrots, there's a sign that says: 'Regular wing clipping is recommended to prevent flying away or any injuries to the bird.' I don't know if a bird who's lived her life in a cage would be able to survive a night, two nights, in the cold.

The intelligent crow in *Science* magazine, the one who spontaneously bent the wire, was born in the wild and only captured once she'd reached maturity. There was another crow kept in the laboratory, who had been raised in a zoo. According to the researchers, he 'rarely attempted the task [of hooking the food] and never bent the wire. He observed the female bending the wire and stole the food from her in three trials.' He hadn't got the details exactly right, as David Attenborough might say. He might learn. The *Science* writers report that: 'The birds are tested together because they are highly social and, when separated, are less motivated to participate in experiments.' But Charlotte is alone. Charlotte tries to shelter from the frigid night under a broken wing. In my mind's eye, I see the shell of feathers lying rigid in the morning grass. A neighbourhood cat—noble, exotic, Oriental—pounces. Breakfast.

When we first brought Charlotte home—the first Charlotte—we'd Googled budgies and marvelled at the goofy, spectacular antics they performed, the vocal gymnastics they produced. Song lyrics, Star Trek quotes, entire bawdy limericks. Different households vied for the most brilliant budgie. 'Meet Joey, the smartest talking bird EVER'; 'Grayson the superbird, so eager to please'; 'Our budgie is worth more than his weight in gold!' A king's ransom; a family's delight. Another clip we watched was titled 'Our Child'. Even in the flurry of welcoming the first Charlotte—the assembling of the cage, the careful placement of the bell and the swing and the water trough— even then, I never thought of her as part of the family. And yet, bird books talk of birds as companion animals: for old people, for lonely people, for grieving people. A girl weeps at a branch she planted for her dead mother, and the white birds perch and witness and provide solace. Or salvation. We stretch out our hand in the rain and the bird comes home to roost.

In a Sunday-afternoon radio broadcast I heard once, a scientist from the Australian Museum was talking about the domestication of native Australian birds. (Later, I printed out a transcript and put it in my boxes under the bed.) The scientist said:

> one of the ironies is that … we watch our endangered animals declining to the point of extinction, some of them vanishing forever, thinking that we're doing the best we can by leaving them in the wild and leaving them alone … [I]n fact by not valuing them, by not getting closer to them, by not integrating them into our lives and ours into theirs, the indifference that we have in effect to their wellbeing, leads to many of them being lost.

The birds sing for us, and we sing for them, hoping to delay death.

Nevertheless, the goose is eaten.

Nevertheless, the bird's carcass is smoked and shrunken or the feet are severed.

Nevertheless, the birds eat the bread crumbs that lead the way home.

Nevertheless, Charlotte flew.

I think about her on that Sunday morning, cramped between a plastic bell and a clump of millet, scratching at the metal walls. Or maybe another vision: chirping with a wholehearted delight, eagerly anticipating a visit from the beautiful girl. A figure appears in the shadowy space outside the cage: a gaoler, a provider. Two doors open. A chance moment.

I wonder what Charlotte imagined. What did she want to find in the space beyond the cage, the vestibule and the back fence?

Call and Response

Nearly one hundred percent of the air passing through
a bird's vocal cords is used to make sound. Humans
use only about two percent.

Don Stap, *Birdsong*

Do you remember that day, years and years
ago, catching the train to the mountains? A
hazy morning, mist in the valleys. Do you
remember the songs of the forest and the
silences between us?

Do you remember last night? Or, to be blunt
about it, too early this morning? Do you
remember what caused me to rumple my body
into you, to roll back, to grunt and then to
flick the covers away?

It happens every year. The start of summer:
an air-ripping cry in the night.

You must have heard it too.

I remember accepting your invitation. I can't recall the actual conversation, but I can still feel the friction in the air after you asked me. We were in one of those dusty spaces outside the lecture theatres: less of a foyer, more like a holding pen. Waiting to go in or loitering afterwards, I can't remember. I remember your question lingering, my need to answer it, my fear of answering. I remember the dust settling when I consented.

It was a weekday, so the train was almost empty. Uni students have all the time in the world. A few figures haunted the far end of the carriage. The train chatted over the tracks. I couldn't think of anything to say. An incomprehensible voice fuddled the names of the stations as we rattled through the outer suburbs and clambered our way up the mountain. When we arrived, the carriage doors chirred open and we stepped out into a shrieking-cold day.

We straggled our way down the main street to the tourist lookouts, passing steamed-up cafes and lumbering beanie-clad pensioners. You were well-prepared for the weather: gloved, and snug in your pleated coat. I put on a brave face in my worn-down duffle jacket. You asked me if I was okay. I squeezed my elbows into my ribcage.

At the cliff tops we were accosted by the grind and hiss of buses and the breakneck shouting of school kids. The children slapdashed around us, sucking in the chilled air, puffing out plumes of white. They proclaimed—to us, to the buses, to no one in particular—that there was nothing to see. They were right. The mist had settled in and there was an empty space where the Three Sisters should be. A pipsqueaking ten-year-old coo-eed into the void. There was no echo.

We weren't there for the view, you said. You knew the way. You led me past the ruckus and found the track to the stairs into the valley. Well, ladders, really: metal frames bolted into the sandstone. You slivered past crumbling rock and disappeared. The icy-sharp railing blanched my palm. I didn't look down. I breathed in the shrill air and followed. The cliff was smeared with moss, sharp horizontal lines. Ashy sediments marking the millennia. I could hear your boots tinkling against the metal rungs. I looked down the precipice. There was a flicker of movement on the ladder even lower, a clang and a clatter of laughter. I saw you hesitate and then squeeze yourself into a flinty niche. A snippet of conversation wafted up: words like *morning, weather, stunning.* When the parka-clad figures clambered past me, I opened my mouth. I meant to say hello, but no sound came out.

Halfway down the cliff—a stratum of silence. Above, the hackling tourists and growling buses. And below—

You were waiting for me in the sandstone alcove. You told me to listen.

I listened.

You can't have slept through it. At the end of the street, no, three houses down, no, in the tree outside our bedroom window. A discordant plea. Two notes, one sliding into the other: a long rounded tone followed by a sudden higher plosive. Rising in inflection like a question, or a passive-aggressive demand. A pause. The grey air is silent. A chance, I hope, to ruffle back under the covers and into cloudy sleep. I sigh into you. Your body huffs and settles, lost in your own dreamscape. We share a few breaths. Then the call gashes the air again. The second plea at a slightly higher pitch, not-quite desperate, but definitely plaintive, woefully hopeful. Release and whiplash stop. Then silence. A third, up another tone in pitch and intensity. The lash at the end coming quicker, more severe, more expectant.

I try to snuggle under your humming body, to use you as soundproofing, but a puff of objection escapes from your lips. You're fast asleep. I'm too half-conscious to apologise, too muzzy to explain. I'm trying not to listen for the next lacerating whoop.

I listened.

We were in another world. Or other worlds, really. Our feet had slopped onto the muddy track at the bottom of the ladders, but we weren't at the floor of the valley yet. The path precipiced downward and we followed.

Every layer down provided new songs.

I didn't know the names of the songs we heard, nor the names of the birds who sang them. It wasn't like I hadn't heard birds singing before, or even these particular songs. I could have bluffed my way through finches, parrots, cockatoos. I could have made a stab at something and call it sparrow or galah or lapwing. I could have scratched out some easy verbs to manage them in my mind: chirp or warble, screech or whistle. On the misty path at the bottom of the ladder, these were inadequate, thin wisps of breath.

You told me to listen, and I was trying to listen.

Release and stop. Silence. Release and ripping stop. I groan into the stuffy mattress. My feet get snarled in the blankets. I kick out. You grumble a few disconcerted, disconnected words. When you twist your torso away from me, you drag the blankets with you.

My humming body is floating, anticipatorily, in the stillness of the air, in the gaps between the whoops. These rectangles of silence are irregular, unpredictable. The room expands with expectation.

Many of the calls were barely audible, like a party at the end of the street, or a television left on in the other room. My mind clutched ineptly at inadequate analogies. My literary mother would be rolling in her grave. One call sounded like the release of a half-filled balloon, the spittly plastic ends flapping together as it zips around the room. One trebled like a baby giggling. Another, a polite cough: short, tentative, as if it was asking permission to join in the fun. Another was a melodious metal detector: slow metronomic beeps and then, as it neared its target, increasing in tempo and delight. It was impossible to get the descriptions right. One was R2D2; another was Monkey from the TV show, whistling for his cloud. Another, an off-kilter Mr Whippy van: half a phrase of 'Für Elise' and then a sudden dissonant clang.

I couldn't have told you where the sounds were coming from. I couldn't tell if they were clasping the spindly branches above or huddled in the undergrowth or hidden in the petrified grottoes. There was an occasional flustering of leaves. High above us, a flash of yellow among the grey.

The path sidestepped an ancient tree.
The bark felt like fur. I smoothed its hide
as I passed.

We moved silently through the quivering
conversations.

We listened. A new melody scented the air.

The next whoop is the shrillest of them all.
I think, for a moment, that the glass of the
bedroom window has shattered. Point blank.
It breaks the room. But the shards bring
revelation. I feel like I've been anointed by
an archangel, like a shaft of truth has pierced
my soul. Or maybe it's more biological, like a
migraine that was gripping my cheekbones has
suddenly detached itself and curled away. The
darkness in the room is dazzling. Everything
feels jagged and clear.

I know what I need to do.

My body is less eager to follow my new
calling. As I stumble out of bed, my knee nicks
the corner of the bedside table. I blunder out
of the room, bumping into the doorframe. I'm
clumsily insistent, evangelical, monomaniacal.
I fumble through the darkness towards the
vestibule. I bang about for the broom and drag

it, scrapingly, down the hallway. The screen door yelps as I shove myself outside. I totter over the tiles of the front porch. The broom clatters.

The nasty noise is unperturbed. The whoop is a provocation.

I peer into the arms of the tree. A cavernous blackness stares back. I grip the splintery handle and smash the broom into the trunk. My arms tighten as the broom cuts the air. I hack the trunk again, and again, and then again.

The new melody was beautiful. A constellation of calls. A chorus of wind chimes, almost too perfect to be natural. Like sonar. Like white coral tinkling underwater. Two tones— though sometimes it felt like three. The higher note held longer. The lower tone used as a springboard. Sometimes insistent, sometimes ethereal. Sometimes two notes came together, clashing, like children landing simultaneously on a trampoline. Sometimes three high notes were held in succession. Sometimes a long gap of silence. Then the paired notes would tinkle again.

And, then—

The broom wheezes through the darkness.
The fractured bark muffles the air, like dust.

And then the other call. Or calls, you might
have said. Harmonious with the quiet chiming
rhythms, working as a counterpoint. A slow
softness at first, like a lyrical cicada: increasing
intensity, until unwavering and clear. It felt
mobile, like it came from nowhere and
everywhere, a siren whirring down a city
street. It thrummed through our bodies. Then,
Doppler-like, the sound changed: a sudden
lash, then silence. We waited. A palpable
silence. A minute, two minutes later, the siren
bent the air from another angle; another slap
as the sound cracked off.

    We sat on the dewy rocks. The fuzzy moss
tousled the hair on my fingers.

    This is what I wanted you to hear, you said.

    Or you might have said. I can't remember.

I huff, exhausted, against the chiselled bark.

In the deepest part of the forest—the hairpin
in the track before it led us back up the cliff—
there was a clearing. Mottled picnic tables,

remnants of a gazebo from another era. We moved, stealthily, not wanting to interrupt the stillness. There were signs planted at the edges of the space, noting its historical or ecological significance. I didn't want words, so I slinked past. But you stopped, tracing the letters with your fingers. Although there was little light down there, the scratchy metal glinted. Then, a whiff of wind created a break in the canopy. A laserbeam of sunshine illuminated the rectangle. The silver spaces around the letters hummed.

The sign declared:

This is Leura Forest. In the bush you may hear the call of the golden whistler, the yellow robin. You might even hear cockatoos soaring above the valley. In the valley, you'll hear the bell and the whipbird.

The whipbird call is a combination of male and female birds. The male calls first and the female with amazing timing answers the male. This is called an 'antiphonal response'. See if you can hear both sides of the conversation.

We didn't say any more about it. We weaved through the valley, listening to the call and response.

The space around the tree feels vacant. The night air feels solid. But it still isn't silent. The whoop returns. More tentative, maybe, but unrelenting, inevitable. I listen. I'm too tired to do anything else but listen. The sequence has looped back to the start: the quiet, slower, dissonant plea. This time, though, now that I'm really listening, it feels listless. Its insistence is provisional. Morose. A pathetic cry. The whoop modulates. Less perfunctory, maybe, but still melancholy.

I scrape my fingers over the whittled bark, through my dusty hair. The whoop moves up another notch: barefaced, acute, ingenuous.

A shadow forms on the front porch. A figure approaches. I feel your warm fingers on my shoulder, the sweaty small of my back. You're whispering to me. Ineptly, I clutch at your dressing gown, grasping at my sobs in the night. The air calms around us. You're breathing in and out. I follow your lead.

The whoop starts up again, a wobbly croak
in the grey morning light.

Do you remember the journey home? Outside
the train, the daylight dimming; inside, the
fluoro lights flickering on. Under the quiet
light, you let my knee move towards yours.
You turned your head and looked at me.

Do you remember the koel last night? Crying
into the void, waiting for a response.

Flocking

There is special providence in the fall of a sparrow. If it be now, 'tis not to come; if it be not to come, it will be now; if it be not now, yet it will come; the readiness is all.

William Shakespeare, *Hamlet*

The sparrows pick at the asphalt. When they pinpoint a crumb, they give a quick muttering gulp, their beaks chattering. They look back and forth, up and down: fretful, fascinated. They hop, nimbly, their tails tipping up. They poke out their rumpy chest; they flick their speckled chestnut cape. A dollop of white amongst the fawn wings. A bronze crown, a toasty underbelly. There's a snatched clicking of song, the head back. They tumble turn into the dust. They pluck and kiss the ground, bristling their wings.

The boy watches the sparrows. I call him 'the boy'; he doesn't call himself that. He thinks of himself as being all grown up, as complete as he'll ever be, his thoughts and ideas all settled and done with. But he's hollow, really: paper-thin, flimsy. The chilly autumn wind sometimes knocks him over.

When the roll is called, the teacher might accidentally mark him absent.

In the expanse of the school quadrangle the birds are tiny; specks of cinnamon on a black plain. Even the dry leaves are bigger. A leaf scratches over the playground, eddying in the breeze, a scrunched-up rip of parchment. It shuffles towards the sparrows. The birds scatter.

A Company of Parrots

In the first year of high school, everyone gets a taste of everything. A term of geography; a module on music. They slop up gooey cakes in the home-ec kitchens; saw into dusty timber in industrial technology; tramp in the mud during agriculture; garble through grammar in French. Everyone has to do drama, no matter what the future may hold for them. Even those who'll vow never to speak in public again. Even those who will think the performing arts are a total and utter waste of taxpayers' time and money. Even the future short-order cooks, the solicitors, the checkout chicks at Best and Less. Even the future accountants. Even the ornithologists.

Everyone knows drama is a bludge. For the first few minutes of class most students muck about, chirruping and chortling. The drama teacher doesn't seem to mind. She's small and spritely. She wears sharp white eyeliner. She's the butt of many students' jokes: her pigmy frame and wobbling chest ample fodder for sniggering. They only ever call her Miss. I don't think the boy ever learns her name. Sometimes the other students come up with titteringly funny pseudonyms for her. Miss TheMark, they quip. Miss IngLink, Miss TheClass. When she overhears, she grins. Sarcasm bounces off her. She bobs about the room, her cardigan caped over her shoulders. Her capering is infectious: despite their wilful ruckussing, she gets the class, one by one, to participate. She whisks them in. They fumble their way through stilted impros; they clamp together as human conveyor belts; they spacejump between skits set at the hairdressers, Mount Everest, a bus stop. And, for half a term, they work through a unit on flocking.

The group—five or six students to begin with, but the whole class by the end of term—has to move around the space together, learning to work as one. They start in the centre of the room. Facing the same direction, in a staggered formation, like an arrowhead. The tip of the arrow leads and the rest follow, imperceptibly slow, inching their way forward. When the students are really concentrating the group can weave through the space, changing direction when the flock allows. It's not easy. The trick, Miss tells them, is for there never to be a leader, really. We should never know who's leading, who's following. Let go of your own thoughts. Breathe as one, she says. They're poised, waiting for the impulse to move. Carefully, elegantly, they curve to the left. The leader now follows. There is no leader. They breathe as one.

Of course, this isn't how it functions in the early stages. There are giggling fits and embarrassed twitches. Nobody knows what to do. Miss reminds them to focus on their peripheral vision. They shiver forward; somebody trips on the aquamarine carpet. They topple in a guffawing heap. Try again, Miss says. They wait. They shimmer. They slide into a rhythm; sense an impulse to the right. They sweep quietly across the floor.

The boy doesn't join in. He's not one for functioning in a group. In any case, he knows the others would only be repulsed by him. They already think he's weird. Miss doesn't notice. She marvels at the movement. She raptures on about synchronicity, about surrendering to the flow.

Miss Tifying, he wants to share with the group. He doesn't say anything.

A Weight of Albatrosses

The boy and his mother are alone in a brown room. She's in the bed, he's perched tenuously on a fidgety chair. It's difficult for her to talk. He's waiting for his cue. Creakingly, she breathes out.

What happened at school today?

Nothing.

There's never nothing, she says, eking out the words.

Nothing much.

In English? she asks.

He knows she likes to talk about books. She taught him to read. He follows her train of aching thought. Writing an essay about the Ancient Mariner.

A smile creases her face. Go on, then.

He whispers the lines she already knows.

He holds him with his glittering eye—The Wedding-Guest stood still, And listens like a three years' child: The Mariner hath his will.

He knows these lines well. A gift from her, reading to him at night. Their positions reversed: him tucked under the blanket, her nesting in the chair. She read him everything. Fairy stories, novels, poems. He'd let the words drift over him, like music. *Let us go there, you and I, When the evening is spread out against the sky. Would I were stedfast as thou art,—Not in lone splendour hung aloft the night. O what can ail thee, knight-at-arms, Alone and palely loitering?*

Now he whispers them to her, every afternoon, in the amber light. He sings to her in the stuffy, chestnut air. *And the good south-wind still blew behind, But no sweet bird did follow, Nor any day for food or play, Came to the mariners' hollo!* They have an hour of this; sometimes more, but mostly an hour. His father says it's best that he doesn't tire her out. A reedy melody; a painful sigh. At the end of the hour, he pecks her on the cheek and slips out of the room.

His father is always on the other side of the door. She's having a good day today, he says, even when she's not.

She's sleeping, the boy says, even when she's not.

His father says, She always looks forward to seeing you.

A Murder of Crows

The group hasn't achieved perfect synchronicity. He's still on the outside, looking in. They gravitate towards the windows then reel away. They lag. He watches a classmate being towed along. She's not in tune with the others: her shoulders are lopsided, an elbow sticks out. A tizz of black hair darkens her face. She flicks it away. Ignore it, Miss says, not unkindly. Let go of your body. The boy considers the other bodies drawling over the carpet. That misshapen boy, spongy and pink, his paunch uddering over his waist. The too-tall girl, shrinking from the ceiling. The rash-haired boy with the messy face, his cheeks a galaxy of pimples. A skirt too short, creeping up a girl's leg. An untucked boy's shirt trailing behind. One student's eyes flit from left to right: anxious, alert. Another student's face is a doughy lump, a slab of tongue worming out of his pale lips. One slouches; another shambles. A boy turns the corner too sharply. He gets elbowed in the jaw; it's a palpable whack. A bruise is bronzing on his cheekbone. Not that way, you doofus, a classmate hisses.

He doesn't make friends. At lunchtimes he hunkers in

a hidden alcove at the edge of the quadrangle, reading or watching the sparrows poke and scatter. He prefers it that way. He's tried. There was that almost-friend in primary school. The girl he talked to, once, in commerce class: she snarled and he backed off. He's not a total basket case. When they're forced into group assignments he's able to engage in tight conversations, innocuous and polite. In those situations he keeps his hands firmly against his body, squeezing his elbows into his rib cage.

He's in this position now, sitting in the corner of the drama room as the others flock away from him. He's acutely aware of his body, separate from all the others. His insubstantial skeleton. The sharpening of his cheekbone, the dull ache behind his eyes. His wispy hair is staticky. His skull is clenched. He's locked inside his own thrumming thoughts. He prefers it that way.

He's aware of an enthusiastic smile warming the room. Miss asks if he's ready to participate. He flees.

A Pitying of Turtledoves

He's shivering in the airless corridor. His hands are picking at the edges of his shorts. The skin on his legs feels ashy.

Miss pokes her head out of the classroom. He can see her wavering, wondering about the best course of action to take. He suspects they've all been told, all the teachers, about his family situation. Sometimes his maths teacher gives him a sad nod when she hands back test papers. Miss looks the same way now.

I have to go, he says.

Of course, she says. If you need to—She flusters. If you're needed at home.

He can sense she's pleased with herself. Miss Understanding.

She smiles and then slides back into the flow.

A Solitude of Space

He doesn't go home. Home is another kind of flocking. A smaller group, maybe, but still a flock. A chorus of three. He thinks about the nightly rituals, the rhythmic recitations. *And the good south wind still blew behind; hung aloft in the night; spread out against the sky.* And not just poetry. The same exchanges, evening after evening. He waits for his cue. What happened in school today? Nothing. It's never nothing. Then later: She's having a good day. She's sleeping. She always looks forward to—

He will not flock. He will not be ensnared in any crowd, not even a gathering of three. He will not be annihilated by the moment.

He walks out of the grounds, not towards home. The streets around the school are booming, but he does his best to shuffle it all out. His jumper is thin. The wind cuts his bare legs. His jaw hums, as if he's been nudged by a classmate's elbow. He straggles into quieter spaces, hedges and fences, parked cars and fluttering leaves. He's ambling, threading down laneways and following hidden paths between houses. The solitude of the middle of the day surprises him. A sliver of a boy, clinging to a fraying grey fence, his fluffy hair shredding in the wind.

He is a flock of one. His mind is a blank sheet of paper, but it's his own to write on.

The street passes over a stormwater drain: a bump in the road, an almost-bridge. On another day, he wouldn't notice it. There's a narrow mesh of fence between two houses; he peers through, looks down at the smooth cement. A sorrowful thin trail of water. A used-to-be creek. There's a gash in the mesh. He eases his way through and swings down. The soles of his feet sting as he lands.

Graffiti swirls the edges of the almost-bridge. It's more of a tunnel. He contemplates the void within. It must run underground for quite a distance, under houses, under parks, under schools. He places a tentative foot onto the oily threshold. He ducks under a frond of straggly vine. His eyes adjust. He thinks there should be an echo but he isn't game to cough or call. The graffiti tentacles across the walls for a few metres in, but then stops, as if reeling from the dankness. The boy sneaks deeper. The smooth cement is stained like eucalyptus bark. He feels like an explorer, mapping out uncharted territory: in the grey density of the bush, on the Antarctic plains, across the expanse of the desert. The silence is profound. When he emerges from the other side, an eternity later, squeezing through rusty wire into the gully of a park, the sky overheard is dark.

He's not far from home. He glides in the back door. His father is waiting, sitting at the kitchen table.

Where have you been?

Deeper in the house, the boy can sense a bedroom door open, just a sliver.

Where have you been?

The boy says nothing.

Where have you been? She always looks forward to—

At these words, these invocations, the boy rips around the room. He rushes his hands across the marble-top table, upheaving a half-full coffee mug. The mug cracks on the floor like broken wood. He flies out of the kitchen, down the hall. This is where they keep the books. He strikes at them, plucking them out one by one. They are bombarded against the wallpaper. Spines splinter, leaves flurry through the air. Scrunchy yellow parchment is ripped at and thrust away. His father is trying to embrace him, to squeeze his arms around the boy's blasting body. But it itches. He scratches back. The boy shrinks down, slipping out of the entangling arms.

He's a hurricane ripping out the front door. A flurry of one.

A Wake of Buzzards

He flails down the suburban street, half a block, maybe, before the fuming dissipates. He stands rigidly in a space between streetlamps, the cold air consoling his skin. He wonders what his next move should be. He considers slinking back to the stormwater drain and hunkering in the dark. But even here, even in this extreme state, he knows that's foolish. He doesn't have anywhere to go. He half turns towards home and trudges back. The front door is still open. There is no way he can go in. He lurks his way down the side of the house, rattling against a watering can. His shoes rasp against the pavers on the patio. He freezes. The bulk of the house is palpably black, but there's a box of light where the kitchen is. Framed in the window is his father, sitting at the marble table. He is staring out. The boy— like all of us when we're standing outside looking in—thinks his father is looking at him. But of course he isn't. He's staring into nothing. He lets his gaze drop to the table. There are pieces of a torn-up book in front of him and he's trying to piece them together. Outside, the air is sharp. The boy hugs himself, rubbing his hands against the sleeves of his papery jumper. He draws in his elbows. His father shuffles the leaves, sorting them into piles. His hands wave over the oniony paper like an incantation. The gesture weaves a perfect circle, signifying everything. His father lifts his gaze again to the window. His hands fall onto the table. The boy watches as his father's face hums and twitches and then cracks open. His father howls. An overwhelming stream of sticky pain. Relentless and hot and melodious.

The howl of someone alone.

An Exaltation of Larks

The boy goes to school. The bevy of students is still twittering and jeering, as if the world hasn't changed. When it's time to begin the flocking, he volunteers to lead the group.

The drama teacher is hesitant. Miss Apprehensive, he thinks.

I'm all right, he says. He knows what he needs.

He stands still in the centre of the room. The flock forms around him. He lets go of his thoughts. He allows himself to be carried along by the flow: from this corner to that, in sweeping arcs over the aquamarine carpet. The flock contracts and expands. They curve away from the windows, and his body turns, too: not before the others, not after, but simultaneously. Synchronously. He feels his skin shimmer as it merges with the others. He can't tell where he ends and the other students begin. He's dissolved. He's embraced by the fleeting, luxuriating movement. The room breathes. The ceiling above them lifts away, the floor below drops, cavernously. They're all carried away. They're flying. It's like water, like air, like clouds. Like music. Like a line of poetry. The flock surges through space, circling and radiating, converging and illuminating. It's seductive; it's frightening; it's beautiful.

He goes home that night and slips into the amber room. He performs all the duties of the ritual. His mother lies in the bed, waiting for the next line. The readiness is all. He tries to love the creases on her face. Afterwards he sits at the marble table with his father.

She's having a good day today, his father says.

She's sleeping, the boy recites.

He looks forward to this communal moment, the last rite of the evening.

Later, the boy falls in with other congregations. Exams and assemblies, interviews and weddings and funerals. He slips away from school, drifts through university. He joins other flocks. A seminar of students, a shuffle of colleagues, the kinship of a new family. He watches other clusters form. A kitchen of cooks, a plunge of plumbers, a balance-sheet of accountants, a flight of ornithologists. He moves unnoticed among crowds, never leading, never following. His relationships are haphazard but harmonious. Occasionally he fades into view, but he tries his best to avoid it. When someone really notices him, the outside of his skin umbers like a bruise.

Do You Speak My Language?

Are the birds making music, or simply mimicking, parroting or aping themselves? Is their song a call and response, a chant, or simply a repetition? Is it a theme and variation, indeed an improvisation, or rather a mechanical repetition, or indeed reproduction?

David Wills, 'Meditations for the Birds'

It all happens in a moment. A slicing of wings through the air. A snatch from the plate by a flat-arrow beak. And bacon and bird are gone, up into the branches of the eucalypt in the far corner of our garden.

Breakfast on the back veranda is part of our weekend routine. Three rickety chairs around a rustic table. Or, more often than not, four bodies stretched on the deck, taking in the sunlight. This morning, the table's been commandeered by the Saturday paper. The travel and real estate sections are splayed over the splintery wood, weighted down by a mug of coffee and the corner of an egg-stained plate. We've all retreated from it.

I've stolen a few pages and am lying on my stomach on the lacquer-brown boards of the deck. The dog, dead to the world, is flopped firmly against my leg. My wife is sitting cross-legged, her back leaning on the glass of the sliding doors. She's sipping her coffee and swiping on her iPad, following esoteric trains of thought. My daughter is balanced on the edge of the veranda, legs dangling, humming a tune under her breath. A strip of half-eaten bacon curls on the plate next to her.

Moments before the kookaburra strikes, my wife is saying, 'Listen to this: they're holding the Fiftieth Annual Bird Calling Contest this year. Can you believe it? You know, those kids with bad haircuts who appear on *The Late Show*?'

I nod affably and say something about Letterman's love of ritual humiliation.

Moments before, my daughter is strumming a rhythm on the boards. *Tap tap tap tap.* A beat I almost-recognise. *Tap tap tap tap.*

Moments before, I'm saying, 'Listen to this: *Who's laughing now? Men at Work lose court appeal.* Can you believe it?'

My wife doesn't even look up from her screen.

'Are you harping on about that *again*?'

Meanwhile, the kookaburra sits on the branch of the old gum tree: poised, sharp, watching.

My wife is right: I can't stop talking about the case. I tell and retell the story: to colleagues, as we're making our way up the stairwell to the office; to neighbours, when we're chatting at the dog park; at the newsagents, when another punning title appears in the paper. The shoebox under the bed is full of clippings with headings like: 'Kookaburra swoops Aussie icon'; 'Riff rip-off'; 'You better (not) take cover'. The press is loving it. A chance for outrage, scandal, the-legal-system's-gone-mad conspiracies, tall-poppy takedowns, underdog talk-ups. After all, the whole thing began in the media.

I remember that night, watching the episode of *Spicks and Specks*. 'Welcome to a special children's music edition,' said a smirking Adam Hills.

'Just what we need,' my wife said, folding an insurmountable pile of tiny socks and T-shirts spattered with preschool paint. *Play School* and *Hi-5* stars grinned out of the TV.

'Have a listen to this,' Adam said. 'Name the Australian nursery rhyme this riff has been based on, as well as the name of the man playing it.'

Charli and Jay and Justine shrugged.

'This bit especially,' Adam said, and tapped out the rhythm in the air with his pen.

The red Wiggle offered, tentatively, 'Greg Ham's the flautist, but … ?'

They all listened again, leaning over their desks, and two

songs disentangled from each other. The panellists' mouths formed words: from one song, from the other.

'It's … it's …?' wondered Jay Laga'aia, before making an astonished link. '"Kookaburra Sits in the Old Gum Tree". "Down Under".' Like the TV panel, the lounge-room viewers were surprised, delighted by the connection. It was remarkable that we'd never heard it before. But there it was: the two songs different; the two melodies the same. My wife wandered off to bed that night, humming the flute riff, gliding into the childhood song.

Two years later, Justice Jacobson of the Federal Court is still humming the tune, but in a different key. He says:

Thus, there remain two principal issues. The first is whether there is a sufficient degree of objective similarity between the flute riff in Down Under and the two bars of Kookaburra.

The second issue is whether, if I am of the view that there is the requisite similarity, the bars of Kookaburra which are reproduced are a substantial part of that work.

Much of Jacobson's deliberations circle around the ambiguity of the word 'substantial', tracing its application through a series of prior cases, and questioning whether or not the word applies to both the original and the infringing work. Jacobson uses what he calls 'quantitative and qualitative consideration' to form his verdict, what he also refers to as 'by the eye as well as … by the ear'. Expert witnesses are called to talk about 'signatures' and 'hooks'. Dr Andrew Ford, expert witness for the applicants, correlates the principal phrase from 'Kookaburra' with the flute riff from 'Down Under'. The first two bars of 'Kookaburra' are its signature. The riff is clearly the hook: 'a short instrumental figure which (with luck) proves to be instantly memorable and recognisable every time the song is played.' Both hook and signature are substantial; they're the essential part, the centre of the song. They're the same tune in both works. To make his point, Ford transposes Kookaburra from F Major to D, to match the impugned work. 'The melody is identical,' he states, 'but the chord that underpins it is different, and it gives a slightly different feeling … it's a bit like shining a different light on it … it doesn't change their nature.'

In a later exchange, Dr Ford is asked, 'And does that separation make them different?' To which he replies, 'No, no, no, they're exactly the same phrases, but we hear them differently.'

I wasn't in the courtroom. I don't know what Andrew Ford looks like, so I can easily imagine him as a bow-tied villain for the prosecution in an episode of *Perry Mason*, twisting his terminology to serve the applicant's line of argument. I only have the clippings to go by: 'Quiz show sparks Aussie anthems battle. Kookaburra conflation undeniable, expert claims.' The media is full-throatedly in support of Men at Work. 'Down Under' is hailed as a de facto national anthem. '"Kookaburra" isn't "owned" by anyone,' Michael Leunig says in a TV interview, hair fluffed up like a koala, 'It belongs to us all.' In fact, Marion Sinclair, the composer of 'Kookaburra', donated the copyright to the Libraries Board of South Australia before she died in 1988. Larrikin Music, the applicant in the case, subsequently purchased the copyright from the Libraries Board. A Facebook page—KOOKABURRA VS DOWN UNDER— AN ABUSE OF COPYRIGHT LAW—is set up so that we can spew out rage and cheer on our battlers. *Larrikan are decidedly UNAustralian. M@W we love ya. its greed for the almighty dollar that is behind all this shit. Shaddup Kookaburra. where are the legal eagles??!!*

Oblivious to these threads, Justice Jacobson proceeds with the case. Objectively, methodically, he analyses similarities of melody, key, tempo, rhythm and structure. On each of these points, he is swayed by the claims put forward by Andrew Ford. Ford observes that there's a clear resonance between the impugned work and the original, 'as though it's a memory of the song, or a reference to the song'. There's only one moment of doubt in the judge's scrutiny. In his final evaluation of the case Jacobson muses: 'The respondents asked a rhetorical question which sums up their response to the claim made against them …' The question posed by their counsel was, 'If both Kookaburra and Down Under are such icons, and the similarities are so strong, why did it take so long for anyone to recognise the connection?'

Even so, there could only be one verdict. As the judges in the appeal case put it, 'the question is one of objective similarity. The aural resemblance need not be resounding or obvious. The relevant test is not the effect upon a casual listener of the whole of the versions of Down Under in the Impugned Recordings …' Jacobson has no doubt that Men at Work stole a substantial amount of 'Kookaburra', both quantitatively and qualitatively. He rules that 'Down Under' has replicated two of the four phrases in 'Kookaburra'—in other words, 50 percent of the song. In his judgement he makes special mention of Greg Ham, the flautist who introduced the riff into the recording. Ham did not attend the proceedings. In publicity photos for the band from the early 1980s, Ham is always larking about: eyes squeezed shut as if he's trying to block out a sudden loud noise; being mock-punched in the face by another member of the group. His expression is contorted, rubbery: part-innocent, part-impish, like he's in on the joke. Jacobson never saw this face. He refers to an affidavit that Ham tendered to the court. Ham, Jacobson tells us, is 'pretty sure' that 'Kookaburra' was part of his school's song book, when he was at primary school in Australia in the late 1950s. Jacobson says:

For present purposes it is sufficient to say that Mr Ham's reproduction of the relevant bars of Kookaburra reinforces the finding of objective similarity. That is the real significance of the failure to call him.

In my opinion, it is appropriate to draw the inference that Mr Ham deliberately included the bars from Kookaburra in the flute line for the purpose referred to above.

I act out this statement, reported via newsfeed, to my wife as I do the washing-up. Suds flick in the air.

'*That is the real significance of the failure to call him.* Can you believe it? Like he did a runner, he's a desperado on the lam from the law.'

I'm aware that I'm cackling like a madman.

She takes a plate from the rack. 'Why are you so obsessed with this?'

I wince. I've never liked the word *obsession*.

'Are you all right?' my wife asks.

'The water's too hot,' I reply.

In the end, it comes down to costs. Even though Larrikin seeks a figure of forty to sixty percent of the total royalties, Jacobson remarks that this is 'excessive, overreaching and unrealistic'. More experts are called, more music is analysed, and a figure is reached of five percent of the proceeds since 2002. Colin Hay, the frontman of the band, calculates that this amounts to 'something like sixty grand'. But he also says, at a later date, 'we lost more than them'. Eighteen months after the appeal is lost, Greg Ham is found dead in his North Melbourne home.

'Check these out,' my wife calls, moments before the kookaburra strikes. She's slid into YouTube, searching for the hooting kids on *The Late Show with David Letterman* and then, deeper and deeper, into archival footage of bird-calling competitions. The dog struggles up from his spot beside me, saunters over to my wife, nuzzles the back of her hand. My wife nudges him away unconsciously; amiably, he waddles into the cool of the house.

'Can you believe it?' my wife is saying, transfixed by the screen. She's found a Super 8 recording of the 1973 Piedmont High School Bird Calling Contest. Teenagers with middle-parted hair and enormous glasses give giggling renditions of wood pigeons and canaries, geese and chickens. Some whistle through cupped hands; others stand back, open their mouths as wide as possible, and squawk the house down. The microphone reverb harmonises. Sometimes the tape gets caught on the reel and the voices change register, jangling forward as if they're anticipating the next moment.

Where Justice Jacobson ponders over the objective similarity between the two songs, these children have no concerns that their calls might not be authentic. You could make—and scientists have made—spectrogram recordings to demonstrate the similarity between bird calls and human imitation. Like Justice Jacobson, the quantitative tools biologists use include comparisons of pitch, tempo, complexity and structural organisation. But bird callers aren't worried about stealing the birds' music or infringing copyright. They're providing a song of unabashed joy, and are being heard by an enchanted, appreciative audience. The song—the imitation and the original—is a gift.

One of the stories I tell my daughter—since the incident with the bacon she's become obsessed with kookaburras—is a dreamtime tale about how the bird got his laugh. I don't know where I unearthed the story. I may have heard it read on *Play School* once: the rocket clock spins to reveal a diorama of a soft toy wobbling in front of an electric-orange sky. It may be from my own childhood: listening, cross-legged, on the frayed carpet of my primary school, to the trilling voice of the teacher. In the story, the morning star asks the kookaburra to help him mark the beginning of each new day. My daughter looks up at a constellation of glow-in-the-dark stickers on the ceiling and picks out the right one to play the part. Every morning the star sits, poised, just above the horizon, but the animals don't notice his quiet twinkling and they sleep through the day. The star realises he needs a proper trumpeter, a call that will wake the heaviest sleeper. So he asks the kookaburra to sing a dawn chorus. When he hears this request, the kookaburra laughs with pleasure. My daughter, not-quite-sleepy, provides the sound effects. The laughter jubilates in the space between the bed and the stars.

'Yes, that's it, that's exactly right,' I say.

'Yes, that's exactly what we want,' the dawn spirits cry.

The kookaburra tousles his mottled feathers. The dawn begins to hum the warmth of a new day.

Consider this moment: in 1934, a school teacher called Marion Sinclair is dozing in a rickety chair in her back garden. There are no iPads, but there might be a weekend broadsheet blanketing her knees, crisp and warmed by the sun. Above her are the sweeping branches of a eucalypt. A kookaburra high above, laughing at the sky. In the space between wake and sleep, a melody takes shape. She uses this to conceive a song called 'Kookaburra Sits in the Old Gum Tree'. Later, she submits it to the Girl Guides Association of Victoria in a competition for 'a typically Australian round'. She wins first prize and the work is published in a Girl Guides' bulletin. The association praises Sinclair and the other contributors for 'a great combined effort of everyone working together for the good of the whole'. In a letter to Sinclair, a member of the Executive Committee of the Girl Guides thanks her for 'the gift of your three rounds to the Association' and 'for your donation of the proceeds to the

Guide House Fund'. Later, Sinclair says of the song that it 'was not composed by me, but merely set down … It is God's song'. She's thinking of the bird, the tree and the enormous canopy of sky above them.

Consider this moment: in 1979, two members of a newly formed band play a bass line to Greg Ham, a classically trained musician. They're rehearsing in a grungy studio in North Melbourne, round the corner from where Ham will later live. It's a fun, satirical song, part pop, part reggae. It talks about drinking beer and chundering; it rhymes 'language' with 'Vegemite sandwich'. Ham giggles and his larrikin face beams. The tune catches in his mind. He's thinking. It needs something, he says to his mates. He picks up his flute and breathes out a musical phrase. It flutters against the jangle of the guitar. Of course he knows that it's been played before: he can remember singing it as a child, sitting on the splintery floorboards of his school hall. He perceives it, not maliciously, as an 'Aussie cliché melody', an iconic reference to Australiana. It's as if the two tunes have always been together. In this cramped studio—sticky coffee cups strewn, egg cartons gaffer-taped to the walls—something miraculous has happened. The men are laughing so hard that Ham sprays a paint-gun of spittle into Colin Hay's face.

Consider this moment: an exhausted mother wafts towards bed. She's just been watching a television music quiz show and she's carrying one of the tunes—two tunes—away with her. In the appeal case, Hay and EMI asserted that the inclusion of the original song:

> was at most a form of tribute to Kookaburra, which might be amusing or of interest to the highly sensitised or educated musical ear, but was otherwise unlikely to be separately noticed by the ordinary listener.

But imagine the surprise, the joy when we do hear it. The gift of recognition.

There's another dreamtime story I tell my daughter. The lyrebird struts through the bush, bragging that he can sing better than all the other birds. When the other birds hear this they're furious and call a meeting to put the challenge to the test. The magpie, the cockatoo, the brolga, the finch. The kookaburra squats on a branch of a eucalypt, a little further away. One by one the birds perform their song. Each time, the lyrebird's mimicry can match it and better it, singing it more melodiously than the original bird.

The kookaburra sits, fat and contented, niggling his feathers. He finds it hilarious that the other birds are trying so hard and failing so spectacularly. He lifts his head and laughs. The lyrebird thinks that the laugh is part of the competition and tries to copy it. This makes the kookaburra laugh even harder, the punked-up white quiff on the top of his head quivering.

The lyrebird opens his beak wider, but can't catch the tune: it's too wriggly, too jangly, too specific to the kookaburra's round rib cage.

The lyrebird concedes defeat, saying, 'That's your song. No one can ever take it away from you.'

Interviewed outside the Federal Court in Sydney, the managing director of Larrikin says he was 'doing his job in protecting lawful ownership of material against theft'. 'You wouldn't steal a car,' my DVD tells me every time I try to watch a movie. In another preview, Geoffrey Rush guilts me into caring about the Australian Film Industry, protecting the rights of artists. In an online article I'll read later, following my own line of inquiry, I'll learn about avian mimicry as a form of 'parasitic deception'. Some birds copy others to gain a tactical advantage: the imitator steals the tune to also steal food, or the roost, or another bird's mate. The original bird hears the call of the mimic and calls back, innocent to the deception. The mimic calls again. The original bird, duped, wanders away from the nest.

Images, too, can offer a false perspective. Dr Ford, witness for the 'Kookaburra' case, is no villain: he's a respected composer and musicologist. He's been composer-in-residence with the Australian Chamber Orchestra, and broadcasts on ABC Radio National. He doesn't wear bow ties: his press photos show him in an oversized woollen jumper, his generous face framed by a furry bushranger beard. Words can be warped, like the stretching of Super 8 tape. Michael Leunig did not say that 'Kookaburra' 'belongs to us all'; in fact, he was talking about 'Down Under', I just transcribed it incorrectly. The kookaburra/lyrebird story is not a dreamtime tale. I found it in the 'Student's Notebook' page of the *Argus*, a popular and conservative Melbourne newspaper. Dated 3 October 1952, the story is surrounded by line drawings that look like they've been lifted from an Enid Blyton book. Above it is a piece about model aeroplanes; to the left, an article about home economics. It's been written for middle-class suburban children: children of the White Australia Policy. Even though it's titled 'Aboriginal Legends: The Kookaburra', I've never seen this story included in any collection of dreamtime stories. It matters where the story comes from.

Moments are never moments on their own. You have to understand the context. My daughter is still swinging her legs off the edge of the veranda, tapping her fingernails on the boards. The kookaburra is still waiting for his moment to swoop.

The case was appealed a year after the first application. One of the many challenges raised by the cross-respondents was a failure by Justice Jacobson to recognise that Kookaburra was published as a 'Round in 4 Parts': if this is taken into consideration, then Justice Jacobson's determination that the relevant phrases constitute fifty percent of the song is no longer valid. Justice Arthur Emmett, one of the presiding judges in the appeal, summarises the argument:

[this] indicates that it was to be sung by four voices or four groups of voices, such that each of the parts is continuously repeated. When sung as a round, the four phrases shown in [Kookaburra] would be progressively heard over the top of each other. Thus, even if Kookaburra were sung through as a round only once, it would consist of seven bars rather than four.

In the transcript of the original case, Andrew Ford (with or without bow tie) does raise the point that Kookaburra is a round. He says that rounds can be a 'tricky and rather amusing business'. Four parts need to work together to create pleasurable rhythms and counter-rhythms. One phrase skips when the others stretch; one busy set of quavers fills the gap where another line rests. In the appeal, much is made of Ford's statement. The judgement document repeats it six times. Sometimes as a complete phrase ('Dr Ford described writing a round as "a tricky and rather amusing business"'); sometimes as fragments, broken down into constituent parts ('a round is a musical work the creation of which … involved the "tricky" and "amusing" business'). Ford's language goes round and round the courtroom: like a record being played by a twelve-year-old boy; like a small girl skipping in a garden looking up into the branches of an old gum tree.

I heard a round sung just last week, when we visited our daughter at her school. (Maybe that's where she's getting the rhythm from? *Tap tap tap tap. Tap tap tap tap.*). It wasn't an official concert, just parents invited along to the classroom so the pupils could show off their good manners and finger painting. My daughter's picture was an A3 affair, a panorama of orange and purple. I made a few conjectures on what it could be representing, and was relieved when she said, '*Daddy. They're just colours.*' At the end of the morning the parents were asked to sit on the springy turquoise carpet. We all enjoyed getting into formation: creaking our legs into the cross-legged position; reminiscing about our own classroom antics. The children formed four ragtag clusters in front of us. They stared at their teacher: eagerly, anxiously. The teacher tapped out a beat on her palm. She nodded, pointedly. The first group took off, then the next, then the next, then the next. My daughter was in the last group. A little flick of spittle sprayed when she hit a consonant.

Jonathan Lethem talks about certain kinds of language, what he calls a 'commons'. He writes: 'That a language is a commons doesn't mean that the community owns it; rather it belongs between people, possessed by no one, not even by society as a whole.'

There was a moment during the performance, right at the height of the round, where it should have been a cacophony. Twenty-four small children, twenty-four spittly mouths, twenty-four bobbing heads. Each with their own worries, their own obsessions: cars or cricket or dinosaurs or budgies. But something made it all come together. All the voices were doing something different, but they were all working together. My daughter looked at me, her eyes glinting.

Kookaburras have two distinct songs: 'joint songs', which are usually only between a breeding pair, and 'group songs', which involve all the members of the flock and are performed during sunrise and sunset. Group songs are stronger: they're usually extended versions of the joint song, but incorporating more laughter, more noise. An ornithologist from Colorado State University recorded the dawn choruses of several flocks of kookaburras in Western Australia. The scientist observed that the song is usually initiated by one bird, *oooah* (or *kooaa* or *hoo-hoo ha-ha*, according to other studies). The rest of the kookaburras follow, several seconds later, one by one, each bird 'probably contribut[ing] its own series of syllables to the chorus'. The song is performed 'vigorously' to create an 'ear-splitting din'.

Kookaburras are also territorial. The dawn chorus is an assertion of boundaries: those who know the carol, who are part of it, belong to the space. Those who don't are rejected, aggressively. 'This is *our* song,' the kookaburras cry. It could also be, then, a form of competition between flocks. At the end of the classroom round, the children dispersed and found their families, preening with satisfaction and clambering into their parents' arms. Each father and mother whispered into their child's ear, secretly and not-so-secretly, 'You were the best, my darling.'

At the end of the Federal Court appeal, it's confirmed that 'Down Under' did reproduce a substantial part of 'Kookaburra', round or no round.

'Listen to this,' my wife says. I don't know where she's wandered off to now: the web is a vast universe. '*Warblish*. What a word. Can you believe it?'

'Warblish,' she tells me, 'is a word used to describe a specific way of articulating bird calls.' It's different from the Piedmont High chirps and whistles; different, too, from an onomatopoeic attempt at representation—'cock-a-doodle-doo'; 'boo-book'; 'hoo-hoo ha-ha.' 'It's when,' she says, pausing to sip her coffee, 'you use words, you know, actual human words, to make the sounds. 'Whip poor Will. Who cooks for you?' She reads out a compilation of warblish calls listed on the website. The indigo bunting: 'Fire, fire, where, where, here, here'; The song sparrow: 'Pres-pres-pres-pres-by-ter-ri-an'; the white-throated sparrow: 'Poor Sam Peabody, Peabody, Peabody.' She's trying to incorporate our daughter into the conversation, but the girl is still swinging her legs off the edge of the veranda, tapping her fingernails on the boards.

'They don't have the one my granddad used to say. There's a bird up in Queensland that he swears calls out: "Shit-a-brick!"'

'*Mummy!*' my daughter squeals.

'Pardon my warblish,' my wife says, laughing.

And then the Kookaburra strikes.

According to Hannah Sarvasy, a researcher in linguistics from the Australian National University, warblish can perform a function that goes beyond simple translation into human language. It can also transform. It turns the birdsongs into time capsules, little stories about the communities they come from: American frontier life ('kettle, ettle, ettle'); Australian bush larrikinism ('Shit-a-brick!'). They can explain a cultural practice or generate mythology. A Brazilian story tells of a group of children who go missing in the jungle, fleeing after their mother berated them. According to the legend, the children were turned into the dusty-legged guan, who calls, 'Our mother scolded us!' There's a similar tale from the Kaluli people in Papua New Guinea. There, some children wander off and are killed by enemies. Their cries are taken up by the bolo bird, who sings the melancholy 'dowo', which means 'father, mother'. We hear the birds, but we're also listening to something else. As Andrew Ford might say, 'the notes aren't different, but we hear them differently'.

In his closing statements in the appeal, Justice Emmett muses that:

> The better view of the taking of the melody from Kookaburra is not that the melody was taken … in order to save effort on the part of the composer of Down Under, by appropriating the results of Ms Sinclair's efforts. Rather, the quotation or reproduction of the melody of Kookaburra appears by way of tribute to the iconicity of Kookaburra, and as one of a number of references made in Down Under to Australian icons.
>
> If, as I have concluded, the relevant versions of Down Under involve an infringement of copyright … then some of the underlying concepts of modern copyright may require rethinking.

In 2013, the Australian Law Reform Commission compiled a report, *Copyright and the Digital Economy*, which outlined some questions and problems inherent in the 1968 Copyright Act. The commission concluded that: 'It is clear that copyright law directly affects a broad range of cultural activity, often impeding access to material for no good policy reason.' It proposed a new way of considering copyright infringement, based on the notion of 'fair use', saying:

Fair use promotes what have been called 'transformative' uses—using copyright material for a different purpose than the use for which the material was created. This is a powerful and flexible feature of fair use. It can allow the unlicensed use of copyright material for such purposes as criticism and review, parody and satire, reporting the news and quotation. Many of these uses not only have public benefits, but they generally do not harm rights holders' markets, and sometimes even enlarge them.

Supreme Court Justice Sandra Day O'Connor, citing the US Constitution, says:

The primary objective of copyright is not to reward the labor of authors, but to promote the Progress of Science and useful Arts. To this end, copyright assures authors the right to their original expression, but encourages others to build freely upon the ideas and information conveyed by a work.

In his article 'Jurisprudence as Musicology: Suing in the Land Down Under', Chris May cites the work of Lydia Goehr, who speaks of an 'originality myth' when it comes to an author's production of a work. Jonathan Lethem, in his essay 'The Ecstasy of Influence', cites O'Connor, and is later cited by May. He says, 'Any text that has infiltrated the common mind … inexorably joins the language of culture. A map-turned-to-landscape, it has moved to a place beyond enclosure or control.' Amplifying this thought, Jim Samson, also cited by May, celebrates the way 'a musical work threads its way through many different social and cultural formations, attaching itself to them in different ways, adapting its own semblance and in the process changing theirs'. They cite, I cite, we all cite, but differently.

An hour ago no conversation had ever linked copyright and bird calls, warblish and the 'tricky and rather amusing business' of composing a round. An hour ago, I unwrapped five rashers of bacon from a sheet of butcher's paper and flicked them into a spitting frypan. The strips danced in the oil, turning from pink to slimy brown. Then they slid onto plates, next to toast and baked beans and fried eggs. They were carried out into the sunlight. A girl, humming to herself, teetered her plate on the edge of the deck. Halfway through the meal—egg smeared on her face and T-shirt, crumbs of toast licked up by the dog—she looked down at her plate at the strip of bacon and saw something else: a country road wending its way between two ridges of toast crust. A stray baked bean became a car. Then the girl became distracted by a fly or a noise or the call of her mother and the objects on the plate became scraps, leftovers to be swept into the bin in the kitchen. Or, in a moment, to become food again, this time for another animal.

The kookaburra, round-chested and alert, will spy it from his vantage point on the branch of the old gum tree. He'll scissor through the air—a streak of azure in his grey-brown feathers—and back up to the branch. In the kookaburra's mind the bacon is a worm, maybe. He whips it in the air, clasping one end sharply in his beak. The bacon/worm slaps against the smooth bark of the eucalypt before it's tossed up and gulped by the kookaburra.

Multiple uses; multiple possibilities.

Of course, I'm not thinking about who the bacon was before it sizzled into the frying pan. I'll save that discussion for another day.

Some birds only have a single song: a finite use; a narrow repetition. These birds have what some ornithologists call 'a preference for predictability' or an 'entrainment to rhythms'— or, as I first read it, 'entrapment to rhythms'. It never transforms into something else, it's never improvised around or altered. It's sometimes easier to follow one pattern, one train of thought. In human communication, there's a kind of repetition called 'priming', which is a tendency to use a phrase or word that has already come up in the conversation. 'Can you believe it?' 'Listen to this.' It's a way of making us feel safe, like we're part of a group. We learn how to speak from the people around us. Young kookaburras learn to laugh by listening to the older members of the flock. Scientists have observed apparently explicit 'laughing lessons' between parent and fledgling. The adult sings the beginning of a phrase and the child appears to imitate: haltingly, ineptly. The ritual is repeated over the course of some weeks until, according to one scientist, 'the juvenile has attained mastery of the laugh'.

Consider this moment: years before a family eats breakfast on the veranda on a Saturday morning, a boy and a man sit opposite each other across the expanse of a marble kitchen table. The man says, 'She's having a good day today.' The boy says, 'She's sleeping.' The father sings the refrain, 'She always looks forward to seeing you.' Learned rituals; entrapments to rhythms.

And there's another song the boy sings: another set of repetitions, another kind of language. In the school terms and holidays of his childhood, he gathers together certain patterns of behaviour. He can't walk on certain colours on a carpet. He has to eat the food on his plate in a certain order: peas, then sausages, then bread. On his way to school he has to cross the road at particular spots and he has to be careful to jump over the slippery cement kerb. He has a record called *Hitwave '81* that was given to him for his birthday. The label in the centre of the record has a cartoony depiction of a tidal wave which matches the bubble-writing font of the album title. If he's careful, the boy is allowed to put on the record in the afternoon when he comes home from school. He watches the label spinning round and round, the tidal wave transforming into a yin-and-yang spiral. He has to play it almost inaudibly so as not to disturb the other inhabitants of the house. He can't play the songs in the track order. The correct order is: 'This Ol' House' *then* 'Stars on '45' *then* 'Down Under'. He lifts the needle and has to ease it down precisely into the groove between songs. It's imperative that he doesn't pick up the end of the previous song or jump to the mid-phrase of the next: if he catches the fade-out of Shakin' Stevens' jangly voice or hits the flute riff mid-phrase he knows something terrible will happen. He doesn't know what will happen if he misses the moment; he knows exactly what will happen.

And at night, in the dark, he looks up at an empty expanse of ceiling. He has his arms straight against the sides of his torso. His fingertips strum his thighs. On the left: *tap tap tap tap*; on the right: *tap tap tap tap*. Repeat. There are words to accompany the tapping. *Tap tap tap tap. Tap tap tap tap.*

'That's your song,' the lyrebird says. 'No one can ever take it away from you.'

And there's another moment: North Melbourne, mid-morning. A corner house, wide colonial awning reaching over the footpath, painted grey. No one's come through the front door for a few days now. Neighbours have noticed that the cat is mewing from the inside. Friends have called, but the phone keeps going to voicemail. Two men are knocking on the door.

Tap tap tap tap. Tap tap tap tap. As though it's a memory of a song, or a reference to a song. Greg Ham says, 'I'm terribly disappointed that that's the way I'm going to be remembered— for copying something.'

The kookaburra swoops. For a moment, the three of us are snap-frozen, wondering if it really happened. My wife and I flick our attention to our daughter. Sharp-backed, wide-eyed, she's on the cusp, trying to decide whether to wail in outrage or shriek with glee. To our great relief, her face transforms into ecstasy.

'Can you believe it?' she squeals.

She jumps down into the garden. The kookaburra has flown back to the eucalypt. My daughter stands on tippy-toes and twists her neck, but she can't see the bird from where she is. She jumps forward. It's curious: it's only a few steps directly to the tree, but my daughter is taking a peculiar route. She hops to the left; she takes a large leap to the right. She's careful to aim towards a precise spot, as if she's trying to land on a particular space between the blades of grass.

Tap tap tap tap, I think. I don't want to think. The adult sings the phrase and the child imitates.

'What are you doing?' I call.

'Well, I can't step *there*, Daddy.'

'Why not?'

'The dog did a *poo* there.'

I laugh. My daughter skips over to the tree. I look up into the branches of the eucalypt. The kookaburra is there, flinging the bit of bacon around and slapping it against the trunk. But there's a young man there, too, face beaming, playing a riff on a flute. He's performing to a koala puppet; its tufty hair looks like Michael Leunig's. Michael Leunig says:

[It's] a quotation or a tribute or a homage if you like, where you quote from the culture you grew up on, is entirely natural and spontaneous and proper. It reinforces and celebrates culture. It's culture making. And I grew up on that song. I mean at school we sang that song day and night. It just goes into you—it belonged to us all.

And the kookaburra opens his mottle-brown wings and flies away.

Further to Fly

What bird, perched on the high-leaved branches of oak or pine, will come to mourn with me …? With cries of woe, I lament before it comes the piteous lonely life, that I shall live for the rest of time, in streaming tears.

Euripides, *Phoenissae*

This isn't a story about what happened to him at the office. There are stories he could tell you about that: the way he plummets from one urgent demand to another; the lumpen dread he feels when confronted with a furious fluster of emails. This is not the story of the loneliness that comes upon him halfway through another pointless meeting. There is a specific story he needs to tell about his workplace, but he'll save that story for another time.

This is a story about what happened on the way home.

He was driving fast, trying not to think about work and listening to a Paul Simon CD, loud. The music probably wasn't meant to be played loud—it was soulful, mournful—but he was comforted by the halo of noise around him. It was the end of a long week. The car was a station wagon, Bunnings-green, with silver trimmings. A Subaru Outback. He'd laughed with his wife that the closest they got to the outback was the Marsden Park Ikea. But it was useful for carting around all the family's stuff on the weekends, and it did have a bit of grunt when he needed it.

He was following the usual line home. The highway ran parallel to the railway tracks: dual lanes mainly, and flyovers that bypassed traffic lights and local shops. There was a segment, though, where the road narrowed and passed a school. On bad days, you could be stuck there forever. Cars crushed up against each other and the air would thicken with exhaust fumes and frustration. Today was a bad day. Fortunately, he had an escape route. Just before the lanes merged, he indicated left and took a sneaky backstreet. Even though he'd taken this road before he always thought of it as uncharted territory, like a secret tunnel under the city. It was houses for a few blocks—weatherboard and brick veneer—then the road plunged through a nature reserve. Quite literally plunged: a steep drop into a tight gully, thick with eucalypts. A diversion of green and grey between suburbs. He never needed to put his foot down there. He'd let the car teeter over the edge and slide down the strip of asphalt. He enjoyed the sensation of leaving his stomach behind at the top of the hill.

The station wagon bounced as it hit the bottom of the hill. Paul Simon sang on, unperturbed, yearning for a river and a lost lover. It was dark in the valley, but he autopiloted the sudden swerve to the right. The tar crumbled at the edges of the road; he kept close to the centre line. He didn't take his foot off the accelerator. A cloud of dust rasped behind him. The trees hung low and dense, with an occasional break in the canopy letting in sharp strips of sunlight. Not quite the outback, he thought, but almost. On days when he didn't feel like hooning he'd imagine stopping in the gully: getting out of the car and resting his palm on the bark of a eucalypt, listening to the call-and-response of the whipbirds. The bark would be cold, like cement.

The road took a series of long bends up the next hill. He skidded around a crumbly corner, letting the bands of light flow over the windshield. One more turn to reach the crest of the hill. As it came over the crest, the car—and driver—looked directly into the setting sun.

He blinked, momentarily mesmerised by the flecks of dust in the air. They were hovering, illuminated. Out-of-focus creatures from another world. He wanted to reach through the windshield and cup them in his hands. And then he was aware of the real creatures in the air, scraping too low and coming directly towards the windshield. He couldn't work out what they were: their wings were flapping too fast, they were a dazzle of red and blue. He only had a microsecond to grab the steering wheel and listen to the shrieking whir as the car spun to the side of the road. He heard something else, too, even over the hissing wheels and Paul Simon's sorrowful tone. Or maybe he just felt it. A sudden thump against the front of the car, like a lump of lead slamming into the bumper.

The wheels had stopped whirring. Paul Simon had been cut off mid-lyric. He sat in the driver's seat, dazed. He rubbed the side of his neck where the seatbelt had slapped his skin. The haze of dust settled around the car.

He wondered what that thump had been.

He had a fairly good idea what the thump had been.

He knew he had to get out of the car and inspect the damage. His red-raw neck hummed painfully.

The car door made a scratchy noise as he opened it, as if a piece of gravel had got caught in the hinges. He edged his way to the front of the vehicle.

There, crumpled into the grille, was a clump of broken bones and feathers. It was amazing how deep it had penetrated, how much it was enmeshed with the body of the car. Globs of dark blood smeared the edges of the impact hole and dripped off the jagged silvery plastic. He thought he should probably crouch down in front of it, investigate more closely. He kept his distance. And, as he stayed still, the bloody lump began to twitch. The smallest, slowest movement, but movement nonetheless. He wasn't sure if it was a wing or a talony foot, but something scratched against the plastic. A whiff of red and blue fluff detached itself from the lump and wafted away. The wing—or whatever it was—flexed a little more. It rested. It flapped, slowly, sadly. The body twisted. The wing was snagged by the broken edge of the grille. The bird—and he knew now that it was a rosella, a red-and-blue parrot native to coastal Australia, a species of bird that often flew past his office window or pecked about in puddles in the park where he took his daughter—the bird tried to twist the other way, but couldn't untangle itself from the plastic.

When he was a boy—a really young boy—he used to go camping with his parents at Jervis Bay. The rosellas were tame there. His mother would break off a hunk of day-old bread and he'd hold it at arm's length. The rosellas would hop over, individually or in pairs, and then as a whole flock. They'd flap up to the bread and clinch his forearm, his shoulder, the top of his head. Their claws would tickle his skin.

The rosella continued to twist against the grille.

He stayed where he was.

The sunlight dwindled and the shadow of the Outback stretched away from them.

The bird stopped twisting, exhausted, and waited for what was going to happen.

This is what didn't happen:

He didn't move closer to the grille, kneel down in the dust

and look into the bird's cloudy eyes. He didn't reach his hand past the sharp plastic and, gently, scoop out the broken body. He didn't take the bird and wrap it in a towel he kept in the glove compartment and he didn't take the bird to the vet in the next suburb. The vet didn't place the red and blue bird on the metal table and, tenderly, fold the wing back into position. The vet didn't tell him that he'd done the right thing and that if he'd left the bird alone any longer it certainly would not have recovered. The bird didn't recover, not even partially, not even with a limp wing or a missing talon. It didn't become the family pet and live in the vestibule near the laundry at the back of the family home, and it never splashed about in puddles when he and his daughter took it to the park.

He didn't remember what his dad had taught him back on the farm when he was a boy: what to do when you find an injured animal in the bush—a rabbit, a dog, a bird—and it's too far gone. He didn't peel the bird away from the car and hold it in the palm of his left hand. With his right hand, he didn't feel about in the blood-matted feathers for the rosella's neck, and, mercifully, twist it sharply and firmly. He didn't help the bird in this way. He couldn't, even if he'd wanted to. He'd never lived on a farm or in the bush and his dad had never taught him this kindness. He'd only seen men on television talk about the best thing for animals in pain, the most humane act you could perform. He didn't perform this act.

He didn't feel a strange energy run through his veins. Filled with this energy, humming and tickling his skin, he didn't reach into the plastic chasm and touch the bird's rib cage. The golden flecks of dust in the sunlight didn't swirl around the bird and, miracle of miracles, the bird did not suddenly stretch out its wings. The crimson and blue feathers glistening in the light and the bird flying off, fully healed, into the bush.

He didn't scoop his hand into the chasm. He didn't even hold the feathery matted mess in his hand and keep the bird warm and safe until it died.

This is what happened:

He got into his car and drove home. He parked in the garage and pulled the roller door shut. The next morning, a crisp and cheery Saturday, he took his car to the detailing place attached to the local shopping centre. When he came back from the supermarket, the car was gleaming wet and clean.

When he drove to work on Monday he stayed on the highway, following clear lines of sight.

The Pecking Order

Who is suffering? No one.

Carol J. Adams, 'The War on Compassion'

At fifteen, my daughter officially became what her grandfather called 'a bloody vegetarian'. She was pretty militant about it. She started a subcommittee of the student council dedicated to making the canteen a meat-free zone, made loud pronouncements in restaurants, distributed animal rights pamphlets around the neighbourhood. 'We're *murderers, Dad*,' she'd say, 'we're *all* murderers.'

I had nothing to say in response. I did what I could to avoid looking at the images on the pamphlets splayed on the hallway table. They'd always catch my eye. Broken wings tangled in cage wire; beaks gasping in an airless metal shed; steroid-altered torsos weighed down by disproportionate pendulous, ulcerated breasts; millions of dead eyes glaring amongst layers of sawdust, woodchips and excrement. I tried, too, not to take in the statistics she'd thrust at me over our evening meal, 'Fifty *billion* chickens are slaughtered every *year*, Dad.'; 'An industrial farm can hold a *million* or more birds, genetically altered to make flesh *fast* before the animal dies under her own *weight*.'

At fifteen, my daughter could see the truth of the world. But, in fact, the kernel of this knowledge was formed much earlier than that.

It happened in a supermarket. I'd say she was about six. (I measure time sometimes by determining which Charlotte was in the vestibule; this was definitely in the era of the second Charlotte.) We were shivering in the meat section, my daughter and I, mapping out the week's dinners. Above us, suspended from the darkened ceiling, was a cardboard mobile of a red barn and cows and chickens, and the words *Old MacDonald's Farm*. After she got bored with jumping up to try and grab one of the black and white cows, my daughter dashed over and started banging a big red button on the wall between the eggs and the meat fridges. She wouldn't stop banging the button, which caused an artificial, strangulated *buck-aaw* to burst out of a speaker in the wall. I tried not to acknowledge the flicked irritated looks from the other shoppers. Next to the button was a childlike drawing of a white hen; between bangs, my daughter would trace the elongated S of the bird's back, from beak to tail. In an effort to distract her, I asked my daughter to fetch one of the punnets from the meat-display shelves. Carting it back, she scrutinised the pink glistening pillow underneath the plastic film, tracing the words on the sticky label. She stared at the silhouette of the bird next to the button on the wall: sleek body; beak, comb and fluffy feathers.

At school, she'd been learning about homonyms. Around the rim of the classroom, the teacher had hung up rectangles of cardboard, with a different definition written in capital letters on each side. 'There's *bark* like a dog,' she'd told me, 'and *bark* of a tree.' There's *left* and *left*, *pen* and *pen*. Up to this moment—the moment poised between the eggs and the freezers, holding a plastic tub of flesh—I think my daughter thought that *chicken* was also a homonym. 'There's a *chicken* in the farmyard, Daddy,' she might have said, 'and there's *chicken* you eat.' The cardboard rectangle spinning slowly in the air.

That night, my daughter looked down at the fleshy pillow, now battered with breadcrumbs and laid out on her plate. She turned her plate so that the fillet was as far away from her as possible. When she finished eating her broccoli and carrots, she pushed the plate into the centre of the table.

My wife and I let her thoughts flutter for a few days. We would take turns offering phrases like 'Just try a little tonight' or 'But that's your favourite.' My daughter's eyes would cloud and the food would congeal on the plate.

'It's not the end of the world,' my wife would say later, when we'd scraped the uneaten food into the bin, or were lying in bed with the lights off, staring up at the shadowy ceiling. 'There are plenty of vegetarian recipes and we can work out other ways for her to get the protein she needs and, really, it's a good thing, it's good to have a daughter who knows what she wants, who cares, who …' The words trailed off into the darkness.

'What's the matter?' I asked.

'I just realised … we've got my parents' barbecue on the weekend …'

'Oh *shit*.'

My wife's family was nothing like my own. We used to alternate Christmases: one year with my father; the next with my wife's parents, and sisters, and brothers-in-law, and aunts, and uncles, and nephews and cousins. The overwhelming silence of my father's barn of a house, the muted gift-giving ceremony, all over in five minutes. As opposed to the chintzy clutter of my mother-in-law's lounge room: the raucous ritual underneath an enormous Christmas tree over-burdened with tinsel; the ritual starting before the crack of dawn, everyone dressed in elf caps or Mrs Claus wigs or 'ho ho ho' T-shirts or aprons that said 'Kiss me, I'm Santa'. After the frenzied ripping and squealing and complaining, we'd struggle through the wrapping paper before going out onto the patio for the even more important event.

Each year's fare would be grander than the last's—one year a pig on a spit; another a surf-and-turf smorgasbord. Every weekend in the lead-up to Christmas, my father-in-law would hold rehearsal barbecues, testing out potential honey-glazes, perfecting the crackling. 'How about that marinade,' he'd say, wiping his brow with a beer. He liked to spice things up, offer a range of choices, the patio table ending up like an oversized meat-lover's pizza. Legs and hocks and racks, barbecue sauce squirting over the potato (and bacon) salad. Pork and beef and venison. 'Rudolf tastes great, Granddad!' a nephew might say. We'd talk a lot about the meat. Was a steak better medium-rare or burnt within an inch of its life? Was a thermometer necessary to roast the perfect turkey, or was it just a piece of useless *MasterChef* paraphernalia? We were all required to provide detailed feedback, rate the quality of the rump over the one we'd chopped up at the previous week's barbecue. Although the way my father-in-law would leer at you, tongs poised, ready to snap, there was really only one response you could give. 'Top feed,' one son-in-law would say. 'Yep,' the second would say, and then I'd murmur, 'Yes, excellent.'

My wife was the middle of three daughters. On the drive to family barbecues, she'd itch in her seat as if transforming into her younger frizzy-haired self: a bodily return to a state of resentment, of long-lost feuds and teenage spats. The hierarchy between sisters was always shifting, dependent on some nuances of power that I could never quite identify. On the way home, she'd mutter about the appalling thing that one of her sisters had the hide to say: each journey home it would be a different sister. I'd watch my own daughter in the rear-view mirror. She'd be looking out the window, but I'd know she was listening.

'Why do you bicker all the time?' I once made the mistake of asking.

My wife sharpened in her seat. 'We don't,' she snapped. Then, as the distance widened between the car and her old family home, she said, quietly, 'It's what we do in our family.'

The hierarchy of sons-in-law, on the other hand, was firmly fixed in place. The superior son-in-law always knew the football score, could keep up with the beer-tally set by his father-in-law, could do the biggest bomb in the pool. The second-seeded son-in-law was working hard to be noticed, had bought himself a Weber six-burner, made sure he knew the right stubby-holder to use, always began know-it-all sentences with: 'I saw on TV that ...' or 'Apparently ...' I could only say, 'Yes, excellent.' I think some of the nephews—scowling at their phones or Marco-Poloing in the pool—ranked higher than me. I think even my mother-in-law did. She was always on the edge of the conversation, clearing up the plastic plates and paper serviettes. Of course, the king of the heap was always the man who slapped a plate of chicken wings in front of you and waited, looming.

'*No*,' my daughter said.

The tongs snapped. The only sound was the hiss of the middle son-in-law's beer. Even the splashing in the pool ceased.

'What's wrong with it?' my father-in-law said.

My daughter's face was blotching with pink. A droplet of marinade splatted from the tongs onto the patio table.

'I'll have some, Dad,' my wife said.

My mother-in-law fluffed her tea towel.

I sat opposite my daughter, willing us both into oblivion. My daughter scrunched up her eyes. My body hummed.

'What's wrong with it?' the lump of a man said.

'Dad, it's just—' my wife said, 'she's just, we're just—'

'*What's wrong with it?*'

And my daughter swept from the table, bolting away to the furthest reaches of the backyard.

'There's nothing wrong with it,' another man said, many years before.

We were sitting, as we always did, opposite each other across the marble table in the kitchen. This was the beginning of it all. (I measure time sometimes by determining how frequently my mother was able to get out of bed; at this stage, she did occasionally emerge from behind the pale door and pad down the hallway. Once or twice she'd join us at the marble table; once, she came and read to me in bed.) In the middle of the table was a chicken casserole.

My father hadn't made the casserole. It had been delivered by one of our well-meaning neighbours. There was a stack of chicken casseroles in the fridge supplied by other well-meaning neighbours, another stack in the freezer, ready to go when we needed them. In the afternoons after school, I'd have to open the front door and take the casserole from the neighbour from across the road or down the street. She'd occupy the doorstep, waiting for me to force the words 'thank you' from my mouth. They'd fall out, dry and hollow, meaning something different from the dictionary definition. It was better when I arrived home late, having planned a circuitous path home from school, and found another Pyrex dish laid out on the welcome mat.

The steam lingered between us. There was a fatty scent in the air. My father didn't say anything else. He couldn't bring himself to say 'please'. I wouldn't mouth the word 'no'. My father's fingers tapped the marble. We sat there in the absence of words, waiting.

I don't remember what made me start eating it.

At school, I pretended everything was the same as it was for every other kid. I did my best to scrape my knees on the quadrangle; to tumble into the classroom over the frayed carpet. But kids worked it out. There was a gap in the way they talked about me. 'He's the one with the _____,' they'd whisper. There was always an empty space around my body as I wandered across the playground, too, everyone repelled

like the bad end of a magnet. I understood. There was a
white humming in my mind that was palpably repellent, a
rhythm that was beginning to form. The phrasing wasn't
there yet. It was still _____ _____ _____ _____, although
sometimes it was turning into *Please don't* _____ _____.
At that point, my mother's appearances on the hallway side
of the door could stave off the humming. But little acts of
control—like stepping over the lines on the quadrangle or
crossing the road at exactly the same spot every day, or playing
a record over and over—meant that everything was going to
be _____ _____.

    I didn't tell anyone about these acts. There was no one to
tell. If another kid was near me when it was time to cross the
street, sometimes I'd walk a few steps along the footpath until
I was alone and then double back, or I'd crouch and pretend to
do up my shoelaces, just in case they worked it out. I'd watch
the beak of the stylus slide down into the correct groove on the
record, but the volume was so low that no one—not the body
sleeping; not the body sitting waiting at the kitchen table—
could hear. At night, in the dark, hemmed in by the blankets,
that's when the humming was at its worst. The only way to
protect myself then was to accompany the rhythm. Arms
straight, palms against thighs, tapping. *Please don't let* _____.
Please don't let _____. Repeat until the grey shadows of morning
stretch across the room.

One morning I was making my way across the chilly quadrangle, tracing a particularly complicated pattern to get me from library to classroom, when I noticed a different shape from the configuration of the bodies. There was another empty space forming around another figure in the playground. 'He's weird,' I heard one kid say. 'He stinks,' hissed another. It was a new arrival at the school: the worst thing you could possibly have happen to you, coming in mid-term, when everything was already settled in its proper order. He had other marks against him, too. He wore a home-made knitted jumper, which wasn't quite the same grey as the official uniform. As I shifted towards him I could see he had a vertical scar that sliced over his top lip. He also had a sneer on his face: I wasn't sure if that was caused by the scar or by whatever he was thinking. He did smell, like he'd weed himself a few weeks before and never changed his shorts. I could feel my body veering away from him, like all the other magnets.

Eventually, though, he and I found ourselves alongside each other more often than not. We weren't in the same class—he was in the year below me—but we'd see each other at playlunch. I'd watch the birds skipping along the edge of the quadrangle and he'd flick out some of his crumbly sandwich bread so the birds hopped closer. We'd sort-of talk: a bit about books we were reading or what was on telly last night. I told him that my favourite show was *The Goodies*; he agreed with me that the giant cat episode was the best one. We became almost-friends. He liked to look over at the other kids and make bitter comments, using words I'd never heard before.

'They're *fascists*,' he'd sneer. 'She's so *bourgeois*.'

I didn't ask what these words meant. I never asked, either, how he'd got the scar on his face, but he did tell me that his birthday was coming up and his mum had said he could have a sleepover if he wanted, if I wanted. He said this out of the corner of his mouth, so that the scar twitched in a strange way. I don't remember saying yes, but I do remember walking to his house after school, pyjamas and toothbrush in my backpack. We left by the incorrect gate, the gate I never allowed myself to go out by, but I squeezed my elbows into my rib cage and kept my palms close to the sides of my legs. I gave my thighs four quick taps. I don't think my almost-friend noticed.

It was a long walk to his house. He pointed out objects of interest in an off-hand way: the big gnarled tree, the lawnmower repair shop, the stormwater drain. I said something about *The Goodies* being on tonight, and he agreed that we'd watch it if we had time. The afternoon light was greying. We walked to the edge of town, out onto the floodplain. The streets here had big gaps between houses, as though there'd once been a house there but someone had erased it. In the spaces were rusted husks of cars growing in the long grass. We arrived at my almost-friend's house. It was made up of horizontal strips of white wood; some strips were a grottier shade of white than others. Against the boards was a stack of bicycles. As we made our way up the cracked cement path, the screen door shrieked open and a midget child galloped out and tackled my almost-friend.

'This is my *fascist* brother,' my almost-friend sneered.

The rest of his family was in the kitchen. The room was cosy: a pot-belly stove was going and the mum was stirring something on the stove. It was the same smell that clung to my almost-friend, but in this room it smelled hearty, delicious. The mum was curly haired and eiderdowny, like the wife on *All Creatures Great and Small*. The dad had just come in from the backyard still wearing muddy gumboots over his corduroy trousers. In the corner was a crib with a baby in it, and the dad was cooing over it. I said a tentative hello and the family replied with some friendly welcoming words, the younger brother talking over the top of everyone else and then the mother telling him consolingly that he could tell me all about his toys later.

'Come and see the chooks,' my almost-friend said.

The chooks were kept at the far end of the muddy, knotty-grass backyard. The coop was tacked onto the side of a nearly-fallen-down shed: a wire caged-in area with a metal gate. Within the cage at least ten brown dishevelled birds strutted, pricking the soggy straw. My almost-friend strode over the puddles and the tufts of grass. I held back as he untangled the latch of the gate: a coathanger wound around the metal frame.

'Are you scared?' a voice behind me said. The younger brother was standing at the back door, clutching a knitted toy in the shape of a cow.

'They're only chooks,' my almost-friend said as he stood amongst the terrifying creatures.

When I stepped into the coop—my hand getting stabbed by the end of the coathanger latch, the mud squelching under my school shoes—the birds flicked their heads and stared at me with their goggly eyes. I hoped they might scatter, but they started, instead, to advance on me. They clucked, loudly. One bird lifted her head and stretched her neck, Godzilla-like. Another lifted a talon. They twisted their heads, peering at me with one eye and then the other.

'They're only chooks,' the younger brother said, clambering in after me.

'Go back inside,' my almost-friend sneered at his brother. 'This coop is for *intelligentsia* only.'

The brother stayed where he was. 'This is my cow,' he said to me, sticking out the knitted black-and-white toy.

'No one cares,' said my almost-friend as he checked the plastic water bottles that were hanging from the top of the cage. Tubes protruded from the bottom of these, like you saw in the hospital wards on *Trapper John, M.D.* A little red plastic bowl sat underneath and some of the creatures were poking at the water. My almost-friend leaped over to the corner of the cage and ripped the lid off a large ice-cream container. He grabbed some pellets that looked like All-Bran and flung them across the straw. The birds' clucking changed pitch, and they strutted towards the pellets, their heads pulsating forwards and back.

'They're tidbitting,' my almost-friend said. 'The weird thing they do with their neck, the weird noise they make, it's called tidbitting.'

One of the birds tidbitted in my direction. Under the watchful eyes of my almost-friend and his younger brother, I kept as still as I possibly could, my hands by my sides. The bird plucked nearly-but-not-quite at my toes. Another bird high-stepped over and took a swipe, not at me, but at the other chicken. The first chicken scurried away.

'We call that the pecking order,' my friend sneered. 'The one at your feet now, she's the boss of the coop.' The creature tilted her head at me, as if she was considering pecking me, too. 'It can get pretty bloody, stabbing at the face and neck with their beaks. Sometimes they all gang up on one chook. They can peck it to death. They don't peck at people, not very often. We had a rooster, it wanted to be the boss of Dad even and my dad had to wear these special gloves and then pin it to the ground whenever it got too cocky. It still wouldn't submit so Dad said there was only one option ...'

The chicken at my feet strutted away. 'Which was ...?' I didn't want to say.

'The stew pot,' my almost-friend sneered.

'The stew pot,' said his younger brother. 'Do you want to play with my cow?'

There's the word 'chicken': pecking at my feet, tilting her head to gaze at me; and there's the word 'chicken': the stringy brown meat bubbling in the pot on the stove.

'Are you sure you're not hungry?' the mum asked me, doling out a second helping to her son.

I smiled wanly but didn't say anything.

'That just means there's plenty for the rest of us, eh boys?' said the dad, then gave a big bear-laugh to show me he was being funny.

The brothers didn't appear to be listening: my almost-friend had snatched the knitted cow away from his brother and was holding it aloft, just out of reach.

'I'll leave some in the pot in case,' said the mum. 'And there's heaps of bread if you want it.'

The younger brother was struggling with my almost-friend, grabbing upwards. 'Give me it!'

'*No!*'

I nibbled at a corner of the crumbly, kibbly bread.

'Give me the cow!'

The mum had turned away to look at the baby in the crib. The dad was watching his sons squabble, amused.

'Why do you want it? Why do you want it?' my almost-friend was saying.

'Because it's mine!'

The older brother flicked it across the room and the boy scrambled after it. 'You're such a *materialist*,' my almost-friend said.

The dad let out a massive hearty chuckle. 'Now where'd you pick up words like that?'

'Chip off the old block,' the mum said, good-naturedly. 'Who wants to wash up?'

The dad washed up and I helped my almost-friend dry. The younger brother wiped down the kitchen table, and the mum picked up the baby and held it in her arms. She undid a few buttons of her shirt and I looked into the sink at the suds draining down the plughole. The younger brother was jumping up at a high shelf in the corner of the room and the dad strode over and took down a pack of cards.

'Do you know how to play Verbot?' the younger brother asked.

I said to my almost-friend, 'I thought we were going to watch *The Goodies*.'

'Oh, luvvie,' the mother said, 'we don't have a television.'

My almost-friend wasn't looking at me. His face was humming.

We all sat down at the table and played cards. During the card game the dad told me about ethical farming and the principles of social equality before the mum told him to quieten down before he bored us all to death. My almost-friend, scowling next to me, didn't say anything, and missed some crucial plays in the game. He didn't even notice when his brother's score surpassed his or when the mum deliberately let him win. And then we all went to bed.

It was strange looking up at a different ceiling in a different room. His brother was snoring in the corner.

'I know my house is a bit weird,' my almost-friend said.

'It's all right,' I wanted to say.

'My dad says that he made a choice, and it was the best choice, for all of us. He says we're all caught up in the *capitalist alienation* machine, no, not machine, the *industrial power complex*. He didn't want to be a *corporate automaton*. I don't either, I s'pose, but I also don't want to have to keep moving towns and I want to buy proper clothes and ...'

His brother snuffled and rolled over.

'I just want to watch telly,' my friend whispered.

A car drove down the street. I watched the lights curve across the ceiling.

'My family's weird, too,' I said.

And I told him everything. I told him about the silences in my house and the stilted conversations between me and my father. I told him about the daily visits from the nurse, and the buckets of vomit my father brings out from behind the closed door. And the times the doctor comes and spends forever in the closed-off room and then when he comes out he won't look at me. And then my father is even more silent. I told him about going into the stifling room and not-talking to my fading-away mother.

And I told him the other stuff, too, the places where I can and can't cross the street and the way I play my *Hitwave '81* record and the humming words forming in my brain and the way I have to *tap tap tap tap*. The words unfurled from my mouth and ascended to the ceiling. They curved through the air like light.

My friend didn't say anything.

'It's all right,' I said to myself.

'It's all right,' my friend echoed.

In the morning, I ravenously ate four pieces of buttered toast.

'I knew you'd get your appetite back,' the mum said.

I avoided an invitation from the younger brother to visit the chooks again, thanked the parents for having me, and took the path past the empty spaces and the lawnmower shop and the gnarled tree back to school.

My friend didn't say anything on the walk.

And then, at playlunch, when I looked for him in the quadrangle, I noticed that the atmosphere in the playground had changed, just a little. The figures were more clumped together than usual and they were buzzing with some new excitement. As I made my way over to the usual corner, a clump of students shadowed over to me. I drifted casually in another direction as if that had always been my intention. I didn't normally like to go this way: the quadrangle here was a tangle of hopscotch lines, scrawled in red paint. The horde moved over with me. I tried to slip past, but one of the boys stuck out his leg and I tripped, slapping my palms hard on the cement, my hands and knees cutting into the red paint.

'Made you step on the crack,' the boy guffawed.

'Tap tap tap tap,' my almost-friend sneered behind him.

My father-in-law said, 'What's got her goat?'

My brothers-in-law snorted and one swigged at his beer. The patio roof thrummed in the summer heat.

'Dad,' my wife was still trying to finish her sentence. 'It's just—she's just—it's just something that—'

'I'll talk to her,' I said.

She was still crouched in the far corner of the backyard, staring into the Colorbond fence. I sat down on the lawn next to her. She wouldn't acknowledge my presence.

'It's all right,' I wanted to say.

Her eyes were dry from staring.

'Darling,' I said.

'I *won't*, Daddy. I *won't*.'

I tried to think of the right thing to say.

'Darling, please,' I said. I looked back at the patio and my relatives-in-law leaning over the platter, my still-wet-from-the-pool nephews licking their sticky fingers. 'Darling, please. It's what they do in this family.'

I thought of families—not just this family—gathering at Christmas time, celebrating together over roast chook, falling asleep together in front of the telly. I thought of the whole *power complex*.

'There are two words,' I wanted to say. 'There's "part": the word you use when you're included, when you're in on the conversation. "I'm part of the whole," you might want to say. And there's "part": when you leave the room, when you're cut away from the rest of the group, when a quadrangle of children sneer at you, when you don't know what happened on *The Goodies* last night, when someone catches you picking the bacon bits out of the potato salad.'

I thought of being on the outside looking in.

'It's what we do in *our* family,' I said to my daughter.

Eventually, I was able to prise her away from the Colorbond and drag her back to the table. I had to use sterner words than 'please', harsher actions than a hand-hold. 'But sometimes,' I told myself, 'it needs to be done, it's for her own good, it's what we have to do.'

She sat at the table; there were four pink marks on her upper arm where my fingers had been. 'I'm sorry, Granddad,' she said, the words falling out of her dry mouth.

Then I watched her from across the table, licking off the gluey marinade to reveal the chlorine-white meat underneath, forcing the stringy flesh into her mouth. Her eyes glinting blackly, looking at me murderously.

My father watched me from across the table, his nails tapping against the marble.

For the rest of primary school, I tried to make myself as normal as possible. I'd see my no-longer-friend in the quadrangle, playing handball with his mates, sneering together. Then one year—halfway through term—he wasn't there any more. I'd walk home, taking a different route each time. I locked away the humming and the tapping for the times when no one was paying attention. When my father served up dinner, the plate clanking down on the marble table, I ate what was put in front of me.

Nocturne

I do haunt you still.

John Webster, *The Duchess of Malfi*

He's never seen a tawny frogmouth, not in real life. He's seen
pictures on the internet. Grumpy, crumpled faces, staring at
the camera, enduring the human gaze. Tufty, downturned old-
man eyebrows. Their beaks are wide and flat, like a schoolboy's
cap. Glumping-round torsos, like Banksia Men or fluffy boom
mikes. He's seen videos of them on YouTube: they yawn and
their mottled heads hinge open like a hand puppet. There's
smooth pink leather inside. There are recordings of their
midnight call: barely audible, low and relentless, *woom woom
woom woom*. A sad thrum in the distance. He's heard accounts
of their wondrous camouflage. The sleeping bird, beak raised;
still and silent, hunched into the rough skin of an ironbark. You
may be rumbling down a bush track in your car and you'll see a
dead branch on the road. If you stop and watch, you might see
it ruffle. It might wink at you: an orange-sapphire eye, watching
sullenly, too doleful to fly away.

The young man is sitting at a narrow desk. Four alabaster walls frame him. There is a blank sheet of paper in front of him. It's that time of night when the air is nebulous and the darkness seems eternal. The palpable silence that overwhelms, when thoughts can be insistent, urgent, insurmountable. A frightening but beautiful silence: as if he's the only one awake in the whole world. He wants to write. Sometimes the words come easily. Tonight they do not.

The man stares at a glimmering screen. He's withdrawn from the warmth of the bed, extricated himself from the entanglement of his wife's limbs. He's shuffled his pins-and-needles feet into the study and slid into the swivelly chair. He's trying to decipher a spreadsheet. The digits are like scratches on a prison-cell wall. They blur together, fluttering over each other. Silent wings polishing the night sky.

The boy is lying on his back in his bed, embalmed under a heavy blanket. His legs feel leaden, his feet are warm and heavy. His arms are tight against his torso. His spindly fingers peck against his leg. He concentrates on the accompanying words. *Please don't let it. Please don't let it.* There's a fifth word in the mantra, one more tap, but he switches hands before his thoughts leap there. He doesn't want to get to the end of the sentence. His open eyes watch the grey streaks of light on the ceiling, the murmuring not-thoughts. He hears a sigh of pain coming from behind a closed door.

The man is reading online articles. He's recently chucked out the shoeboxes under the bed, but he's still bookmarking webpages, collecting and connecting ideas in his mind. The sluggish air blankets around him. He's skimming over political catastrophes, ecological crises. A bushfire smoulders; a presidential rival says, smearingly, that where there's smoke, there's fire. A desert encroaches on fertile land, swathes across the shoulder of Africa. There's a chasm deepening in forests in Brazil, in Myanmar, in New Zealand. Closer to home. The man reads about forest dieback on the east coast. The trees wither from the top downward. The cancer spreads through the branches, discolouring the leaves. There are multiple catalysts: logging and insects and even birds. He learns about the bellbird's involvement in deforestation: a memory is tainted. He decides not to tell his wife about his discovery. He delves deeper. The birds scare away the other species, those who'd normally eat the grubs. The grubs multiply and suck away the sap. He scans the pictures. A gash of grey emptiness. The shards of tree trunks lacerate the sky. Economies crumble, cultures are annihilated. Humans and bellbirds shriek into the void.

It's another night, not that long ago. The baby is screeching, unrelentingly obstinate. The man hesitates in the doorway, emerging from a jagged sleep. The baby's head is splayed open. The tongue curls in her purple mouth. The man is sullen and sore. He's not aware of the strumming fingers on his thigh. The baby keeps crying.

The boy wakes, petrified, in the night. He's much younger now. He's sweating and the sheets are jangled round his legs. He cries out, *Please don't let it. Please don't let it.* A figure shadows in through the open door. He shudders with recognition, yearning for her quiet presence, clinging to her comfort with frantic loneliness. *Please don't let it. Please don't let it.*

She soothes him. She smooths his matted hair. She whispers into the pale light. His mother is reading to him.

The man has moved away from newsfeeds. He's reading poetry. He knows that he should go back to the spreadsheet, which is still waiting, untouched, in another window. He knows that the shimmering words are forbidden territory. He's not allowed to be a poet. That door was shut to him. His father, annihilated, packed all the books away. Old books: their spines splintered like bark, the pages streaked with age and one moment of childish fury. They had to go: their gloomy shadow weighed down the hallway. Online, though, the poems are airy, feathery. He reads new poems, sparkling pinpricks of light. He bookmarks these to read another night. He finds familiar poems, ones he knows by heart. Poems about birds and night and loneliness. *And the good south wind still blew behind, But no sweet bird did follow; Not in lone splendour hung aloft the night; Let us go then, you and I—*

They're sitting in a neon-lit hospital waiting room. His father is telling him something. It feels like a recitation, but it's one he's never performed before. The boy is scrutinising the man's face so he doesn't have to listen to what's being said. One side of his father's face sags, as if he's had a stroke. The side of the boy's leg thrums. *Please don't let it. Please don't let it.* He stops. He knows his father doesn't want to say the words. He feels his father non-entifying in front of him. He can see the tongue retreating. The poor sap. The words drip—no, they waft—from his mouth. Shadows of nothingness, hollowing out the iron air. The two of them, father and son, watch the words together. *Please don't let it. Please don't let it.* The sentence is finished. The father has nothing more to say. The boy knows his father wants the silence to be appreciated, that it's best to sit there, in the too-brightness, rigidly wordless, side by side on the plastic bench. But he can't contain the ache filling the cavity in his chest. His head hinges open.

He veers away from poetry. He clicks on links, following whimsical lines of flight. Poems to paintings; paintings to myths. He encounters the story of the Bird of Sorrow. It's not a story from his childhood; it's a tale he's never read before.

It's Turkish. Another desert, cold and unrelenting. A happy princess witnesses her governess sobbing in the corner.

What makes you sad? she asks.

I have sorrow, the governess says.

What is sorrow? the princess asks.

The governess fetches a glistering cage containing a grey, speckled bird. It's a nightjar. The girl is left alone with the bird and the bird speaks to her. Set me free, princess, the bird trills. I promise to return, always. Foolishly, inevitably, the girl opens the cage door.

Later, when the princess is playing in the palace gardens, the bird returns, cleaving the air. The bird snatches and carries the princess away over the desert.

The princess, terrified, cries out into the wind, Why are you doing this?

This is sorrow, calls the bird. And there's always more to come.

The princess is dropped onto the sand, left to fend for herself. She scratches her way to a dusty village. There, she finds work in the local inn, clearing the plates and goblets from the drunken revellers. She settles in to a new life. The innkeeper's son is handsome; the life is simple but satisfying.

Alone in the kitchen one afternoon, she is humming happily when the bird of sorrow appears at the window. The bird swoops in and smashes the saucers and cups, the plates, the bottles of wine.

Cowering among the broken porcelain and glass, the girl asks, Why are you doing this?

This is sorrow, calls the bird. And there's always more to come.

The girl flees. She finds another position, working for a tailor. He's handsome; she can sew: they fall in love. She loves to watch him thread the needle; they have a child. One morning she's in the sewing room fixing a hem on a rich woman's gown, rocking the baby's cradle with her foot when the bird appears at the window. She scratches at the princess's face, shreds the fabric, grabbles at the baby and carries him off.

The girl calls out, Why are you doing this?

This is sorrow, cries the bird, and carries the baby away, never to be seen again.

The young man sits with a blank piece of paper. He sees the past. He knows the future. There's always more to come. He taps his pockets. He feels the rustle of the pill packets. He knows what to do.

The computer screen comes in and out of focus. The man's eyes droop with sleep and sadness. He needs to slip away from this capsule of sorrow. On his slouching path back to bed, he deviates to his daughter's room. He peers in and watches her soothing, sighing sleep. He leaves the door open in case she calls out.

He's never seen a tawny frogmouth. But he has read, late at night, two lines from a poet:

This is how frogmouths disappear.
They raise their beak and petrify.

A branch of sorrow on the road ahead. But this bird doesn't want to snatch you away; she has no desire to scratch at your face. She's hoping that you won't recognise her lying there. That you'll pass by, contented and oblivious.

Magpies

A good territory may well be matched by good occupants. Plenty of experience, high levels of vigilance, and strong group cohesion (effective teamwork) may be the most important qualities that mature individuals can bring to maintaining a territory.

Gisela Kaplan, *Australian Magpie*

This is what happened at the office.

I can't get to any of my emails today because we've been forced to go to a group dynamics workshop. I don't need to give you any more detail than that. You can imagine. I'll let you decide for yourself what the facilitator looks like: if she's ratty-haired or poised; if she delivers her point about roles and responsibilities with a flourish, or if she wavers between each thought, her words clagging the corner of her mouth. The tables in the conference room might have been divvied into small clusters, flowing with butcher's paper; or they might have been managed into a large rectangle that's now tacking us to the walls. There'd be a lopsided hole made by the shape of the tables in the middle of the room, and we'd all be rolling our eyes at one another across the expanse. You can see the textaed jargon-terms razor-bladed into the whiteboard, but the specific words aren't important. I want you to look instead at two of the people in the room who are the focus of this story. Two members of my team.

The first is our team leader. She's dynamic, inspiring, zealous: a stickler for detail, a cutter-to-the-chase. Her polished hair is shrewdly scraped back and her earrings glint. Her jacket is tailored precisely: v-shaped around the neck, bold at the shoulders, slender at the waist. A permanent silhouette. Only occasionally do you see flashes of the white blouse underneath. Her eyes dagger about the room. She's been essential to the department since it started and she's always been proud to represent it. When the facilitator proposes a discussion topic, any discussion topic, our leader's incisive solutions resolve the matter. She pivots in her chair and adjusts her collar.

The second person is not polished or decisive or inspiring. His name is Peter. He's probably in his fifties; he might always have been in his fifties. He's a bit sloppy. Today he's wearing a lumpen jumper over his shirt and tie and there's a glob of breakfast on it. There's a shred of unshaven beard in the bend of his jaw. He's kind of foul. We're always on task-and-finish working groups together, but I never want to make eye contact with him. I try to make small talk in the stairwell up to our department. He has terrible teeth: brown and clumsy.

Peter talks a lot about stationery. His office is next door to the cupboard where we store the Post-it notes and the extra suspension files. He's often passing my office, his clotted body clutching another ream of paper for the photocopier. He's very dutiful. Right now, he's listening carefully to the facilitator's sales pitch, nodding his head politely. He's even taking notes.

At one moment, after a succinct summary of core competencies from our leader, Peter offers his extemporaneous thoughts on the matter.

Our team leader stiffens. You can feel the hair bristling on the nape of her neck.

'Peter, *that's hardly the point.*' The outburst is a bayonet. We all reel from it.

Our leader is unruffled. Systematically, mathematically, she extracts the fallacies from his flabby argument. She peels away the oversights. His ideas are not proactive or innovative or sustainable. She's absolutely right. Peter tries to smooth down the cowlick in his hair. He turns away from her pinprick gaze. The facilitator interposes, but quickly retreats. Nobody else moves.

I won't say we're used to the behaviour. It's always a surprise, even when you see it coming. It comes in high and fast like a sniper's headshot; it spikes in deep like an arrow. Up close, she can bite sharp and quick, serrating a suggestion or ripping into a memo. She can also sting in from a distance: via email or with a shout, whirring down the corridor. Some of us are targeted more than others, but she's always got her eye on Peter. He tries to avoid her, I think. I see him peeping furtively out of the stationery cupboard and bolting for it, running the gauntlet, waving his hands above his head. But she senses his presence. 'Peter—a minute?' she calls. Her black wings open and he's assaulted by the flash of white shards.

We all know about magpies. We all have anecdotes about When Magpies Attack. Mine happened when I was very young— during my first year of school, I'd say. There were poplar trees between the classroom and the oval. I wandered down during playlunch and the bird roared down at me vertiginously, viciously. Its stiletto beak actually drew blood—at least that's what I remember. I know I howled. The deputy called my mother in, so it must have been when I was very young indeed. My mother swooped in and scooped me away.

My daughter regularly brings home notes from her school, warning that 'Magpie Season' is upon us. These scrunched-up pieces of paper provide handy hints to reduce the risk of assault. They include:

- Avoid areas where magpies are swooping, and make a cardboard sign to warn others.
- Walk quickly and quietly away if you see a magpie swooping, trying to keep an eye on the magpie as you do so.
- Make a hat from a cardboard box or an ice-cream container and scribble on a pair of eyes.
- Carry a stick or an open umbrella above your head.
- Above all, if you're swooped by a magpie, do not stop. You are in the magpie's territory and he will keep on swooping.

We have other handy sources of information about the magpie. There's the Sunday-arvo barbecue banter: know-it-all insights, informed by the scent of burned sausage and the comforting beer in the stomach. Usually commencing in spring, these insights are foraged from slivered articles in the local newspaper and half-watched segments on TV science shows. *Apparently*, the conversations begin. Apparently, magpies are super-intelligent, even more clever than crows. Apparently, they can distinguish one human from another and carry this memory for years, even decades. According to scientists, magpies can communicate this knowledge to other magpies in their community. They target some individuals for swooping and not others. I heard this one story, someone says, squinting from the sizzle on the hotplate, about a man who threw sticks at a magpie in his garden when he was a kid.

Hoppy, he called it, because the bird only had one leg. His mother used to lay out hunks of bread on the lawn for the poor bird. Years later, fully grown up, he comes back to visit and Hoppy's son scimitars through the air and takes his revenge. It's not about provocation, someone else says. He takes a swig of his stubby. You can just be walking by and *bang!* Man, those beaks are sharp.

Then what's the reason? Why do they pick some people and not others? Everyone wonders, and the sausages are turned over to reveal their charred underbellies. We believe, smugly, that magpies won't attack us. But we're all scratching the tops of our heads, soothing old wounds between the hair follicles.

A magpie once settled in the centre courtyard of the building I work in. She built her nest in the crook between two branches in the courtyard's solitary leafless tree. She swooped for weeks: any time people wanted to smoke or eat lunch or take a diagonal shortcut. Eventually, security came and escorted her away. Our team leader pointed out that this was an incorrect strategy. As the cage passed the gathered crowd, our team leader snipped, 'It'll only come back. They're sharper than you think.'

She was absolutely right. I don't know where security released the magpie, but a few weeks later, there she was, pitched on the flat roof of our building, vigilant as a prison guard.

Our team leader keeps a strict routine. First thing in the morning it's emails and then a briefing with her PA. Then she does the rounds. 'This office has a lot of moving parts,' she often says, 'and it's essential to touch base with the team.' She clears a path down the corridor as we all scamper to our desks. She works the plot systematically. She looms. You never know what she's going to do next. Sometimes she's jocular, throwing her head back and jubilating. That can be more terrifying than her stern head-tilt; in me, it induces a hollow replica of a laugh, spindly and embarrassed.

Despite the pain, it pays to stay at your desk: poised, alert. As soon as she passes, though, we tend to disperse. I hear her pontificating to a colleague further down the corridor. I strike off another action item and abscond.

Our building is one of those sixties blocks, a cube with the middle cut out of it. Cancerous concrete with a gravel roof. Our department is three floors up, so you don't always have time to sneak down to the courtyard. My colleagues tend to linger in the stairwell. It's your basic cement chasm, echoey and cold, the white paint peeling off the metal railings. It's not unpleasant. We install ourselves on the steps and gossip. It's a half-escape. It's like we're working up the courage for the real liberation, the total bolt.

Sometimes Peter joins us, and we engage in polite, awkward chitchat. I sit on a lower step, not wanting to get a whiff of his sour breath. Most of the time, though, he doesn't hang around. He seems to prefer walking down to the ground floor and back up again. He tells me that he's trying to lose a few kilos. He's rubbing his wobbly jumper. So up and down he goes. He calls it his daily regimen. When he's out of earshot—or when we assume he's out of earshot—our conversation turns towards him. I know *she's* awful, we say, but a lot of the time he does bring it on himself. If he just learned to placate her, if he just kept his trap shut …

There have been times in meetings when Peter has floundered over a piece of policy. I've seen our leader's hackles rise but before she has a chance to strike, another colleague cuts in to Peter instead. I've done it myself. If I do it, I think, I can explain his mistake in a reasonable way, in a friendly way. Another colleague joins in, just as pleasant, just as helpful. We're providing a buffer, we reason, a safe zone. Our team leader sits back, smoothing down the front pocket of her jacket.

We're still chatting when he plods back up the stairwell. As he passes, his head flicks to us: furtive, disappointed.

It's lunchtime and we've all been called to a systems review meeting. It's a small meeting—our leader calls these a 'huddle'—in the glass-walled conference room next to her office. We were ordered to submit our reports in advance of the meeting, but we still don't really know what it's actually about. I'm shuffling at my office door. I don't know if I should print copies of my reports or not. I want to make the right impression: the big boss is coming, the boss above our team leader. Better to be primed for all contingencies. But I also remember the rant our leader bombarded us with at our last meeting about resource management and greening the office. I decide against the printouts.

I slip through the glass doors. Our leader is pitched next to the big boss. She's touching her hair conspicuously and nodding as the big boss talks to indicate how intently she's listening. Between them is a platter of catering. It's fancier than the too-dry, too-wet sandwiches we normally get. There's a chopped-up baguette, some pickles, slabs of salami and cubed feta, lettuce and sliced cucumber, and, in the middle, some chicken wings. The big boss takes the corner piece of the baguette and affixes some salami to it. Our leader lifts a chicken wing, daintily.

The big boss announces he's only got forty-five minutes until his next conference so we'd better get a hustle on, hadn't we. We settle. The first report—an update on a new policy— has already swung into action before our team leader twigs that Peter is missing.

One of my colleagues mutters something about seeing him loitering near the stationery cupboard.

Our leader looks askance at him and the colleague is silent.

I'm sent to fetch Peter. My murmuring colleague is right.

He's not in his office, and I can hear whistling emanating from the stationery cupboard.

It's not quite a melody: it's the absent-minded sub-song of someone happy and on his own.

The door is plastered with bits and pieces: almost-risqué cartoons, postcards from gloating colleagues, clippings from the social pages showing our not-game-enough-to-be-debauched Christmas parties. It's pretty ratty: the clippings are frayed like hessian bags; the sticky tape is sallow. The whistling—the sound of a flat kettle boiling—continues from within. I'm wondering if I should knock. I opt to make a vague scratching noise with my throat.

The whistling stops and Peter peers out. He tells me he's sorry, he lost track of the time, he'd just come in for a minute and he'd noticed … He opens the door and for a moment I'm blinded by the light behind him. There's a large window above the shelves letting in a multitude of sky. Peter, a blobby shadow, tells me he just thought he'd do a spot of spring cleaning. When my eyes adjust I see how organised everything is. A density of stacked manila folders, their rounded corners aligned. Glue sticks in a row like soldiers. Hoarded boxes of staples stacked, neat and compact, in a pyramid. I think he's waiting for me to pay his tidiness a compliment. I turn back to the glass room and he shuffles after me.

We haven't missed anything. A lively conversation is taking place between our team leader and the big boss, a flustered colleague shelved on the sidelines. The big boss is evangelising about breaking through the clutter, about focus, about consolidation and maximum impact, about attention to detail. He's telling us that without attention to detail we can't drill down to the real problems, we can't take it up to the next level, we can't get to the bleeding edge.

Our leader concurs, absolutely, unequivocally. Nobody, it seems, knows how to follow procedure. Nobody knows how to leverage an opportunity. She's licking her lips. Despite her desire to impress, she's making a bit of a mess with her lunch. She's hooked the end of the chicken wing and has snapped the sticky bone at the join. She turns it upside down and the marinade drips. The big boss notices. He snorts and tells her that she needs a serviette, no, several serviettes. He laughs at the splotch of sauce she's got on her blouse.

Her lips tighten.

'Peter?' she hackles. 'Isn't your report ready?'

Peter looks up from his notepad and gives one of his grotty good-natured smiles. He dithers out stapled photocopies of a gritty spreadsheet, one for each member of the team. He's sorry he didn't have time to submit it earlier.

Our leader snatches and pokes at the report as Peter commences a zigzagging account of budget analytics and potential streamlining models.

We're not listening. We're waiting, our eyes fixed.

'*Peter*,' she piques, with a *Taxi Driver* tilt of the head, 'look at the error in the third column.'

Peter contemplates the splotchy ink. He doesn't think … he could be …?

She maintains her binocular gaze, her smooth head thrown back, her chest expanded. She's steely and still. We all duck and cover. It's much worse than her usual attack. This is what she means about procedure, this is what the big boss means when he's talking about clutter, attention to detail, updating systems.

She whirls in her chair. 'I mean honestly, Peter, this is ridiculous. How could you make such a fundamental fuck-up?'

Yes, yes, Peter says, his head down, the cowlick exposed. Yes, yes, he knows.

'Well, if you *know*—if you *know*—*then why did you do it?*'

We don't say anything. Peter faces away from the team. His head isn't bowed, but he's not making eye contact with anyone. His nose is pointed at the glass walls. For the rest of the meeting, you can sense him trying not to shudder.

A colleague passes my office en route to the weekly round-up. I delete some send-all emails and follow. We haven't had a chance to debrief about the Peter incident—we all left the meeting shell-shocked and silent—but now isn't the time or the place to raise the topic. Only a moment later we're at our team leader's door.

She waves us into her office. It's a vast room, trimly furnished: a white desk, neat bookcases, a small cleared table for intimate conferences. There's a strip of windows along one wall and they're open today, letting in late afternoon sun and airy sounds. She's recounting a story the big boss told her about someone in another department. It's not an unfunny story, and she's telling it expertly. At the punchline, she lifts her head and laughs. I catch a glance of her pristine-white blouse.

She doesn't mention Peter. He's meant to be at the meeting.

We discuss the action items for next week. We follow a routine of points. There are a few moments when we encounter a task in Peter's domain: we skirt around it, hoping our team leader won't notice. She notices.

'I think I should say—' she begins.

And, absolutely, unequivocally on cue, there's the sound of breaking glass. A cry from a colleague, confused, rattled, using Peter's name and words like 'Don't—' and 'What are you—?' A whoosh and a scream. A kerfuffle of feet. One of my colleagues is in the doorway, saying, 'I think—I think—'. Through the open windows, there are other voices rumbling, calling from the cavernous space below.

I think Peter may have—the voice is saying.

I don't know much about magpies. Peter did, though. I joined him on his journey up the stairwell once. I was coming from the carpark; he was slowly trudging through his regimen. I don't know what made us get onto the topic of birds. He's an ornithologist, he told me. Well, an amateur ornithologist. A twitcher. He went on to tell me how he always goes bushwalking on the weekend, binoculars at the ready. But he doesn't have to venture far to watch his favourite bird. The magpie is a much-maligned creature, he said. Everyone harps on about their aggression, their steely beaks, their yellow eyes. They're not aggressive. Their swooping behaviour is limited to four to six weeks in the year, and they're always only defending their hatchlings. We think of the attacks as unprovoked, but, for them, we're invading their territory. There are statistics to show that magpie attacks count for something like 0.01 percent of human injuries from animals. Magpies are beautiful. Did you know they're one of the few birds—in the world—to engage in play? Did you know they have facial expressions? They can fluff the feathers below or above their beak to show fear or anger or surprise. They're capable of binocular vision, so they can look you in the eye. They sunbake! They lie on their back, wings outstretched, and it looks like they're dead. But one eye is always in shade under the beak, keeping watch. They have a complex social structure with a tight hierarchy, but they also work cooperatively. They forage side by side and, if there's a predator, one bird will warn the others. Their calls are a warning for other animals in the wild. They're the police of the bush. Magpies can even forge close connections with humans. Peter told me how he'd cared for an injured magpie once. He thinks a cat had got her. He gathered her up and fed her droplets of water. When her wing was healed, Peter released her into the wild. But she didn't go far: in fact, she built her nest in his backyard. Peter loves to watch her fretting the grass, plunging her smooth beak into the ground.

Look, I've been playing with a metaphor here, but, like most metaphors, it doesn't always stay still. I've never been very good with analogies. I started writing this story with a simple correlation: magpie-attacks-human-equals-workplace-bullying. Thanks to the conversation with Peter on the stairs, though, I've moved from a simple metaphor to one where the analogy shifts, mid-swoop. Peter is sometimes the small boy, walking between the poplars, howling when the beak-knife pierces the top of his head. Then he becomes the magpie, expertly fashioning an elegant nest: the outer layer rough with plastic, rope and hessian bags; the inner layer ordered and scrupulously cared for, insulated against the wind. Sometimes he's a marginal member of the magpie clan, ostracised, not permitted to eat or drink. Crouching for hours in front of a tree, beak touching the bark. Sometimes we're all magpies.

In a book I read, a scientist describes an experiment in which she placed a stuffed eagle carcass in the bushes. One magpie spotted it and called the alarm. Then all the magpies mobbed the stuffed eagle, picking it apart, beaks clapping and wings flapping furiously. We've all been there.

And as for our team leader—

We've all stumbled down the corridor, seen the shattered glass in the stationery cupboard, the two black scuff-marks on the shelf. We've all flown down the stairwell and splayed into the courtyard. Security has got there before us and is attempting to cordon off the area, but we can all see the carcass. It's mangled, splintered, frayed. I've seen something like that before. I'm paralysed, staring at another broken body. We're all paralysed. Except for our team leader. She swoops towards Peter. Security tries to warn her away but she persists. 'It's my job,' she cries. 'It's my responsibility.' She peels away her black jacket and folds it over him. She's careful not to move him. She knows exactly what to do. She's the one who went to the first aid course last year when we all deleted the email. She tells everyone to stand back. She whispers into his grazed ear. She listens. 'He's alive!' she calls. 'Get the ambulance here!' She feels along his rib cage, his pelvis, the open edge of his thigh bone. All the time she's warbling to Peter, soothingly, a sub-song, a song a bird might sing when he is sitting on his own. She glances at one of us and a colleague offers her a water bottle. She sprinkles droplets of water over Peter's forehead, making sure to keep them away from his mouth.

When the ambulance arrives she lets them do their job. We watch as the paramedics shuffle Peter onto the stretcher. I don't want to look as they carry him towards the ambulance. His blood-splattered eyes twitch. One eye is open under a broken nose. Teeth are barbed through his bottom lip.

Our team leader is watching, too. There's blood on her white blouse.

I step forward. As the courtyard darkens and the siren fades, I have to comfort her.

And No Birds Sing

Like a whisper in the feathers there,

    in the wings'

Great wind, like a whirring of words,

    but I could not

Say the shape of them.

    W.S. Merwin, 'The Annunciation'

It's a silence that overrides all others. It's as if the whole room is on mute; no, the opposite: as if the volume is up so high that you can no longer hear it, it's become a bone-splitting unfathomable fuzz. He's not sure if he's in a dream; he's fairly sure he isn't. There's a dull ache separating his body from the rest of the room. He's not sure, yet, what the room is. It could be a scrubbed-clean kitchen with a white table in the centre. Or it could be a sparsely furnished, chalky-walled granny flat. It could be the void of a courtyard in the centre

Alaotra grebe
Tachybaptus rufolavatus

Atitlán grebe
Podilymbus gigas

Aldabra brush-warbler
Nesillas aldabrana

Colombian grebe
Podiceps andinus

Mariana mallard
Anas oustaleti

Kauai akialoa
Hemignathus obscurus

Stead's bushwren
Xenicus longipes variabilis Stead

of an office block. It could even be an empty school quadrangle, a chip packet wafting over the asphalt, or a silent ravine on the journey home from work. He knows it isn't any of those places. He knows where he is; it's on the tip of his mind, but there's a smooth surface between himself and that knowledge.

There are bodies in the room with him. In the other beds, he can sense a series of broken-winged humans. Other figures float past, coming in and out of focus. Their mouths open and close, but what they're saying can't be heard over the humming silence. They tuck and untuck the starchy white sheets that pin him to the bed. Once, one of the figures moves to the edge of the room and lets in a sudden flood of light. It cuts across the face of the man in the bed opposite him. He's sleeping; he has a grotesque, frightened expression, a twisted frown. For the next stretch of time (An afternoon? A lifetime?) he watches the light deaden over the frightened man's face.

A woman and a girl appear. He knows who they are. The woman's face is flat, like she's wearing a veil. The girl is scared. He wants to comfort her but he can't work out how to

South Island
piopio
Turnagra capensis

Kākāwahie
Paroreomyza flammea

Long-tailed triller
Lalage leucopyga

Sunda teal
Anas gibberifrons remissa

Glaucous macaw
Anodorhynchus glaucus

North Island
piopio
Turnagra tanagra

Niceforo's pintail
Anas georgica niceforoi

San Benedicto
rock wren
Salpinctes obsoletus exsul

151

get out of the bed. The woman and the girl sit on two porcelain chairs that are next to the bed. There is some half-hearted opening and closing of mouths. He knows he's supposed to do something. The girl has a large book on her lap: her hands are like mittens, or paws, resting on top. Between her paws the cover image of the book comes into focus: a black bird flying over a white sky. The woman's mouth moves. The girl doesn't speak.

Or maybe he isn't in the bed. Maybe he's under the pale light of a desk lamp, looking at his computer screen, swivelling in his chair. It's a windy night. A gush of air shakes the window frame; through the window he can see the leaves of the eucalypt in the backyard glinting as the air reverberates through them.

He's transcribing a list he's taken from the internet. He has a stack of paper to write on. It's that kind of paper they used to use (Fifteen years ago? Twenty years ago?) for printers, the type bordered by strips of perforated circles. Each page is attached to the last; the ream comes out of the box in one long zigzagging ribbon. He's writing the words on the paper in

Laughing owl
Sceloglaux albifacies

Wake rail
Hypotaenidia wakensis

Laysan rail
Porzana palmeri

Cyprus dipper
Cinclus cinclus olympicus

Maré Island thrush
Turdus poliocephalus mareensis

Grand Cayman thrush
Turdus ravidus

Daito varied tit
Sittiparus varius orii

black texta. He doesn't know why he's doing this; he knows exactly why he's doing this.

He writes:

The Alaotra grebe (Tachybaptus rufolavatus), a duck-like bird with a yellow face and black cowl, was formerly found in Lake Alaotra in central Madagascar. The introduction of predatory fish and human poaching are believed to be the primary causes of its extinction. It was officially declared extinct in 2010.

He writes:

The Atitlán grebe (*Podilymbus gigas*) was declared extinct in 1989. Endemic to Lago de Atitlan in Guatemala, it was similar to the pied-billed grebe (*Podilymbus podiceps*) but with a reduced wingspan and flightless. Extinction was due to a variety of factors: introduced fish, reed-cutting, tourism development, lowered lake levels after the 1976 earthquake and even political unrest. The murder of the park ranger during the coup of 1982 significantly hampered conservation efforts.

He writes:

Mcgregor's house finch
Carpodacus mexicanus mcgregori

Grand Cayman Jamaican oriole
Icterus leucopteryx bairdi

Assumption Island white-throated rail
Canirallus cuvieri abbotti

Ryukyu wood pigeon
Columba jouyi

Pink-headed duck
Rhodonessa caryophyllacea

Isle of Pines solitaire
Myadestes elisabeth retrusus

The Aldabra brush-warbler (*Nesillas aldabrana*) had pale feathers on its slender frame, with short wings and a long, pointed tail. It was threatened by habitat alteration by introduced species, such as rats, cats and goats. It was last sighted in 1983, and searches in 1986 confirmed its extinction.

Running his finger down the long list on the screen, there are some names he doesn't recognise: the Niceforo brown pintail (*Anas georgica niceforoi*), the Laysan honeycreeper (*Himatione sanguinea*), the slender-billed grackle (*Quiscalus palustris*). Others are more familiar: the passenger pigeon (*Ectopistes migratorius*), the great auk (*Alca impennis*), the slender moa (*Dinornis torosus*). The last name on the list is the dodo (*Raphus cucullatus*), but he knows that there were birds before this. And, of course, there will always be birds to come.

He doesn't know what to do with this list of vanished birds. He has a desire to shred his ream of outdated paper or to scrunch it up and shove it into the recycling bin. He also has a desire to read it all out aloud, like a mantra or a eulogy. The Latin words form in his mouth. There's a certain rhythm to the

Hawai'i 'ō'o
Moho nobilis

Canarian
oystercatcher
*Haematopus
meadewaldoi*

Paradise parrot
*Psephotus
pulcherrimus*

San Clemente
wren
*Thryomanes
bewickii
leucophrys*

Iwo Jima white-
browed crake
*Poliolimnas
cinereus
brevipes*

Norfolk starling
Aplonis fusca

Laysan
honeycreeper
*Hiimatione
fraithii*

incantation; he can feel the tap of it thrumming against his leg. He continues to write down the information: the San Benedicto rock wren (*Salpinctes obsoletus exsul*), declared extinct in 1952; the laughing owl (*Sceloglaux albifacies*), 1950; the wake rail (*Rallus wakensis*), 1945. He chants out their stories; dots of his spit pixelate the computer screen. Outside the room, the wind has picked up; the eucalypt thrashes from side to side. The black mamo (*Drepanis funereal*), 1907; the huia (*Heteralocha acutirostris*), 1906; the Auckland Island merganser (*Mergus australis*), 1905. The air is rasping. The Bonin woodpigeon (*Columba versicolor*), 1889. Something is calling him on the wind. His chanting increases in volume. The O'ahu 'ō'ō (*Moho apicalis*), 1837; the mysterious starling (*Aplonis mavornata*), 1774. He's using his voice to drown out the bawling wind.

A woman, clumsy and fuzzy-headed, comes in from another room in the house. He gasps, as if he's suffocating, or drowning. It takes a while for him to decipher the words coming out of her mouth. She says she can't have another night of this, please, you're starting to upset—

Laysan millerbird
Acrocephalus familiaris familiaris

Red-moustached fruit-dove
Ptilinopus mercierii

Japanese bush warbler (Daito)
Cettia diphone restrictus

Robust white-eye
Zosterops strenuous

Molokai 'ō'o
Moho bishopi

Passenger pigeon
Ectopistes migratorius

Carolina parakeet
Conuropsis carolinensis

His gasps turn to sobs. The chair swivels away when she tries to put her arms around him. He can't stop sobbing.

Canary Islands chat (Alegranza) Saxicola dacotiae murielae

Or maybe he isn't crying in the middle of the night, trying to ignore the rattling window. Maybe he's blinking at another computer screen, as he takes another capsule for the ache that's murmuring behind his eyes.

Chatham bellbird Anthornis melanocephala

The atmosphere in the office is listless. If he chose to listen, he'd hear hushed conversations in the corridor. It's been two days since his colleague's broken body was taken to the hospital. No, longer than that. (Three weeks? Six months?) The whispers say he's doing well, he's paralysed, he'll be coming back, he's going to be fine. The words aspirate the walls of the corridor like Spray n' Wipe, cleaning away the frantic rushing towards the stationery cupboard, the cries and the shrieks when they wrenched the door open and looked down into the courtyard below.

Chatham fernbird Bowdleria rufescens

Euler's flycatcher (Grenada) Lathrotriccus euleri flaviventris

Slender-billed grackle Quiscalus palustris

The door to the stationery cupboard is closed now. The ratty collection of newspaper clippings has been peeled off.

A well-dressed woman returns from visiting hours at intensive care. She's

Black mamo Drepanis funerea

a reduced figure: still implacable, still sharp, but smaller, paler. No one has the energy to blame her; no one talks about the moment when she comforted the broken body in the courtyard. She's not culpable. She nods at him in the corridor, and once she leans over the conference table in a meeting and lets her ivory hand slip over his. The air conditioning emanates a throbbing kind of silence.

Huia
Heteralocha acutirostris

Auckland merganser
Mergus australis

As he passes the closed door, he thinks he can hear something, or someone, humming tunelessly behind it. He feels his ribcage tightening.

Choiseul pigeon
Microgoura meeki

Eventually he and a colleague decide to open the stationery door. He knows that this happened sooner rather than later, that an office can't run without stationery indefinitely, that professional cleaners were called in to wash it all away, swiftly and efficiently. But this isn't how he remembers it. He must have dreamt it. He doesn't think he dreamt it. The metal handle turns stiffly and the weight of the door pushes back. He and his colleague shoulder the door open. Papers, reams and reams of photocopying paper, have been blocking the sweep of the door. There's an

Guadalupe caracara
Caracara lutosa

Chatham Island rail
Cabalus modestus

New Zealand little bittern
Ixobrychus novaezelandiae

audible reek: sweet, like a piece of uncooked chicken left too long in the fridge. He blinks into the sunlight. The glass in the window is still jagged, the wind skirls through the gap. Feathers have attached themselves to the sharp edges of the glass. The colleague says that birds must have broken in and he now sees the evidence of this: not just the feathers, but the white liquid splodges over the envelopes and the manila folders, and the leaves and twigs in the corner, intertwined with strips of paper and Post-it notes. He breathes in the mess. The image is both beautiful and appalling. It's wild and raw and claustrophobic. His colleague doesn't know where they're going to begin to clean this mess up. His hand is sticky from the birdshit.

There's a curling rush of wind coming through the window. As it flows over the glass, it whistles.

His colleague nudges a cardboard box on a high shelf and tilts its contents. It's a box of that paper they used to use for printers. The paper slinkies to the floor in one long ribbon.

The wind doesn't sound like wind. It

Greater 'amakihi
Viridonia sagittirostris

Tristan moorhen
Gallinula nesiotis

Hawaii mamo
Drepanis pacifica

Greater koa-finch
Rhodocanthis palmeri

Kona grosbeak
Chloridops kona

Ula-ai-hawane
Ciridops anna

Lesser koa-finch
Rhodocanthis flaviceps

sounds like music. He can feel the friction of it against his skin.

Bonin grosbeak
Carpodacus ferreorostris

He folds up the paper and lifts it back into the cardboard box. His colleague makes a joke about obsolescence.

Bonin woodpigeon
Columba versicolor

As he hefts the box out of the cupboard he steps on something. The crack of it creaks like bone. When he goes to scrape it off in the bathroom he discovers that it was a tiny egg. The shell is white and brittle.

Cuban macaw
Ara tricolor

Or maybe he's not in a toilet cubicle, holding back a sob and trying not to listen to the wind calling. Maybe he's driving home, or walking the dog, or carrying a baby in his arms, or shaking hands after a successful interview, or listening to a woman asking him if he'd marry her. Maybe he's climbing the stairs in a university library.

Hawaiian rail
Zapornia sandwichensis

Figures ghost past. It's not a dream; he's fairly certain it's not a dream. He's in the first year of his degree. He's a young man. He doesn't think of himself in those terms; he doesn't think of himself in any way if he can help it. He keeps moving upwards. In the distance, beneath him, at the bottom of the stairwell, he can hear

Rodrigues parakeet
Psittacula exsul

New Zealand quail
Coturnix novaezelandiae

something: a kind of music, a sort-of song. Maybe it's wafting in from the library lawn, a local band shrieking over the dozing students. Maybe it's coming from another source. He quickens his pace up the stairs.

Labrador duck
Camptorhynchus labradorius

He knows he's on the fly—he's allowing himself to articulate that thought—he knows he's fleeing from the house he grew up in. He's eaten his last meal at the marble table, he's no longer avoiding eye contact with the mausoleum of a man on the other side.

Coues' gadwall
Mareca Strepera couesi

Stephen Island rockwren
Traversia lyalli

He's absconded to the city. He's found himself a flat and lives on his own. He'd blanched at the idea of colleges, crammed in with all those other bodies. The flat is out the back of a brick-veneer house. A family lives in the house. A crumbly-cement ramp leads the way past the house and the Hills Hoist in the backyard. He has to nod at the family in the house if they say hello, but once he's closed the front door, it's just him. It's only a room with a bathroom attached. Four white walls. A scabby kitchenette is tacked onto one wall; a narrow desk lies opposite. There's an even narrower bed under the window. He chooses

Seychelles parakeet
Psittacula wardi

Himalayan quail
Ophrysia superciliosa

Kioea
Chaetoptila angustipluma

not to attach anything to the chalky walls. He cooks plain meals—two-minute noodles, eggs on toast—on the coiled stovetop. He rests his hand on the Formica counter. It feels like someone's squeezed too much Jiff on it.

Reunion starling
Fregilupus varius

He's enjoying the emptiness, the space of absence.

At night, though, lying in the bed, he hears the song. It's like the family has the stereo on, or there's a party at the end of the street. He feels his body separating from the world around him. No, the opposite of that: the air is solidifying, as if someone has made a Styrofoam mould of the granny-flat air.

Spectacled cormorant
Phalacrocorax perspicillatus

Norfolk kaka
Nestor productus

It's almost impossible to lift the Styrofoam away, or, when he does, to sneak down the lopsided path. Then he has to work out a way of loitering in the dusty space outside the lecture hall without anyone noticing. He realises he hasn't spoken to anyone for three weeks, no, longer. (A month? A year?) He sits in tutorials like he's a marble sculpture; he says nothing when he hands over the money to the person in the shop who sells him the two-minute noodles. He keeps his head down when he walks past the Hills Hoist.

Great auk
Alca impennis linnaeus

Black-fronted parakeet
Cyanoramphus zealandicus

And at night he listens to the song calling in the distance.

Ryukyu kingfisher Todiramphus miyakoensis

He goes to a lecture. He's allowed himself to take one elective, something different from the numbers and charts he needs for his career. The elective is 'An Introduction to English Literature'. He doesn't know why he picked it; he knows exactly why he picked it. The lecture is on *The Waste Land*. He does try to read the poem, beforehand, sitting upright at the narrow desk, the book laid out in front of him, the spine pressed flat on the smooth surface. He used to know another line from Eliot, something about empty skies and anaesthesia. But the words in this poem detach from the stanzas like leaves from a tree. The lecture doesn't help. A figure stands at the front of the asphyxiating room pronouncing a litany of sources: Shakespeare and the Fisher King and Sanskrit. The lecturer's mouth opens and closes. He plucks the ideas and pins them down in a senseless order. They almost make sense, but there's something missing, like they're an unfinished sentence or a list without a heading. Late at night, as he listens to the music at the end of the street, the words

Chatham Island banded rail Gallirallus dieffenbachia

Kangaroo Island emu Dromaius baudinianus

O'ahu 'ō'ō Moho apicalis

Mauritius Blue-pigeon Alectroenas nitidissima

unpick themselves again. They waft above
the bed. The bit about the sailor, Phlebas the
Phoenician. The words shape themselves into
a pattern:

Mascarene
parrot
Mascarinus
mascarin

> *A current under sea*
>> *Picked his bones in whispers.*

Lord Howe
gallinule
Porphyrio albus

The whispering words fall into the rhythm
of the distant music.

In a tutorial, a translucent-skinned girl
tells the story of *To the Lighthouse*. They never
get to the lighthouse. The girl augments her
presentation with information about the
author. The shallow grey water of the Ouse.
Her body was missing for three weeks. The
rocks, cold and polished like marble, sewn
into the pockets. The colourless girl flutters
when she quotes the handwritten note left
behind. At night, these words join the melody
of the music, swirling like a whirlpool above
him:

Snail-eating
coua
Coua delalandei

Kosrae starling
Aplonis corvina

> *I hear voices and cannot concentrate*
>> *I have fought against it but*
>>> *cannot fight any longer*

Kittlitz's thrush
Zoothera
terrestris

One afternoon he wanders past the suburban home and sees three rectangles of faded terry-towelling fabric stiffening on the Hills Hoist. The father calls out from a window at the back of the house that it's such a glorious day, that he should really get down to the beach if he can, the water's a bit icy, but once you're in it's lovely. He keeps walking up the ramp and shuts the flimsy door.

Kosrae crake
Zapornia monasa

Upland moa
Megalapteryx didinus

The music is coming in waves now. When the wind is blowing in the right direction, it sounds like howling.

On his way home from uni he walks past the supermarket and goes into the chemist. He uses his two-minute noodle money to buy packets of pills. He listens to the packets rustle in his pocket as he walks home.

Mysterious starling
Aplonis mavornata

The rustle doesn't quite drown out the moaning music. He tries to fight against the current.

Réunion flightless Ibis
Borbonibis latipes

Or maybe he's not sitting at the narrow desk, scratching words onto a white sheet of paper. Maybe he's with his father, packing away the books from the hallway, stripping the sheets off the bed, carrying a box of clothes out the front door. The house is filled with the

Tahiti sandpiper
Prosobonia leucoptera

scent of eucalyptus and bleach. With this scent comes the neat story, eulogised by his father in the hollow church, then repeated for the days that follow. Something to say to people when there's an empty space in the conversation, when people's hands go to their mouths after a faux pas. Something to say to yourself as you're walking to school; something to fold away and put at the bottom of your suitcase when you're flying the coop. This was my mother. Her habitat was limited to a darkened room in a suburban house in inland New South Wales, Australia. Her existence was primarily sedentary. The introduction of cancerous cells into her breast, lungs and bones are believed to be the primary causes of her extinction. He thinks he can take this story to the city with him and it will all be all right. He convinces himself that this is enough.

He knows it isn't enough. He knows that this is a story he's telling to protect himself. A cover story, like a list of names and dates to paper over the real experience. The passenger pigeon population dropping from three billion to one in the space of seventy years: one corpse lying rigid at the bottom of her cage

Society parakeet
Cyanoramphus
ulietanus

Rodrigues
solitaire
Pezophaps
solitaria

Mauritius grey
parrot
Lophopsittacus
bensoni

Rodrigues
night-heron
Nycticorax
megacephalus

Rodrigues rail
Aphanapteryx
leguati

in the Cincinnati Zoo. Or a sailor on Eldey Island in 1844, crushing the last great auk egg into the ground with his boot. Even these are stories, ways of cleaning up the moment of disappearance, like stuffing a dodo and placing it on display behind glass, as if it still matters. They're not real. They're not what it's like to really face the music.

Rodrigues parrot
Necropsittacus rodericanus

Where he really is, is in a hospital waiting room. He's a boy: he'll always think of himself like that. His father has finished his sentence. He listens even as he tries to drown it out. His head hinges open.

Rodrigues turtle-dove
Nesoenas rodericanus

He wails. His wailing washes over everything, like a flood, like a sudden whoosh of wind. It's a sireny song. It destroys like a bushfire. It scorches the walls. His wailing reverberates over everything, over forest, over fields, over time. He wails on his back veranda, by the side of the road, in the vestibule staring at an open doorway, at a barbecue over a plate of chicken wings. He wails, teetering on the rocks looking at the ocean, thinking of Phlebas the Phoenician. His wailing bellows through the bush, screaming its way around the thin rasping trees. Even the birds will hear it.

Rodrigues owl
Mascarenotus murivorus

Réunion solitaire
Raphus solitaria

The wail will always be there, washing over his skin. He will never stop wailing. There is always more to come.

Mauritius night-heron Nycticorax mauritianus

He wails in the stationery cupboard. He can't stop. His colleague places an ivory hand over his.

He wails silently in the dusty space outside the lecture theatre. A young woman asks if he's all right. He doesn't remember what words he sobs out to her.

Mauritius shelduck Alopochen mauritiana

He wails in the hospital, this hospital, right now. The afternoon light is shafting through the open window, but he can't hear any birds singing. The woman wants to hold his hand, he knows this. But the wailing is like a Perspex bubble around him. The girl is terrified, her face mirrors the face of the man in the bed opposite. She claws at the fairy tale book in her hands. He wants to stop wailing but it pours and pours out of him. It's a scream that overrides all others.

Mauritius duck Anas theodori

Then, without warning, the girl's body dashes towards the bed, like a sudden gust of wind. Her body crashes into his. Her body is like a barnacle on his skin; her head knuckles into the cavity between his collarbone and his chin.

Red rail Aphanapteryx bonasia

He keeps wailing. She clings to him. He wails and wails. The rhythm changes. It undulates. The wails fluster and feather in the air. He feels his hand being taken. The woman's hand is warm.

Mascarene coot
Fulica newtoni

Then the room empties out. He can see it washing away, polishing the light.

After a long time (An aeon? A childhood?) the girl untangles herself. She goes back to her book. The covers span open on her lap.

Broad-billed parrot
Lophopsittacus mauritianus

Even though it's just a fairy tale, he listens to his daughter's voice as she begins to tell her story.

Slender Moa
Dinornis torosus

Great elephant bird
Aepyornis maximus

Dodo
Raphus cucullatus

Aves Admittant

The past is not for living in; it is a well of conclusions from which we draw in order to act.

John Berger, *Ways of Seeing*

Years and years from now, I'll be working as an island ecologist undertaking research on Cabbage Tree Island and my dad will come along as a volunteer assistant. It'll be part of my postdoc. He and Mum will have been so proud of me: taking me out for pizza at the end of high school; for a massive banquet lunch after the BSc graduation; a hatted restaurant to celebrate the conferral of the PhD. Just Dad at the last one. 'We always knew it would be birds with you,' Dad will have said, many times, over the years. 'I mean, all those Charlottes ...'

It's a small island, only about thirty hectares, a k and a half from the entrance to Port Stephens. Its isolation will be perfect for my research: away from human population pressures and with a strong history of recovery programs. There are multiple species of birds on the island. Terrestrially, the standouts are the birds of prey (Peregrine falcons, white-bellied sea eagles) with occasional rainbow pitta and blue-faced honeyeaters and an abundance of grey shrike-thrushes. The most common seabirds on the island are the wedge-tailed shearwaters, the short-tailed shearwater, and, in two crevices in the rocks, a colony of little penguins. But I'll be interested in the Gould's petrel. They're a small gadfly petrel—wingspan seventy centimetres; weight 180 to 200 grams. They're trans-Pacific migrants; back in the 'teens, geolocative studies traced their pelagic distribution, a counter-clockwise sweep of the ocean, into the Tasman, round to Hawai'i and back along the lower equatorial latitudes. They return to the breeding colony in October, about a month before laying. My supervisor will have been going there for years—when he's there, winding his way up the gullies, it'll be clear that the island is in his blood. This trip will be my third; I'll have come as a volunteer, tagging on to my supervisor's project, before unearthing my own research. I'll be monitoring the incubation process of the GPs, noting any depletion of residual population or decrease in successful fledgings. When I use the words 'depletion' and 'decrease' in the car ride up to Port Stephens, I'll ignore my dad's scrunched-up face and the way he grips his seatbelt.

From the mainland, the island looks like a humpback whale with a mossy coat. It's on a tilt, the tail submerged and the body rising, poised to leap into the air. A dense rainforest grows on its back, on the leeside. Around the island is a ring of frothy waves, like the valances that my grandma—my mum's mum—used to have around her bed base. I'll smile at this thought and tell my dad about it, but he'll stand on the pontoon in the marina, staring at the swelling water in the bay. His mind will be somewhere between terror and panic. That'll be fine— as long as his thoughts don't go to that other place, wherever it is—that place where he always wants to go.

My supervisor will give a yank on the cord of the outboard motor.

'Come *on*, Dad,' I'll say. 'We haven't got all day.'

On the trip over, my supervisor will be squatting in the stern of the Zodiac, one hand steering, the other sweeping back his scraggly, flailing hair. His gnarled face will be pink from the spray. I'll be sitting against the prow, my back to the gusting air. My dad will be cowering below me. As we ride the crest of a wave, my supervisor will be chatting to us, but we won't be able to hear him over the thunder. As the base of the boat thumps against the water, my supervisor will hit what seems like a punchline and laugh into the wind. The boat will scud and curve around the island. On the ocean side, we'll see fractured cliffs dropping sharply into the sea. I'll note that these crags haven't yet been affected by the sea-level shifts. My dad will look, eyes-wrinkled, into the sun.

We'll circumnavigate the island and come back to the western side. My supervisor will steer the dinghy into a small cove of serrated rocks.

' … using the island as a cage,' my supervisor will say into the stillness of the harbour.

I'll have heard this story before, so I'll laugh and then say, 'He doesn't mean *us*, Dad.' It's a yarn my supervisor loves to spin about the introduction of rabbits onto the island. 'It was a controlled experiment,' he'll say, 'part of the Intercolonial Rabbit Commission's attempts at eradication. Henry Parkes offered a reward of twenty-five thousand pounds—we're talking like twenty million bucks in our money—and this French bloke, Louis Pasteur's nephew …'

My father will be glaring at the orange rocks. I'll leap across first and my supervisor will chuck across the packs, still yabbering about the rabbit experiment. In 1906 Jean Danysz established an inoculation station on Broughton Island, northeast of Cabbage Tree. He wanted to see if rabbits infected with a pox virus would survive. They did, and ravaged the undergrowth. Somehow they made it to Cabbage Tree, too.

'Your turn now, Dad,' I'll say.

He'll look at me across the sliver of black water. The Zodiac will bump against the rocks.

He won't move. Not for the first time, I'll wonder why I invited him.

While we're waiting for Dad to change out of his wet shoes, my supervisor and I will sit on the uneven rocks and look back to the mainland.

'Listen to that,' he'll say, and we'll hear the call of a white-bellied sea eagle. 'I heard they were nesting.' The lines round his eyes will expand and contract.

When Dad is ready, we'll climb up into the forest. We'll be following one of the steep, narrow basalt dykes that run west to east across the island: a fold in the hill marked out by a line of cabbage palms. We'll clamber up an almost-track, trying to avoid being stabbed by the spurs of the palm stems. We'll pass a metal sign, salt-bleached, that says:

NO UNAUTHORISED ENTRY. Access to the island is closely monitored. Maximum penalty $660,000 or two years imprisonment, or both.

My supervisor will be a few bounds above, still nattering about the rabbits and Danysz's trials with microbes of chicken cholera. 'He found that it wasn't contagious to rabbits,' he'll call down to us, 'but the rabbits certainly—here. This is what I'm talking about.' He'll crouch next to a tall round-trunked tree and reach into the mulched leaves. 'Birdlime,' he'll say, looking up the length of sturdy trunk. 'The rabbits ate the understorey so the birdlime fruit fell to the ground, so birds were exposed to the seeds which should have been entangled in shrubbery. Here.' He'll offer a birdlime calyx—a thin, grooved tube, like a withered frangipani—to my breathless father.

Dad won't want to accept it, but he will take the calyx in his hand, and I'll watch him stretch the viscous syrup between his thumb and forefinger.

'Gums up the birds' wings so they can't fly,' my supervisor will say. I've seen pictures of the affected birds: the calyx sticking out of their feathers like pierced arrows. 'Eventually, the bird starves to death.' My supervisor will tramp higher. 'When ecologists came here in the eighties,' he'll call, as we follow, 'the forest was jammed with birdlimes.' He'll chuckle at his pun. 'So bad that the nesting pairs were down to less than 250. So it wasn't just a matter of eradicating the rabbits. We didn't need to make a drastic change. All we needed to remove was thirty-four plants and their seedlings in the breeding ground. By the mid-nineties the undergrowth was regenerating and the population upswinged to—here we are.'

On a ledge on the hill, camouflaged among the trees, there'll be a fibreglass structure, like a mutant pumpkin. It's called the igloo. Apple-green, it has round porthole windows and window shades like eyelids. My supervisor will unclamp the padlock from the door. Inside will be a cramped space, just enough for two storage shelves: one holding sunscreen, WD-40 and Aerogard; the other a ragtag library of bird books, collected shells, and bird skeletons and feathers. Around the edge will be three compact bunks for us to sleep on. 'Home sweet home,' my supervisor will say.

My father will waver next to the trunk of a cabbage palm.

My supervisor will have clambered into the igloo. I'll finish his story for him. 'That was one of the success stories. By the late nineties we had more than a thousand breeding pairs.'

In the hush of the rainforest my dad will ask, 'And now?'

My supervisor will be clattering about inside. 'That's what we're here to find out,' I'll say.

We'll get to work immediately. My supervisor will be doing his own side project in the other gully. When I ask him about it, he'll mutter some words I won't catch—it'll sound like a scientific name, a phrase in Latin. Before I get the chance to say 'What?', he'll have moseyed away over the fig-tree roots. 'Aves' something. 'Bird' something. I'll gather up the materials we need—head torches and the nest record sheets—and my father and I will head in the opposite direction.

Gould's petrels are the only gadfly petrel that don't burrow. They nest in natural cavities under the toscanite scree or among the buttresses of fig trees. Sometimes they nest beneath dried cabbage-tree fronds that have fallen to the ground. On Cabbage Tree we've got a good record of the nests. We've been demarcating them for years. Each nest has its own indicator tied to a metal stake—those pink, blue, green, yellow numbered pendants they use to tag cattle. The data sheet my dad will carry into the bush—laminated in plastic but a bit frayed—will be based on a list compiled by the team way back in the nineties, but it's still accurate. Gps form long-term partnerships, and nest sites are used by the same birds in successive years. The birds fly off after fledging. They return to almost precisely the same spot they were hatched from. Dad and I will be tracking down a series of nests: looking to see if they're still intact; if there's anyone at home and, if so, one bird or two; is there an egg or, even, has it hatched? With the change in mean temperatures over the last ten years I'll be wanting to gauge its effect on breeding times and cycles.

The nests are often clumped together, sometimes within a few metres of each other. Not all the nests will be marked: there was a decision in the noughties to focus on the breeding cycle of only the known-aged birds: the birds we have banded and followed for years. We don't know exactly the lifespan of the GPs, but we have a bird—R025—that was banded way back in the 1980s, even before my supervisor's time on the island. As we zigzag up the hill, hopping from rock to shaky rock, we'll have passed several potential nest sites, but I won't have told my dad about them. I'll know that this knowledge would paralyse him: he'd stand there, among the mat rush, petrified that he'll accidentally crunch an egg.

We'll traipse higher, passing fronds of palms that spindle on the ground like large paper spiders. Tangled roots will hang down from the canopy. Even as we undertake our work my dad will pussyfoot anxiously over the rough ground, clasping the data sheet like it's his protective coating. The record sheets allow us to locate the nests: next to each listing is a set of coordinates that places the site in relation to its nearest neighbours. We'll have a system in place: my father will be acting as the 'driver', calling out the name of the next nest while I'll scramble over the scree searching for it. They're not always easy to find: the undergrowth will be taking hold and sometimes a nest will be well hidden among the bushes. 'Green 265,' Dad will cry thinly, 'south of Yellow 027, three metres; west of Blue 568, five metres.' He'll reach out and grab a native plum tree to steady himself. I'll spy the tag—it'll indicate the hollow in a fallen palm trunk—and crouch down to reach into the dark space.

As we work I'll tell Dad about another Gould's petrel success story, what my supervisor calls the second recovery program. It'll be why I want to include the species in my research. When I'm an undergrad my supervisor will give a lecture on the programs established by his team back in the early 2000s. 'The creation of conservation reserves won't in fact save species from extinction,' he'll claim, 'We need highly focused and effective recovery actions.'

After the eradication of the rabbits and the reduction of the birdlime threat, my soon-to-be-supervisor developed a targeted translocation plan. Near-fledged birds were taken from Cabbage Tree to form a satellite colony on nearby Boondelbah Island, a small circular crag.

Under the sleepy lights of the lecture hall, my soon-to-be-supervisor will shape the island with his hands. The other students will be playing games on their smartpads, but I'll be listening. My nearly-supervisor will tell me about Boondelbah Island: its cliffs to the north and a basalt dyke to the south which has eroded to create a deep ravine and ocean bay. He'll explain how his team of ecologists are constructing artificial nests: boxes of Brunswick-green plastic, the entrance tunnel a section of polyethylene pipe. The project was not without its challenges. Birds selected for translocation needed to be taken after they had reached maximum mass, but before they emerged from their burrow. Birds chosen closer to fledging would have reduced the mortality rate, but the older the bird, the greater their philopatry—their ability to return to the nest. 'They GPS themselves,' my supervisor will say with a grin.

A friend will type something on her pad and the words 'lame who uses gps anymore' will pop up on my screen. Despite the risks, the majority of birds adapted to their new environment. The second iteration of the program met with a 100 percent success rate, with all nestlings successfully fledging after transfer. The removal of the young appeared to have no discernible effect on the breeding productivity of their parents: in fact, with the dispatching of their young, the pair could leave the island in more robust condition.

Sitting in the stuffy lecture hall, watching my nearly-supervisor flap enthusiastically, will change me forever. The undergrad years will have been a dark time for me: class after class on extinctions and yet more extinctions; encroachments on habitats; birds drowning in oil spills or choking on plastic. I'll feel myself slipping into a world I don't want to inhabit—a world I've seen on my father's face and in my father's stories. But this man will be telling me a different narrative, one where even plastic can transform into something productive, something protective. 'The irony is,' he'll say, 'GPs could not only breed successfully in plastic nest boxes, but breeding success in these artificial nests was greater than in natural ones. And the use of plastic greatly increases the lifespan of the nest.'

My father's map will have directed us to one of these boxes. A stake in the ground will confirm that we've arrived at R346. The box will be half-submerged amongst the toscanite. I'll lift the rock we use to secure the lid and open the box. I'll hear a body shift underneath. I'll open the internal lid and stick my hand in. Many GPs are placid; this one not so much. 'Ah yes, Reddy 346,' my supervisor will say, casually, later that night, 'he's the crankiest on the island.' My arm will recoil from the bite and R346 will give a disgruntled squawk, but then we'll both compose ourselves. The bird's round black eye will look into mine.

'Come and have a look, Dad,' I'll say. My father will keep his distance. As gently as I can, I'll clutch him around the wings, my palm against the oily grey back, my fore- and middle-fingers around his neck. My other palm will steady the bird's bat-wing feet. I'll take note of the number on the metal band around his leg. The ashen face will tremble and the smooth black beak will twist. Inside the box, amongst a few shredded palm fronds, will be the egg, gleaming and smooth. Before I replace the struggling bird, I'll say, 'Come and have a look, *Dad.*' But his white face will twitch like the bird, and his feet will remain rooted amongst the rocks.

It'll be the same face he'll make, the same stance he'll hold, a month before our visit to the island. The sale of the house will have gone through and he'll be standing in the backyard under the shade of the old spotted gum tree. I'll have spent the morning doing the final wiping down of the surfaces and the sweeping of the veranda. He'll have stood in the garden looking at the tree. I'll have been patient, understanding, fulfilling the promise to my mother to humour him, to protect him. But everyone has their limits. '*Dad*, you have to do *something.*' He'll still not budge. So my decision to ask him here won't really be an invitation, more of an enforced recovery plan. I'll draw up the list of essential items for him and fill his backpack and shove him into the car for the journey north. I'll cajole him into the boat. All the while, he'll be like a branch of petrified wood. All the while, I'll wonder why I'm doing this.

Towards the end of the afternoon we'll need a break so I'll lead him right up the hill, through the dense trees until we emerge into the sunshine at the top of the cliff. It's a spectacular view: you don't realise how claustrophobic it can be under the canopy until you face the expanse of the grey ocean and the flat blue sky. Dad won't want to go too close to the edge so he'll hold back, half-submerged in the bush. I'll stand on the rock shelf so I can get a better view of Cathedral Rock. It's actually a separate islet linked to the island by a boulder field: a tower of basalt adjacent to the island, like a craggy lighthouse. I'll want to see if the Peregrine falcon is nesting there this season. I won't be able to see the nest, but there'll be enough guano splattered down the sides of the tower to indicate her residency. My father will crawl out a little further and he'll wedge himself next to me. The wind will be light and the air fresh and clear. I won't expect a conversation from him, and I won't get one. Together, separately, we'll look out at the ruffling water.

A boat will come round the southern tip of the island. A small trawler, maybe two or three figures hidden under the red roof of the deck. We'll watch as the figures cast their nets. Bait fishing, most likely, before heading out to deeper waters hoping to find a school of larger fish. The figures on the boat probably won't see us, or maybe won't care that we've seen them. But they'll definitely see the man who'll step out onto a rock ledge further along the cliff, his long hair waving in the breeze like a halo. His chest will be puffed out; it'll look like it could be possible for him to stride over to the pinnacle of Cathedral Rock. My supervisor will take his sunglasses off his forehead and use them to flash the setting sunlight into the eyes of the men below. He'll call out, 'It's illegal to net so close to shore.' They won't be able to hear, but they'll get the message. My supervisor will give the men a friendly wave and then jump off the rock back into the forest.

That night, over rice and vegies, I'll be looking at my father and my supervisor sitting on canvas chairs leaning against the igloo. Mosquitos will fizz in the night air. We'll be able to hear the bark of the penguins in the bay below and, once or twice, the whistle of the GPs. My supervisor will have his hair tied back so you can see the line of grey running through it like the bride of Frankenstein. My dad will have collected a few dog-eared books from the igloo library and will be searching for birds that he's familiar with. They won't exactly be talking to each other: Dad will locate a bird from a book and my supervisor will spin a yarn about it. 'The interesting thing about magpies,' he will say and then launch into an anecdote about how the female does all the work: selecting the nest site, building it, incubating the eggs and feeding the young. Birds of paradise? The male is a tease, flashing a dance to win over the female, fluffing his wings up and fluttering them like a Victorian lady's fan. But in the end, the female is left to raise the chicks on her own. It'll be clear that my supervisor is enjoying himself, embellishing the stories like a bird of paradise's dance. Maybe my dad will be happy, too—well, as happy as he can possibly bring himself to be. I'll remember the moments of near-happiness of my childhood, little ports in my father's storm before he drifted off to the other place—wherever it is he drifted off to. My dad will fish out a kookaburra from the books. The page will be loose—the book's seen better days—and Dad will hold the picture of the bird like an offering. 'Now, their social group is interesting,' my supervisor will say, scratching the back of his neck. 'It normally comprises a dominant pair and a collection of helpers to feed the young: older siblings, usually, or maiden aunts. But unlike other cooperative breeders, when the dominant pair dies the helpers don't inherit the territory.'

I'll flick a buzzing bug away from my face.

'As for the GP,' my supervisor will say, without even needing a cue from my dad, 'the incubation and natal periods are completely cooperative.' Incubation for the Gould's petrel takes six to seven weeks. The parents take turns to forage for food. The male takes the first shift, which is sometimes thirteen or fourteen days long. The female waits on the egg without leaving it—not even for food. 'They can go without food for extended periods,' my supervisor will say. 'They can manage a loss of a third of their body weight. Like camels. The ships of the ocean,' and he'll laugh at his joke. 'The search for food takes them as far away as South Australia. It's the convergence of warm and cold oceanic fronts. More nutrients can be held in suspension in cold water; more food lives in the warmer currents: phytoplankton, zooplankton, shrimps, squid. One flies there and back and the other waits. Then it's her turn: all the way to the bight and back again.'

I'll see a question forming in my dad's mind, the same question I asked when I first heard the story. I'll ask the question for him. 'Why do they travel so far? Couldn't they choose somewhere nearby?'

'They've been doing this for thousands of years,' my supervisor will say. 'Things were probably a lot closer when they started.'

In the morning, over muesli, my supervisor will still be spinning yarns. He will be recounting an event from 1995, what he calls the pilchard 'hiccup'. During that season there was a major drop in breeding success: less than twenty percent, as opposed to the normal more than fifty percent success rate. It was the pilchards, he'll explain. Fish farmers introduced frozen pilchards into their schools; these had a pathogen—a kind of herpes. The pathogen spread to oceanic pilchards. From the pilchards to the kingfish—'and then it followed the food chain,' he'll say, carrying his wiped-clean bowl into the igloo.

My dad will be sitting on the edge of his foam-mattress

bed, hunched by the curve of the igloo ceiling, listening.

'Of course, that's got nothing on the megastorms of the 2020s. There, the depletion was—'

I'll take a swig of canvas-flavoured water and say, 'Come on, Dad.'

We'll be spending the day in the smaller basalt gully to the north of the igloo. My supervisor will tramp alongside us for a few minutes and then disappear into the scrub, off to his mystery project. The figtree roots and blocks of crumbling granite will create a mazy path. The northern dyke is narrower but lighter than the southern site—there are some gaps in the canopy and, at the opening of the gully below, you can see the orange rocks of the shoreline and the glistening ocean. We'll be skidding downhill, stepping between wide-leafed ferns and dead palm fronds. I'll be hoping we'll find a hatchling in amongst these leaves: it'll be too early in the breeding cycle, but it's been documented that the seasons have been shifting, incrementally, over the last fifteen or so years.

On this particular morning my father will seem less gangly, less tentative with his calls. He'll stumble over loose rocks but this won't freak him out. When he nearly steps on a nest and the bird emits a peep of protest his face won't blanch. When I reach into the nests and ease out the birds he'll still keep his distance but he'll be paying more attention. I'll say, 'See here—look at the nasal cavities' and glide my finger along the curved black beak and he'll nod and almost move towards me. With another bird, I'll show the underside of the GP, the pure white of her chest, a sharp contrast to the sooty top of the wings. When they fly, the heat of the white feathers gives the bird a subtle lift. The bird will peek her head around, white face framed by a slate-grey cap, and she will clack her beak in Dad's direction. He'll barely flinch.

At one point during the mid-morning, I'll look over at him. A greeny-yellow glob of sunlight will have made its way through the branches, warming his face. His eyes will be closed and his face will be smooth, pale, like it's shifted into neutral gear. I'll want to say something to him, make a sappy comment like, 'It's good to have you here.' But I won't. I'll consider saying something my supervisor always says, which is, 'It's a place for the birds. Our presence here is a very minor one.' Instead I'll say, 'Where next, Dad?'

When my mother dies I will, of course, be sad, devastated, but I'll also have had time to prepare for it. It will have been a proper goodbye. When we're together—at home, at the hospital, in the hospice—Mum and I will talk about her death as part of the larger scheme of things. She'll give me her necklace with the moonstone pendant and ask me if I want to keep any of her clothes and scarves, or would it be all right if she donated them to the women's refuge? We'll piece together some memories from my childhood, and hers, and we'll compile a list of invitees for the funeral. There'll be an obvious gap in the conversation, something that Mum is circling round, and I won't be eager to lead her towards it. She'll dip into silence. Eventually, very close to the end, we'll be in a rectangle of sunlight in the hospice courtyard. A lime-green hospital blanket will be tucked round her angular skeleton.

'Look after your father,' she'll say. 'You know he's always been ... ' She'll be clutching at the air.

As I'm growing up, we'll never talk about what my father has always been. I'll love him—of course I'll love him—I'll love the stories he tells me and the family trips to the beach or that time Mum and I will visit him in the bush and we'll explore the ruined schoolhouse together. But each time he drifts away to that place—wherever it is that he goes—I'll lose something of him. He'll come back and he'll read me another story—or I'll read him one—but it'll feel smaller, more distant. He'll feel eroded. It'll just get so exhausting. Eventually, I'll close off thinking about him. This is what always happens—we get caught up in new entanglements, the lure of other lives. I'll move into share houses and fawn over girlfriends and become immersed in new ideas. But it'll be a bit more than that. Sometimes when I call home Mum will say something like, 'Your dad's been a bit ...' and I'll deflect the conversation. When we get together for family dinner or Christmas it will be friendly, polite, detached.

Getting everything arranged for the funeral will be a

challenge. He'll be like this pool of dark matter in the centre of the house; it'll feel like I have to step over him to get to the kitchen or back to the bedrooms. I'll have to manipulate him into his suit and drag him into the chapel at the crematorium. I won't discuss if he wants to do a eulogy. After the minister speaks, there'll be a cavernous pause. No one will look at him. Slowly, achingly, he'll shadow his way to the lectern. It'll start as a mumble, not directed to us. It'll be a jumble of memories, cramped and convoluted. It'll be too much about the details. The wrong details. He will say nothing about her as an English teacher, her volunteering at the refuge, the fundraising work she used to do for Planet Ark. Just a meandering anecdote about a bushwalk they took once in the Blue Mountains: her taking him into the depths of Leura valley and getting him to *listen*, really *listen*. 'I always said she rescued me,' he'll say. He'll falter, surprised that he said this out loud. After a few minutes his voice will warble and another sentence—something about a flock of birds he once saw down at Little Bay—will hang, unfinished, in the air.

'Look after your father,' my mother will say.

I won't know what to say back.

He'll be standing in front of a silent crowd, open-mouthed, palms pressed into the blond-pine lectern. I'll get up and take him back to his seat.

The nest record sheets will take us further downhill, over piles of slippery basalt. There'll be less of a canopy here and the sound of the ocean will echo in the hush of the forest. The last nest we'll survey will be in the middle of what seems like a volcanic crater, an amphitheatre of jagged rocks. My supervisor will say that this depression was artificially created. During the Second World War, as they were preparing for the battle of the Coral Sea, troops used the island as a training ground, shooting up the branches—and probably the birds—for target practice. We'll still find ordinance fragments in the undergrowth; there'll be a collection on the shelf in the igloo. My supervisor will mention he thinks the indent might be a shell crater. 'It's too perfectly round,' he'll say, 'the edges too perfectly level.' It certainly does feel different from the knotted jumble of roots and branches surrounding it. As we step into the crater, we'll be captured by the glare of the noon sun. The flat blue sky will seem solid, like Perspex.

We'll find a stone ledge and sit in the sun for a few minutes. 'Dad,' I'll say and find myself talking about the life of the Gould's petrel just after fledging. I'll be threading an obvious analogy, but you've got to start somewhere. After fledging, the young birds leave for three to five years, sometimes longer. During this time, they don't return to the island. It's believed they spend the entire time at sea on their own. Like many birds, they even sleep on the wing, shutting down one hemisphere of their brain during flight, keeping the other hemisphere connected to the alert eye. The half-awake half-asleep bird courses her path, on air currents, searching for fish in the middle of the ocean. We don't know what makes them decide to return to the island. As a scientist it's not my job to speculate on what they must think when they find themselves spiralling above the cabbage trees. But sometimes I like to imagine what it must be like to dive into the forest and pinpoint the exact location of their hatching, to find your way home.

My father will listen to my story. He won't say anything, but I'll sense a kind of subdiscussion taking place in his mind: his hand, I'll see, will twitch, as if it might be lifted up and rested on my shoulder. I'll almost place my palm over the back of his hand.

On our way back to the igloo we'll decide not to clamber back up the hill. 'It'll be easier to slide down to the ocean and skirt our way round the rocks,' I'll tell my Dad. But in fact it'll be slower-going than I'd imagined. The wind will have picked up and we'll keep getting sprayed by the choppy water. My dad will seem even less sure of himself on the wet wobbly rocks. We'll cling to the boulders and lurch our way round the perimeter of the island.

We'll find ourselves in a recess in the rocks, momentarily protected by the wind. I'll suggest that we have a bit of a breather and we'll crouch on the pale-green and saffron lichen. There'll be a sugary-sour smell ingrained into the rocks. My father will be peering at something that has been scrawled into the deepest corner of the alcove. It will be a black ovoid shape. Inside the oval will be a smaller oval and then a smaller one, and in the centre a fat black dot. A lopsided target. Spray-painted on, and probably recently. The official status of the island is that it's a nature reserve and the only access is approved by Environment and Climate Services, but we'll know others come here. My supervisor will tell me that sometimes he'll find shards of fish scales on the rocks near the landing site, and he once came across a rusting yellow penknife lying in the sun. Another time he'll find the lock on the igloo door jimmied and, inside, the floor scattered with the leaves of bird books. Once, even, he'll discover three breeding boxes knocked over, palm fronds and feathers strewn over the hill. In the alcove my dad and I will notice a cairn of tarnished beer cans, and chinks in the rock face between the black lines of the target. Next to the cans there'll be small collections of bones, a few desiccated carcasses. I'll scrutinise the leathery cadavers and note that some of them are the size and shape of a petrel.

'It follows the food chain,' my father will say, his words reverberating against the rocks. He'll be as surprised as I am that he said it out loud.

That night, in the dark, I'll be lying in my narrow shelf bed. Dad and I will have turned in early—it'll have been an exhausting day. My supervisor will have stayed up; he'll be outside sitting on one of the canvas chairs listening to the noises of the evening.

The darkness will form a solid frame around my body.

I'll hear the sound of the canopy creaking above the igloo. Or maybe it'll be something else: the sound of someone quietly tapping the side of the bed. The tapping will form a sort-of melody in my mind. I'll find myself slipping into a place I don't want to go. I'll be thinking:

Tap tap tap tap: the rabbits rip up the forest understorey.

Tap tap tap tap: pilchards dead from herpes float in a black sea.

Tap tap tap tap: the nets drag away the last remaining fish.

Tap tap tap tap: the bullets ricochet off the rocks.

Tap tap tap tap: the storm waves batter and erode the cliff face.

Tap tap tap tap: the island floats further and further away from the continent.

'Dad, *please*,' I'll cry into the darkness. 'Will you *go to sleep*?'

We'll be groping our way up through the palm fronds. My dad will be plodding behind me. 'Pick up the pace, *Dad*,' I'll want to say. We'll be back in the first gully, surveying the last section of the data sheets. We'll have doubled back a couple of times: Dad will have missed a few of the markers on the page or I'll have overlooked a stake in the ground. Edging down the gully, I'll lose my footing on the scree and take a tumble. I'll stretch out my arms in front of me and my hands will scrape against the bark of a cabbage tree. I'll wait for my father to say something, but he'll just stand there, gormless, looking at his own feet.

Most of the birds will have been quiet that day—a few flutterings, but mainly they'll have been docile clumps of feathers. Some nests will be empty. My dad will make a note on the sheet. Most birds will be brooding, an egg warming underneath. No hatchlings. I'll place another bird back into her box. My dad will yawn—a big, full-face yawn—and that'll set me off yawning too.

'Just a few more to check, Dad,' I'll say.

He'll nod, but it'll be like he's not really there.

The night before, I'll have crawled out of bed to get away from my father's insomnia.

'It's such a balmy night,' my supervisor will murmur as the canvas chair outside the igloo scrapes against the earth beside him.

I'll tell him the stories that have been tapping in my brain. He'll listen, and nod, and scratch his eyebrows. He'll wait until all the stories are finished.

He'll let his fingers follow the thread of grey in his long hair. He'll say:

'If you were in dire straits, if the island was up shit creek, and all the birds were dying, which would you pick?'

'Which bird, or which species?'

'Which bird. You have ten pairs left, say.' His tone will be careful, measured, as if he's said this out loud before.

'I don't want to think that,' I'll say.

'We may have to.'

The mosquitos will shimmer around our faces. The canopy above us will creak. *Tap tap tap tap.*

We'll head west, up the mossy slope. We'll squeeze our way through a teepee of knotted vines. Dad will direct me to another metal stake. A yellow cattle eartag: Y271. The nest will be in a natural rock cavity, held within the lazy curve of a fig-tree trunk. A ragged-mouthed portal.

I'll reach my hand inside and my fingertips will brush against downy feathers.

'Dad,' I'll say. He'll be standing between two tall cabbage-tree trunks, holding the data sheet against his chest like a security blanket.

'Dad,' I'll say again, 'you'll want to see this.' As gently as I possibly can, I'll draw out the nestling. The chick will wriggle, fluff its wings. Grey and soft and fragile. It will look like those clumps of lint we used to scrape out of the door of the dryer. I'll cradle it between my hands.

He'll edge his way closer. He'll steady himself, his palm pushing into the rough bark. His mouth will open and close. The bird will twitch its dodo-curved beak.

I'll offer him the chick to touch but he'll teeter back. 'I can't,' he'll say.

'*Please*, Dad,' I'll say. The body will feel warm and alive in my hands. I'll hold the bird out in front of me, like an offering. The golden-green light of the forest will make the feathers glow and hum. 'Please, Dad,' I'll say again.

I won't know why it'll seem so vital for him to touch the downy bird. I'll know exactly why. This bird will fledge and fly and transcend. It will follow the rim of the Pacific: trace the currents of the Tasman Sea, hairpin along the coasts of South America, trace the scent of fish along the line of the equator. It will sleep and soar and dive and drift. And then it will return. It will circle the island and fly down through the canopy and land, right here, right on the spine of this fig-tree root. It will be part of a flock of a thousand birds, or two hundred, or ten. It doesn't matter. It will return.

I'll offer this living being to my father. His face will contort. 'Please, Dad.' He'll lean forward, his fingers clutching at the air. In my hands, the feathers will be soft. He'll bend down and reach out his hand.

The chick will flick its neck, twist its beak.

His hand will recoil.

'Dad,' I'll say.

'I can't, I—'

'*Dad.*' I'll feel the body struggling in my hands.

'It's too—I just—'

'Come *on*, Dad.'

His arms will be dithering in the air.

'I can't. We can't. All those things—the rabbits and the poisoned fish and—'

'And the birds *survived*, Dad. This one will survive you picking it up and feeling its feathers.'

But the pebbles under his feet will scatter. He'll say, 'I can't—I can't—' and he'll scurry off, over the crumbling rocks, away from the breathing bird in my hands.

I'll find him out on the clifftop, looking over the expanse. The wind will be pounding; he'll be sheltering inside a cleft in the rocks. Absent-mindedly—or maybe full-mindedly—he'll be stroking the palm of his right hand with his left thumb.

I'll ease myself into the cleft beside him. 'I'm sorry,' I'll say.

He'll squint at the ocean.

'I put it back in the nest,' I'll say. 'Everything will be all right,' I'll add, redundantly, possibly untruthfully.

We'll wait in the constricted space. The wind will whip over the top of my head. I'll wrap my arms around my chest. We'll watch the grey waves rumple.

He'll say, 'I'm sorry.'

'Dad,' I'll say.

'Do you remember Charlotte? The first Charlotte?'

'That was *years* ago, Dad.'

He'll be staring at the ocean like he's carrying the weight of the world on his shoulders, or around his neck. 'I'm still so sorry—I didn't mean to—'

I'll see him going off to that place—wherever it is—that place where he always wants to go.

'And there's always more to come,' he'll want to say.

'You can't keep telling the same story, *Dad*,' I'll want to reply.

Instead of that conversation, we'll huddle in the crack between the rocks and listen to the hollow cry of the wind. He'll look into the sky in that crumpled way he always does.

Over the ocean—a long way off—a single bird will be flying. It will be arcing its way towards us, skimming low against the slate-grey water and then up into the pink afternoon sky. It will tilt, stretching its wings vertically, so its span looks like a shard of frosted glass. It will turn away, and the white of its belly will be replaced by the grey of its back. It will fly close, shadowing over us and then diving down into the forest.

'*Aves admittant*,' I'll say.

Looking at the bird, my father will say, 'I'm sorry about—' He'll sweep his hand, palm up, in a circle. A gesture that incorporates everything.

In the heaviness of the night, my supervisor will spin another yarn. This one will be about Roman augurs. 'They used birds to predict the future,' he'll say explaining how they surveyed the arc of a bird's flight—or its entrails. Whenever a matter of importance needed to be resolved, the city would call upon the College of Augurs. The augurs would make their way to the top of a hill at dawn and ask the gods for a sign. They'd sit and watch the birds. With a stick, they'd draw a series of lines on the ground. Two straight lines intersecting each other—north-south; east-west. The spaces would correspond to different quadrants of the sky. If the bird flew in a particular direction, in a particular way, into a particular quadrant, then the augurs could make a prediction. The pronouncement would either be *aves admittant* ('the birds allow it') or *alio die* ('another day').

'We're doing the same, in a way,' my supervisor will murmur. 'Using the birds—and the island, and the water—to see what the future will be. But we can't wait for another day. It may be a future without them. Or without us.'

'I don't want to think that,' I'll say.

'We don't have a choice,' he'll reply.

He'll shift in his seat. 'We'll do what we can,' he'll say. 'When we translocated the GPs to Boondelbah, way back when, I wasn't a hundred percent convinced it would work. It was a painstaking process. We had to weigh and measure them, assess their plumage to determine their age, shift them into nesting boxes, ferry them over in the Zodiac, feed them by inserting segments of squid and fish into their oesophagus. Then we had to wait. Not just for the fledging, but for the next breeding season, or maybe the one after that. Even then, it wasn't plain sailing. The worst day for me was when we saw what happened to the first hatchling to die. A fledgling had returned with a mate and set up a nest in his natal box. We watched the brooding process: the disappearance of one for a week, two weeks; the other nesting, still, silent. Then they'd swap. When the egg finally hatched it felt like the birth of my own child.' He'll be quiet for a few moments. The lines around his eyes will tighten.

'What happened?' I'll ask.

'A rockfall destroyed the nest box.'

The forest canopy will breathe above us. The lines on my supervisor's face will expand and contract.

He'll look at me. 'You know what we did?' he'll say. 'We replaced the crushed box, put another plastic container in its place. The next season the brooding pair returned and produced another egg.'

Above us, we'll hear the whoosh of a bird on the wing, a quiet whistle as it calls in the air. Coming home, or flying away?

And then he'll tell me about his side project, what he's really been doing on the island. He'll have spent the last two days not watching the flights of the birds, but tracing the rim of the island, measuring the sea level, noting the shifts in water temperature. 'These last three years,' he'll tell me, 'the tides have been different. Cabbage Tree is doing all right at the moment, but Boondelbah lost thirty-four breeding boxes with the flooding of the basalt valley. The islands are going,' he'll say, 'one by one.'

I'll think of my nestling flying home to a swelling ocean, only the crown of Cathedral Rock reaching out of the water. But maybe there's something we can do. Translocation has worked before and it might work again.

We'll talk through logistics, the precarious processes. I won't yet be convinced, but my supervisor will say that he's going to try, if the birds allow it.

'But where …?' I'll ask.

My supervisor will tilt his head towards the north-east. 'Broughton looks good, for the moment.'

'And then?'

'Another island? And another after that?'

On the clifftop, my father will be sweeping his hand, palm up, in a circle. He'll say, 'Doesn't this—doesn't all of this—make you angry? Doesn't it sadden you?'

'We don't have time for sadness,' I'll say to him. 'Come on, we've got work to do.'

The Flight of Birds

Yes, I've looked everywhere
You can look without wings.

Maxwell Anderson, 'It Never Was You'

There's an old fairy tale—sorry, one more story, I promise only
one more story—about a farmer so protective of his wife that
he decides to take her out onto the moors and hang her. Is he
jealous? Is he paranoid? The story doesn't tell us; it doesn't
need to. He is resolute in his decision to hang her. Nothing
she can say will soften his heart, the story says. The farmer
reaches for a hempen rope from the rafters of his cottage,
drags his wife by the elbow through the stone doorway, out
into the cold night. It's a lonely farmhouse, and the moor is
desolate. The wind is bitter. The farmer spots a solitary tree on
the horizon silhouetted against the midnight blue sky. As the
man and his wife trudge towards it—dragging, pleading—a
flock of birds sweeps over them, battling against the wind. The
story doesn't tell what kind of birds they are. Maybe they're

crows, sharp-beaked and intelligent, their black wings barely trembling as they sweep overhead. Maybe they're sparrows, tiny specks of brown quivering against the brisk night. I like to think of them as seagulls. The farmhouse could be tressled on a clifftop and the wind could be an ocean squall. The seagulls lift off from the gnarled rocks below. They glide across the empty sky, over the lumbering couple, their white feathers glimmering in the moonlight.

The farmer and his wife reach the tree. It's a dead husk, grey and leafless, like a skeleton's hand reaching out of the ground. The birds have settled on one of the branches. They stare down at the couple silently with only the occasional twitch of a wing. The farmer puts the noose around his wife's neck; she's too exhausted to struggle any more. Her face is spattered with tears. The farmer throws the rope up towards the strongest bough, the one where the birds are perched. The rope arches over the branch but doesn't stick: the rope slides over the birds' silken wings. The farmer tries another branch, higher up. But the birds ripple up and land on that branch too; once again, the rope slips and coils itself to the ground.

The man sees another solitary tree, sharp against another horizon, across the expanse of the moor. He drags his wife towards it—stumbling, weeping. The wife's head is still in the noose. The birds fly with them. The farmer and his wife reach the tree: it's another hollow, barren shell. The birds settle on the branches and, try as hard as he might, the farmer cannot fasten the rope. He hefts the rope again and again, but it slithers over the birds' feathers and falls to the muddy ground.

It's lighter now and the wind has dropped. It's that pale time of morning before the day begins. There's one more tree to be seen across the expanse. The farmer sets off, pulling his wife along. The birds soar high in the air, off and away. Maybe the birds have forgotten the wife; maybe they've caught the scent of a fish on an ocean wave and left her to her fate. The farmer and his wife shuffle and sob towards the next dead tree. Much to his relief, the branches of the tree remain birdless. As he flings the rope up there's a great whirr of wings; the birds whoop down, as if from nowhere, and the rope falls once more. The man tries again.

He is sweating, his arms are aching. His wife is quiet, as still as the morning. The farmer looks at his wife. The first rays of the dawn break over the moors, over the clifftop, over the ocean. The rays catch the wife's face. She's smiling as she sees the birds' wings fluttering in the early morning light.

I don't remember how the story ends. Maybe the woman's smile makes the farmer's heart soften and the couple—repentant, forgiving—wander back to the cottage, hand in hand, exhausted. Maybe he succeeds, and the rope is fastened to the bough of the next tree. Or maybe the birds plunge and, wings flapping wildly, surround the wife and lift her up into the air, away from the wasteland of the moors, away from her husband and her barren life, never to be seen again.

The young man has not heard this story and is not interested in fairy tales. At this moment, he's not interested in anything. His mind is a blank; well, not quite a blank. He's trying to keep focused on the task at hand. He's sitting on a rattling, sweaty bus. The bus is not important to his story: it's just a means to an end. A way to get from his empty granny flat to the ocean. His destination.

He's had his destination mapped out for some time. He may not read fairy tales, but he has read *The Waste Land* and knows all about Phlebas the Phoenician, who forgot the cry of gulls and now swells in the deep seas. He's heard the story of Virginia Woolf lining her pockets with rocks to weigh her down in the water. The young man doesn't have rocks, but his pockets are laden with packets of pills. Their plastic cases rustle like dead leaves. Some of the cases are already empty. They're just painkillers but there are enough of them, he hopes, to be productive. The plan is simple, obvious: once he's drowsy enough he'll take the plunge.

The bus reaches the end of the line: an exposed, grassy headland; a carless carpark. It's on the edge of the city, an empty place overlooking some sharp rocks and the open sea. The brakes on the bus hiss and the young man—the only passenger—stumbles off. Even though the sky is vast above him, the air bites. He holds his elbows tight against his ribs. The ground feels uneven and the blue horizon lopsided. The young man lurches forward. At the far end of the carpark is the way down to the rocks and the sea. He has to stagger down a wooden staircase. The structure feels unsafe. It clutches the cliff like temporary scaffolding, like matchsticks that might snap.

At the base of the stairs he plonks himself down, groggily, and takes off his shoes and socks. It's probably not the time to be worried about grit in your sneakers, but it's an old habit. He's been here before, several times, scoping out the possibilities. He looks out at the grotty expanse of sand. On the weekend it's swarming with children and bikinis, but today it's uninhabited: there are only a few chip packets and cigarette butts to indicate human visitors.

Of course, there are birds. Seagulls. Two or three of them, tapping the sand and prodding the stubbed-out cigarettes. The young man ignores them. The birds flap a little when he hobbles past, but for the most part they ignore him too.

He wanders haphazardly over the sand. The beach is not his destination. He's picked out a spot round the next headland. He has to scramble over some rocks. There are maybe one or two birds hovering high above, but the young man has his head down and his thoughts on other things. He's reached his destination. Well, not quite his destination, he thinks. The water pulses against the rocks. The young man sits.

The horizon is sharp today, even when seen through the young man's hazy eyes. A thin strip of midnight blue; an overwhelming sensation of bright blue above. Some days the sky can seem deep and dense, a whole spectrum of blues, a depth of space. The young man doesn't see that today. The sky is flat, a monochrome screen at the end of the ocean. The sun is too bright, the blue is too blue, and this moment feels like an overexposed photograph. He sits on the hard rock and stares at the flat sky.

The ocean approaches and retreats. The tide's coming in. He'll sit here for as long as he has to.

It takes him a while to notice the seagulls. They've flitted down one by one, chosen roosts on outcrops nearby, or on the flat shelf that separates the young man from the grabbling water. The birds are interested in him, it seems. They twist their necks stiffly and make small awkward jumps towards him. Of course, these are not the birds of a fairy tale: sleek, intelligent, benevolent. They're a dishevelled collection, ripped and ravaged. To the young man, the seagulls' feathers look moth-eaten, tinged with dirty yellow. Their red beaks are faded, sun-bleached. One bird is missing an eye: the black jagged hole glares. Another is missing a foot: it's been severed by a net, or hacked off by schoolkids, the young man imagines, or tries not to imagine. He keeps his mind focused on the pills and the swelling ocean.

He puts his hand in his pocket. A flash of movement ripples through the flock. They teeter over the rocks. The footless bird makes the littlest movement, the slightest tilt of the head, the tiniest hop on its single foot. It gives out the feeblest noise— more like a bleat or a cough than a squawk. The young man can't bear to look at this battered creature. He feels sweaty and dizzy. He wants to lash out at the bird, at the birds, to rip off all their feet and pluck out all their feathers. He feels hemmed in by the birds and the flat, overwhelming sky and the ocean shuffling towards his feet.

And then it happens. As if they'd choreographed this moment, all the birds unfurl their wings. They lean to the left, they lean to the right. Then they all glide skywards. For a moment the young man isn't certain if they levitated or if the rocks dropped from under him. They're all in the air above him, sharp against the blue sky. They form a synchronised circle that wheels above the young man's head. Even the one with the missing foot flies smoothly, turning this way and that, letting the sun catch his wings at different angles. Even the one with the gaping eyehole can drift and swoop through the air. In fact it's impossible to tell which bird is which: they are all perfect, all elegant, all miraculous. The birds move as a group, concertinaing in and out like a lung. Sparkling in the light as they turn, flipping from black to blinding white. The young man watches in awe at this sight, as the birds soothe the sky, their white feathers glinting. Then they soar out to sea, swifting down to the water and up into the air again. Then they're specks against the sharp horizon. Then they're gone.

The sun's in his eyes. He blinks. He looks at the space where the birds used to be and the dark blue ocean rolling—relentless, mesmerising—over the rocks.

When he's ready, he makes his way home.

The young man, exhausted, sleeps on the bus, dreaming of seagulls. Years later, he will hear the story of the farmer and his wife read to him by a child, carefully and quietly, so as not to wake the patient in the bed opposite. He will remember sparking strips of white against an open blue sky.

Field Notes

Field notes have been described as 'jottings': 'quickly rendered scribbles about actions and dialogue'.[1] Certainly the field notes I came across during my archival research could be called 'scribbles'. Narrow notebooks with scratchy black pen marks, sentences half-finished interrupted by diagrams attempting to represent a bird's call. Field notes are provisional: conjectures hazarded before the definitive meaning is determined. Field notes are personal, private: they are accounts of what happened to the note-taker when the thoughts were being made. Field notes, then, are also about process: 'Writing, rather than the written'.[2]

Strictly speaking, what follows aren't quite field notes: they were written retrospectively and they don't have the scrawling energy of a note written at the moment an observation is made or a thought is struck. What they are focused on,

---

1   Emerson, Fretz and Shaw 2001, 356.
2   Haas 2017, 23.

though, is the process of writing *The Flight of Birds*: a tracing of the oscillations between (sometimes contradictory) ideas; the marking out of discoveries made, digressions explored and surprises chanced upon. More importantly, they are discussions about the points of encounter between two 'fields' that made the writing possible: the discourses or disciplines we call 'fiction' and 'animal studies'. Neither of these fields have one single path running through them: they contain multiple, sometimes meandering tracks; they even crisscross and wind around each other. To labour the metaphor further, their paths sometimes run parallel to the fence line and sometimes jump the fence entirely. These field notes map out some of the ways I traversed the fields, moving from one field to the other and back again. In particular, they demonstrate the relationship between the subject matter and the form of my writing, and the ways the key concerns of animal studies stimulated or—to put it a better way—*animated* my writing. They are part of a broader discussion about the role of fiction in engaging with the lives of nonhuman animals and the ways that fiction as a critical practice might contribute to the crucial discussions instigated by thinkers in animal studies. More specifically, these notes are an account of how I re-evaluated my creative project: from asking the question 'How can I write *about* birds?' to 'How can I write *with* birds?'—or even towards the more significant question: 'What might a bird's story look like?'

Encounters on the Bridge

The first birds I noticed were three black cockatoos flying overhead as I walked over the highway bridge near North Wollongong railway station. I was a jumble of worries. The everyday anxieties about being late or the latest work crisis were tied up with long-term fears about the future: economic, political, ecological. Cars clanged and hissed as they passed me. I could see schoolkids pinching and shoving each other on the train platform below. Doors slammed in the carpark. Underneath the train tracks was a stormwater drain, tentacled with graffiti, the remnant of a creek. As I plodded along, the cockatoos wafted down from the open sky and hovered at eye level. They were so close I could have reached out and touched them. As I watched them suspended in the air, I could see their charcoal wings were fringed against vibrant blue, the dirty-yellow smudge on the side of their faces, the glinting beaks, the black eyes ringed with silver. Then, one by one, the cockatoos dropped lower, under the bridge, and flew away. They were bewitching, remote, oblivious. They were in another world.

This almost-encounter with the cockatoos stayed in my mind's eye for some time before I knew what to do with it. I'd be walking the dogs or sauntering to the station and I'd linger on the crest of the bridge, hoping they'd soar past again. They didn't, but I did start noticing—by sight and by sound—the multitude of birds in my neighbourhood. Members of the

Illawarra Birders group have sighted over 350 species of birds in the area, citing over seventy species of birds as 'common'.[3] Pelicans and silver gulls in the harbour, white-faced herons and sooty oystercatchers on the rocks; galahs and kookaburras in the garden, catbirds and brush turkeys along the track up the escarpment. Unlike the office worker, Peter, in the story 'Magpies', I'm not a twitcher. I often don't know the right names for birds. A man I met when I was out walking one day berated me when I referred to a pied currawong as a magpie. The birds I'd see poking at the rubbish near McDonald's, I'd call 'those yellow-faced birds with their legs on backwards' (I think they're masked lapwings). I distinguished bird songs by placing them in the categories 'the calls that I like' (the warble of the butcher bird, the soft coo-coo-coo of the wonga pigeon) and 'the calls that shouldn't be blaring at four in the bloody morning' (the wattlebird and the koel and the one I can't identify that goes 'dak-DAKK dak-DAKK dak-DAKK', interminably).

And my imagination still circled around the bridge above North Wollongong station. To bring in another metaphor (and I will admit to the problems of metaphor later in these notes), my mind was spinning a tangled web. The web was messier than the ones I'd get caught up in on my evening walks with the dogs. These threads wove in and around me as I began to

---

3   The Illawarra Birders group, in collaboration with Wollongong City Council, has complied a document that records the diverse avian life of the Illawarra. See https://bit.ly/2Dfwbsd

conceive of the project that became *The Flight of Birds*. They formed unbreakable knots of inspiration, they frayed and confused my thoughts, they even lured me to places I hadn't imagined.

I can pick out four threads that came out of my knotted thinking. The first thread was the desire to see what birds see, to engage with what the cultural geographer Steve Hinchliffe calls 'making oneself available ... to the world of the bird.'[4] This was more than just a self-centred wish to escape my petty worries, to soar away from my earth-bound human existence. I wanted to respect birds as agents of their own experience. The second thread seemed to pull in the opposite direction. Literature is full of cross-species confrontations that emphasise the impossibility of understanding nonhuman animals, particularly birds. In his poem 'Poor Matthias', Matthew Arnold writes that: '[Birds] live beside us, but alone [from us] ... What they want, we cannot guess'; more recently, the filmmaker Ceri Levy says of birds: 'They are poetic creatures that almost work in an ethereal space to us. Inhabiting our world, but also inhabiting some other, unseen space, a place we can only glimpse ... one that we can never exist in.'[5] Could it be possible for me—as a writer, as a human—to inhabit the world of birds? Or would I always be ruled by my own anthropocentrism?

---

4   Hinchcliffe 2010, 34.
5   Arnold 1945, 457; Brower 2013, 60–61.

The third thread was to make a correlation between the particular and the planetary. The place where I saw the black cockatoos is coloured by my own fears about the future of the planet. Wollongong is a post-industrial city, an intersection of what we could call 'nature' and human attempts to control it. The city is framed to the west by an ancient crumbling escarpment; to the east by the expanse of the Pacific Ocean; to the south and north by steelworks and coal mines. Central to many discussions between friends and colleagues in this place is the issue of environmental change: what we have done to cause it and how it might affect our surroundings.[6] These conversations usually focus on the overwhelming scale of what we're facing, and our incomprehension of it. We could call this feeling a kind of planetary grief, a sense of totalising helplessness. We exemplify Isabelle Stengers' recognition that 'Amongst us there are those who know they ought to "do something" but are paralysed by the disproportionate gap between what they are capable of and what is needed.'[7] In the environmental sciences, birds are often used to predict changes in ecosystems, acting as what has been called 'barometers of changing habitats and environmental health'.[8]

---

6   Some of these conversations are recorded in *100 Atmospheres*, a multi-authored book by MECO [forthcoming] Open Humanities Press. See also the writing of the Illawarra author, Catherine McKinnon, whose work *Storyland* depicts a projected image of Wollongong transformed by extreme weather and sea-level rises.

7   Stengers 2015, 22–23.

8   Caballero and Ekeberg 2014, 498. See also Raghuram et al 2016; Vollstädt et al 2017.

In my thinking about birds, I began to imagine stories that might portray the ways our everyday actions are indicators of the way we treat our planet on larger scales. A suburban road cuts through a bird's natural habitat; a quick trip to the supermarket makes evident the violence we inflict on other animals; people's treatment of their family pet shows up the hierarchy of the animals we value, and those we do not. Perhaps I could also tell stories that, even if they don't reduce the ecological crisis, might ameliorate the sense of totalising paralysis. A moment with one bird—or three swooping under a North Wollongong highway bridge, or a flock soaring over the ocean—may allow us to engage with planetary grief in an active and productive way: our care for other species might make the need to 'do something' more imperative.

From these thoughts, you can see the fourth thread being woven: I wasn't just watching birds, I was beginning to devise stories around them and, perhaps, with them. The stories I imagined were, to use Adam Trexler's words, a way of representing 'the emotional, aesthetic, and living experience of the Anthropocene'.[9]

Four thoughts intertwined with each other: a desire to understand birds on their own terms; a questioning of my own position in relation to birds; a sense that the particular can't be separated from the planetary; and a hope that telling stories about another species might draw attention to the planetary,

9   Trexler 2015, np.

overcome anthropocentrism *and* give agency to birds. Too much netting over the birds of the Illawarra, perhaps.

In order to help me unravel the tangled web, I started taking note of the ways that others have written about birds. Of particular importance were the scholarly investigations from the broad disciplinary area that has come to be called animal studies.[10] Interestingly, as I read through these writings it became evident that the threads running through my imagination are also woven into the active discussions in animal studies. Central to the field is an imperative to make problematic the dominance of human vision. Philip Armstrong points out that scholars in animal studies 'are interested in attending not just to what animals mean to humans, but what they mean themselves; that is, to the ways in which animals might have significances, intentions and effects quite beyond the designs of human beings'.[11] Susan McHugh's complex readings of works like *Animal Farm* and *Babe* challenge the notion that 'animals are only literary as human subjects' and rethinks the textual

---

10 I acknowledge that some critics prefer other disciplinary markers, such as 'human–animal studies' and 'critical animal studies'. I have chosen the broader 'animal studies' to highlight the field as a site for multiple questions springing from multiple discourses and disciplines: from animal rights and critical animal studies, to animal ethology and ethnography to literary, geographical or philosophical animal studies. For a more thorough survey of the multiple modes of animal studies, see McCance 2013, Marvin and McHugh 2014, and Herman 2014.

11 Armstrong 2008, 2.

animals as 'something other than metaphors or as more than just humans in animal suits'.[12] In doing so, we may be able to respect animals on their own terms.

Nevertheless, questions still arise about our position as humans and the effect it has on the animals we are thinking or writing about. McHugh, in discussion with Garry Marvin, concedes that 'it is important to remember that we cannot talk, write, or even think about animals in any sense except in the context of humans, if only because we can never get away from ourselves'. Marvin expands on this, writing: 'I am very wary about what I ... can say about animals per se, outside of how they figure and are configured in the human imagination or in terms of human relationships with them ... How does one avoid anthropocentrism when the only languages available to write about animals are human languages?'[13] As in all critical discourses, we must always be aware of the dangers of speaking for others.[14] But critics in the field also challenge the idea that human language is 'naturally' anthropocentric. In her examination of animals and ecological ethics, Val Plumwood makes an important distinction between physical locatedness and ideological interests. By marking out the difference she demonstrates that anthropocentrism is a discursive position as

---

12 McHugh 2006; McHugh 2009a; McHugh 2009b; McHugh 2017, 18.
13 Marvin and McHugh 2014; McHugh 2017, 17, 14.
14 For more detailed discussion, see Linda Alcoff's 'The Problem of Speaking for Others'. Alcoff 1991–1992.

opposed to an intrinsically human trait. Plumwood illustrates the ways anthropocentrism uses the same hegemonic controls as other centric epistemologies such as sexism or racism. These dominant discourses internalise oppressive modes: they link an ideology to a body. I'm a man, *therefore* I must be androcentric; I'm European, *therefore* I must be Eurocentric; I'm human, *therefore* I must be anthropocentric. Of particular note is Plumwood's analysis of the stories we tell of others as 'unknowable', as in the assertions from Arnold and Levy I have cited above. These kinds of (non)interpretations create a polarising structure: we are known; the Other is mysterious, unreadable. They lead to further 'inevitable' conclusions: the Other is 'inessential', 'unworthy', 'not worth noticing'.[15] Plumwood asks us to view human–nonhuman relations not as dichotomies of exclusion but as interactions that permit the location and interests of both groups: through this reconception we might be able to 'go beyond' the ideological presumptions of our 'locatedness'.[16]

Several thinkers in animal studies propose models to think beyond the human discursive position. For instance, Wendy Woodward offers a mode of re-reading animal stories that

---

15   Plumwood 2002, 130–134, 106–109, 99, 104.

16   Plumwood argues that our thinking about nonhumans may be said to 'involve some form of enlargement of or going beyond our own location and interests, but it does not require us to *eliminate* either our own interest or our own locatedness'. Plumwood 2002, 132–133.

emphasises the encounter *with* rather than the speaking *for*. We need a commitment, she argues, to a 'deterritorializing of our own subjectivities'. Using Derrida's interaction with his cat as her starting point, Woodward (re)positions animals in human stories as 'agentive' and advocates for 'the naked truth of every gaze', human and nonhuman. Through the gaze, nonhumans, like humans, can be seen as 'irreplaceable living being[s]' rather than 'exemplars' of a species.[17] In what ways, Woodward asks, can we sympathise with animals on their own terms?

Animal studies also makes explicit the link between the lives of animals and planetary concerns. Many critics expose the 'carbon hoofprint' of killing animals for food (eighteen percent of global greenhouse-gas emissions, and increasing).[18] As critics like Plumwood and John Sorenson have noted, the killing of animals and the subjugation of land for farming has also led to significant biodiversity loss and ecological collapse.[19] This devastation has an emotional as well as an environmental effect. Writing about animal killing and extinction, Deborah Bird Rose conceives of our species 'howling into, and from, an extremely complicated place: the shadow of the Anthropocene'.

---

17 Woodward 2008, 2–4; 166. See also Derrida's 'The Animal that Therefore I Am (More to Follow)' 2002. Derrida's encounter with his cat has been read in many different ways: it is, as Cary Wolfe puts it, 'a moment either famous or notorious, depending on your point of view'. Wolfe 2008, 36.
18 I borrow the phrase 'carbon hoofprint' from McHugh 2010, 187.
19 Sorenson 2014, viii, xi; Plumwood 2002, 2–3.

She continues: 'Our howling starts from within, from empathy, grief and much more, and it reverberates beyond us'; 'we howl in the dark for the loss that surrounds us now, and for all that is coming'.[20]

Even more interesting for me is the fourth thread running through animal studies, which has already wound its way into the discussion: the hypothesis that the kinds of stories we tell might counter the violent ways we interact with animals. Thom van Dooren muses that 'telling stories has consequences: one of which is that we will inevitably be drawn into new connections, and with them, new accountabilities and obligations'. McHugh concurs, stating that: 'The future of such communities hinges on aesthetic perhaps more than on any other transfigurations of biopolitical life—that is, on just this sort of creative cultivation of the conceptual places where individuals, species, and other living agents meet.' Fiona Probyn-Rapsey makes the case that telling stories about animals can provide a space for animals' agency to be affirmed. She proposes that 'telling "stories" of animals and telling animal's stories turns "behaviour" and/ or "instinct" into culture'; or, to put it more directly, 'The idea that *they have stories* complements the idea that *they have subjectivities.*'[21] This final thread leads us back to the first one: that animals matter on their own terms.

---

20 Rose 2013, 1.
21 van Dooren 2014a, 10; McHugh 2010, 197. Probyn-Rapsey 2014, 4.

Perhaps, then, it's two threads winding round each other: the interrelation between stories about animals and animals themselves. Van Dooren and Rose, talking about moments of encounter between animals (including humans), make the claim that 'animals, sites, and stories all shape, and are shaped by, entangled and circulating patterns of intra-action'.[22] The black cockatoos navigate the bridge and the railway posts and human figures, weaving a spatial 'story' through the air; the human, meeting the silvery gaze of the birds, replies with his own story. Stories aren't just recountings of events but manifestations of convergence and divergence: between subjects, across species, through ideas.

As I began to construct the stories within *The Flight of Birds*, the alertness to this intertwining relationship became crucial to the broader philosophical approach I took in my project: I began to consider the ways that writing practice might contribute to animal studies, not just as an object of study but as a critical act in itself. Before I discuss the specific 'applications' of the ideas of animal studies to my stories, I will outline the ways that I believe fiction as a critical practice can work with animal studies in an active and productive way.

---

22   van Dooren and Rose 2012, 1.

Encounters in Fiction

Of course, not all animal studies scholars think of fiction in a favourable light. In his memoir *The Philosopher and the Wolf*, Mark Rowlands asserts that storytelling is one of the most destructive aspects of human culture, justifying acts of violence towards and domination against those we determine are inferior or unworthy. It is this conceptualisation of storytelling that has led Dawne McCance to declare that 'fiction is not the place in which to deal with ... things on an ethical level.'[23] Despite these assertions, other critics in the field do see a place for fiction in the discourse of animal studies. Woodward argues:

> [we] can tell stories of animals which are salutary and ethical due to the sympathetic imaginations of the writers and their characters. This sympathetic imagination [can then] be extended to the 'real' animals in all their embodiedness and in all their presence so that humans do not denigrate and mistreat them as inferior others.[24]

The study of literature has been central to the project of animal studies in the humanities, whether as readings of animal metaphors in works like Mario Ortiz-Robles' *Literature*

---

23 Rowlands 2009, 2; McCance 2013, 135.
24 Woodward 2008, 168.

and Animal Studies or in the more complex analyses of the interrelations between discursive and actual animals in the work of Woodward, McHugh and Cary Wolfe. Ortiz-Robles draws attention to the ways we might use fiction to 'imagine alternatives to the way we live with animals'; more radically, McHugh views the animal–literary nexus as a site for 'intervention'. Her work reconfigures literary analysis to demonstrate that human–animal relations 'raise representational concerns about the interrelations of textual and political forms' within our broader culture. These kinds of deployments with literature as a form of reading certainly can be seen, as David Herman puts it, to 'question assumptions about the primacy of the human—and call for a rethinking of practices based on such assumptions'.[25]

But how might writing as a *practice* be deployed to activate the critical imperative to 'conceptualise and respond to "real", embodied nonhuman animals'?[26] One way might be to include creative strategies alongside critical ones; in other words, to write fictocritically. Anna Gibbs establishes that fictocriticism deploys fictional devices to 'stage' theoretical positions; Stephen Muecke puts it more simply, saying: 'Fictocriticism tells a story and makes an argument at the same time'.[27] It's been described as an 'undisciplined' form, a mode of writing that moves

---

25 Ortiz-Robles 2016, xi; McHugh 2009b, 491; McHugh 2006; McHugh 2011, 28, 126; Herman 2011, 159.
26 Woodward 2008, 8.
27 Gibbs 2013, 309; Muecke 2008, 113.

between different registers and genres—formal and informal, disinterested and personal, factual and fictional.[28] It's a mode I've adopted in at least two of the stories in *The Flight of Birds*. Both 'Six Stories about Birds' and 'Do You Speak My Language?' move between two discursive modes: fictional narration placed next to scholarly and archival material like articles in *Science* or High Court transcripts. The 'fictional' element is often deployed at the moment when an idea becomes too urgent for the writer to embed it in the world of the story. Rather, the writer must use storytelling devices to immerse the reader in the ideas: to provoke what Helen Flavell describes as 'an empathetic engagement' with the theoretical material.[29] Think of the way Virginia Woolf in 'A Room of One's Own' violates 'the first duty of a lecturer—to hand you after an hour's discourse a nugget of pure truth to wrap between the pages of your notebooks and keep on the mantelpiece forever' and instead tells the more engaging story of Judith Shakespeare, which releases them to 'draw … their own conclusions'.[30] Fictocriticism, then, has what Gerrit Haas calls an 'interventionist edge': an intention to engage the reader with a political position in an intimate way through fictional tropes. Haas traces the 'marginal/ised provenances' of fictocriticism as it is currently understood, particularly the way its formal approaches borrow from feminist, postcolonial and queer theories. He states

---

28   Haas 2017, 102.
29   Flavell 2004, 296.
30   Woolf 2001, 1–2.

that fictocritical writing 'directs attention to our dominant textual practices and the particular functions they often serve within our wider discursive practices, such as differential identity formation in relation to the world and others'.[31]

Several critics in animal studies take this approach. The most obvious example is J.M. Coetzee's *The Lives of Animals*, which presents a range of ideas crucial to animal studies through a framework of the fictional world of Elizabeth Costello.[32] But the writing of Freya Mathews, Deborah Bird Rose, Alphonso Lingis and Ian Wedde (to name only a few) also place personal anecdotes and storytelling modes alongside more conventionally scholarly analysis.[33] Indeed, even Rowland's work, which directly questions stories as productive tools, can be seen as a form of fictocriticism: in the same way that he and the wolf Brenin 'walk together', sharing and challenging each other's world views, so too does Rowland's text let storytelling travel alongside more overtly academic theorisation. These creative approaches provide critics with different ways to explore the complicated ideas at work in animal studies.

Discussing *The Lives of Animals*, Cora Diamond proposes that Coetzee creates a space for his readers to approach

---

31 Haas 2017, 99, 19, 9.
32 Coetzee 2016.
33 See Mathews 1997; Rose 2013; Lingus 2003; Wedde 2007.

the 'profound disturbance' we feel when faced with animal death and the killing of animals in a much more embodied and sympathetic way.[34] Unfortunately, the explicit mode of fictocriticism does not always have the desired effect. Marjorie Garber suggests that, rather than sanctioning a more embodied engagement with the ideas of animal studies, Coetzee's strategy might in fact 'insulate' the reader from Costello's views—they are, after all, only the ideas of a fictional character. Similarly, Elizabeth Anker finds the shifting registers in the text a 'struggle' and 'hopelessly muddled'.[35]

In order for fictocriticism to function as a useful rhetorical approach in animal studies, perhaps a more integrated approach to the fiction–theory nexus needs to be taken up. As Marvin and McHugh put it: 'To account for these nonhuman agency forms, we have to change our ways of doing academic work and, at the same time, work to shift notions of what constitutes creative practice as well.'[36] Arriving at a more expansive way of thinking about fictocriticism, the poet and performer Hazel Smith promotes 'a fusion and exchange of critical and creative writing'. 'Ideally,' she writes, fictocritical writing should create

---

34 Diamond 2008, 53, 56.
35 Garber in Coetzee 2016, 79; Anker 2011, 184. Granted, Anker also concedes that 'it [is] precisely their ostensible confusion that lends them value, reflecting the same productive antagonisms that have spawned the multiplying scholarship on Coetzee's text'.
36 Marvin and McHugh 2014.

'a symbiotic relationship between theory/criticism and creative work, so that they feed into, and illuminate each other.' With Roger Dean, a composer/improviser who specialises in music cognition, Smith envisions a way of using critical material in a creative work in a more immersive way, an approach they call 'research-led practice'. In research-led practice, the practitioner begins with a theoretical concept or scholarly idea and then investigates it using creative practice as a methodological strategy. In this conceptualisation of fictocriticism, theoretical ideas manifest themselves in a creative work not in dialogue with (or opposition to) the fictional mode, but fiction becomes a critical practice in its own right. The theory is *in* the writing: a thinking *through* writing.[37]

This mode of fictocriticism—what I call 'implicit fictocriticism'—may be a more productive way to engage with these particular ideas of animal studies than the more explicitly fictocritical approach. According to Smith and Dean, in implicit fictocritical writing ideas can be transformed to inspire new ways of thinking about ethical dilemmas, and perhaps find alternative ways of interacting with the worlds around us.[38] This can include the nonhuman world. As an example of implicit fictocriticism, consider Coetzee's novel *Disgrace*, which as Wolfe notes can be seen as an alternative version of *The Lives of Animals*. In his comparison of the

---

37 Smith 2005, 204, 205; Smith and Dean 2009, 7.
38 Smith and Dean 2009, 3.

texts, Wolfe observes that, like *The Lives of Animals,* a significant concern of *Disgrace* is 'our moral responsibilities to nonhuman animals'.[39] Unlike the explicitly fictocritical approach taken by Coetzee in his representation of Elizabeth Costello, though, the tactic in *Disgrace* is to present the theoretical ideas through scene and action. For instance, late in the novel the narrative concentrates on the trauma the protagonist David Lurie faces when he participates in the killing of 'superfluous canines' at an animal welfare clinic. Coetzee describes Lurie's reaction:

> He had thought he would get used to it. But that is not what happens. The more killing he assists in, the more jittery he gets. One Sunday evening, driving home in [his daughter's] kombi, he actually has to stop at the roadside to recover himself. Tears flow down his face that he cannot stop; his hands shake.[40]

Wolfe submits that the trauma is all the more powerful because it is presented not as a declaration of an idea, but an embodiment. 'It's an "unspeakability"', Wolfe argues, 'not only the unspeakability of how we treat animals ... but also the unspeakability of the limits of our own thinking in confronting such a reality.' It's theory *through* experience, *through* writing.

---

39   Wolfe 2008, 5–6.
40   Coetzee 2010, 142–143.

As Coetzee says elsewhere, 'There are no bounds to the sympathetic imagination ... we understand by immersing ourselves and our intelligence in complexity.'[41] While I think this distinction between the two texts is probably too simplistic (I am as moved by Elizabeth Costello's articulated grief as I am by David Lurie's mute howl), I do believe that there is room for more implicit fictocriticism as part of the rhetorical strategies of animal studies. In this, I echo the sentiments of artist and activist Sue Coe, who states that: 'It's never one thing that creates change. It's multiple exposures to different facets that creates a different heart.' Such an embedded fictional approach to the complexities of animal studies might also support McHugh's call to 'locat[e] narrative as a zone of integration' whereby 'the content questions regarding animals and animality arise inextricably from this play with narrative form.'[42]

In *The Flight of Birds* I have used McHugh's notion of a 'zone of integration' as a crucial strategy to conceive and shape the stories I tell with birds. Each of the twelve stories that comprise my novel takes as its starting point a question or concern raised by critics in animal studies (or related fields) and tries to present a different facet of the idea *through* fiction. Some of the texts and ideas I draw upon will be well known

41 Coetzee 2016, 35, 62.
42 Coe quoted in Aloi and Bennison 2011, 109; McHugh 2011, 2.

to readers in the field; some sit perhaps at the edges or even cross the fence from other adjacent fields: animal behaviour and ethology, posthumanism, art and literary theory. In the writing I've undertaken what Haas calls 'speculative and rhetorical exercises' around a particular concept.[43] It is not my intention to challenge or undermine arguments raised in the field of animal studies; rather, I aim to take these arguments and explore what happens when they are transposed into fiction. Each story is a 'testing place' taking different, even contradictory, propositions and exploring the ways they might be amplified in the fictional space.

By taking this experimental approach, I'm drawing upon a formal strategy that can also be found in and around animal studies. In her investigations into art and animality, Elizabeth Grosz speaks of thinking speculatively when it comes to engaging with animal practices.[44] Grosz's project resonates strongly with *The Flight of Birds* for other reasons, too. Her tactic is to subvert the view of human as a more privileged form of animal, and human art as a practice reliant on this privilege. She asks: What happens when 'we place the human within the animal'? Under this hypothesis, art becomes 'the consequence, the unexpected, unpredictable effect, of the coupling of a milieu or territory

---

43 Haas 2017, 144.
44 Grosz 2011, 170. She admits elsewhere that 'the beauty of being a philosopher ... is that I can make these bold conjectures. If they don't work, okay, I've learned something, but I think it's really worth exploring all the range of possible explanations of what art and creativity and construction are'. Copeland 2005.

with a body': a result of an experience and, more importantly, an encounter in a place. By thinking about creative practice *as* animal practice, Grosz suggests that we may be able to see beyond 'the concepts, meanings, and values art represents' and instead immerse ourselves in art's 'capacity to affect and transform life.' We agree to contemplate 'what art does' as well as 'what it means.'[45] An acceptance of Grosz's approach in relation to my project moves me beyond the initial questions I asked on the bridge (How can I write about birds?) to speculations about the lived knowledges of birds.

In the next section of these notes, I will outline the particular 'speculative and rhetorical exercises' I undertook in each of the stories in the novel. The stories can be divided into two kinds of experiment. The first set of stories ('Flocking', 'Further to Fly', 'The Pecking Order', 'Magpies', 'And No Birds Sing' and 'Aves Admittant') are direct applications of ideas emerging from animal studies in their creative exploration of the relations of violence and care (sometimes simultaneous) between humans and birds. The second set of stories ('What He Heard', 'Six Stories', 'Call and Response', 'Do You Speak My Language?', 'Nocturne' and 'The Flight of Birds') ask broader questions, following Grosz's approach. Can we place the human within the animal? Can we think beyond the differences between humans and birds and begin to immerse ourselves in the world of birds? Or, to pose it as a writer's question: What might a bird's story look like?

---

45   Grosz 2011, 170; Grosz 2008, 44: Grosz 2011, 186.

Like all experiments, the stories don't always turn out the way I expected. Sometimes the ideas are overshadowed by the human characters' (and writer's) anthropocentric blind spots. Sometimes a critical point loses its urgency when absorbed by fiction. They are undoubtedly human stories and it is possible to read the represented birds merely as projections of the protagonist's psyche. Nonetheless, there is a concerted attempt to devise tactics to break this human control, and to discover glimpses of other subjectivities. As Plumwood says: 'Considering your own interests does not imply that you cannot also consider others' interests.'[46] I don't pretend to provide solid proofs, irrefutable answers to the questions I've posed. Indeed, one of the benefits of writing as a critical practice is that it provides sites of provocation rather than resolution. It allows for encounters.

Encounters in Flight

What He Heard

This story is my first attempt at putting into practice the question 'What might a bird's story look like?' It is informed by Jakob von Uexküll's notion of 'Umwelten' as described in his 'A Stroll Through the Worlds of Animals and Men' in which von Uexküll argues that the earth comprises habitats formed by

---

46   Plumwood 2002, 128.

the sensory values of particular animals or groups of animals.[47] An Umwelt creates a different 'relationship between a living subject and its object', unique to each animal's consciousness.[48] Part of the point of the story is that it is extremely difficult to get away from our own perceptions and preconceptions of the world. In other words, our understanding of our environment is tied to our own hegemonic 'centrisms'. The dog views the environment in the bush in terms of 'scent lines'. The human transforms the bush to reflect his own anxieties: eucalypts become 'talon-scratched', rocks are 'ossified'. But the story is also about reckoning with other ways to engage with the world, 'manifold and varied as the animals themselves'.[49] An Umwelt contains within it different sets of relations between species such as birds and flowers, and ticks and mammals. These change according to the needs of the agents contained within it. Building on von Uexküll, Grosz writes:

There are no stable objects, equally and always perceived in the same way for all living things; no one

47 von Uexküll 1957. Although not written for the field we now call animal studies, von Uexküll's text has inspired critics across animal ethology and critical theory, most notably Deleuze and Guattari's thinking around deterritorialisation and reterritorialisation, and Grosz's extensive use of the Umwelt to argue for connections between Darwin's notion of sexual selection and art as a form of animality.
48 von Uexküll 1957, 11.
49 von Uexküll 1957, 5.

sun, moon, or stars, just as there is no single space or field, time or rhythm, no universal within which we can locate all living things. One and the same object on entering different Umwelten becomes different. Each species perceives what it needs and can use from its world.[50]

What happens, then, if we consider a relationship to the space which is different to the human? Can we creatively imagine another animal's Umwelt? One of the things I determined very early on in the project as a whole was that I couldn't attempt to represent a bird's voice: this, I believe, could only lead to the clumsiest kind of 'speaking for'. Nevertheless, I was interested in providing spaces where we might imagine a nonhuman environment. What I have tried to create in 'What He Heard' is a meaningful space for the lyrebird to inhabit that also provides us, as humans, with an opportunity to perceive it. The story contains the only scene in the work as a whole where a human is not present.

The lyrebird is scratching the dirt in the gravelly corner. He lifts his head. His larynx vibrates. Out of his beak come three short notes. The second is microtonally higher than the first and third. This is followed by a long high trill. The noise he is making is

---

50 Grosz 2011, 175–176.

not full of sadness or pain. The lyrebird is not thinking about lost or abandoned children. His head pivots. The dwindling light points out a speck in the dirt. The lyrebird pecks and then he sings his song again.

Granted, the story is still written by a human and using a human mode of communication. But part of my strategy to avoid anthropocentric representation has been to allow for the bird's perspective to be acknowledged, even if it can't be realised. What the lyrebird is thinking is not depicted. Rather, readers are given the viewpoint in terms of negatives: 'the lyrebird is *not* thinking about lost or abandoned children'; his song 'is *not* full of sadness or pain'. Readers are kept on the outside of the lyrebird's pivoting head, but are given the opportunity to speculate on what the bird *might* be thinking. We could use this, as von Uexküll suggests, 'to build up the animal's specific world with them'.[51]

Six Stories about Birds, with Seven Questions

In order to consider what a bird's story might look like it is also necessary to determine the shape and function of human stories about birds. We can compare the two and show up the ways our stories undermine our relationships with birds, even those stories that aim to strengthen the connection. In this explicitly fictocritical work I uncover the myriad ways we

---

51   von Uexküll 1957, 13.

frame birds so that they are, to use Plumwood's conception of instrumentalism, 'denied, subsumed in or remade to coincide with human interests'.[52] The birds become helpers and punishers in fairy tales; sacred objects or fashion accessories or symbols of power in the stories we tell about our past; markers of spirituality and transcendence in our poetry and music. Even in ostensibly 'objective' scientific discourses, birds are remade within human structures of knowledge.

A larger framing device for 'Six Stories about Birds' is Adrian Franklin's essay 'Relating to Birds in Postcolonial Australia'.[53] Franklin carefully traces European settlers' interactions with Australian birds, before moving on to the founding of organisations like the Australasian Ornithologist Union in 1901 and the Gould League of Bird Lovers in 1909, with animals being seen as exemplars of the exotic bush to specimens that can be recorded and controlled. More important for my project is his examination of contemporary Australians' relationship with birds. Franklin presents a complex account of human–bird interactions: some establish an anthropocentric hierarchy of owner and pet; others present a potential for mutual care. In this they echo Grosz's vision of a spectrum of human–nonhuman interactions, from 'worlds they sometimes share with us, [to] worlds waiting to be invented, [to] worlds that may inform our understanding of our own inhabited worlds'.[54]

52 Plumwood 2002, 109.
53 Franklin 2007, 121–122.
54 Grosz 2011, 173.

'Six Stories about Birds' is also the place where I begin to explore a stylistic strategy around naming conventions in the novel, one which calls into question the decisions we make to name (or to not name) different animal species in fiction. My decision not to name the characters in 'What He Heard' (instead, referring to them as 'the man', 'the dog' and 'the lyrebird') may not be noticed by the reader, but the apparent inconsistency around naming in 'Six Stories about Birds' is more overt: humans remain unnamed, but the budgerigar is given the name 'Charlotte'. The decisions made by writers to name or not to name characters has been considered by literary theorists in many different, sometimes oppositional ways. For the purposes of my project I have drawn upon two critical arguments. The first is the premise that the act of not naming characters renders them powerless. Sam Sacks traces the ways that unnamed characters is a trope in a range of narratives about disempowered subjects: in dystopian fiction, in political parables, and in stories that focus on 'those treated as background extras in the primary story lines of history'.[55] In a slightly different way, D.A. Miller points up a hierarchy of value implicit in the naming conventions in realist writing. He argues that realism divides characters into two categories: 'narratable' and 'non-narratable'. Narratable characters are those central to the narrative world, whose histories and thoughts must therefore be included in as much detail as

---

55   Sacks 2015.

possible; while non-narratable characters are those whose histories are not elucidated, whose thoughts are not explored or, in some cases, whose names are not even worth knowing.[56] In the early drafting stages of *The Flight of Birds* it became clear to me that the protagonist's grief places him in such a state that precludes his own sense of worth; as such, he does not deem himself worthy of narration. (This will become explicit in later stories like 'And No Birds Sing': the narration is full of provisional statements like 'He's not sure'; 'It could be'—so much so that the character almost-admits that 'there's a smooth surface between himself and th[e] knowledge [of himself]').

But if I wasn't going to name the other protagonists, why name Charlotte? Other critics argue that the act of naming another subject (real or fictional) can in fact be seen as a form of domination, what Sigrid King calls naming's 'link to the exercise of power'.[57] Historically, certain political organisations have used the naming (or, more accurately, re-naming) of oppressed groups to assert a discursive authority over them: European governments in the eighteenth and nineteenth centuries changing Jewish names to regulate tax collection; US slave owners changing Africans' names to indicate ownership. The names inscribed on the individuals were often ironic (Washington, Jefferson) or belittling (Niemand/nobody, Wanzreich/rich in bedbugs). In fiction, writers use similar

---

56 Miller 1981, 110–113.
57 King 1990, 683.

tactics to push their characters into comic positions (Dickens' 'Barnacle' family in *Little Dorrit*, for instance), expose their shortcomings through ironic counterpoint (in the same novel 'Edmund Sparkler' is a dimwitted social climber), or even to denigrate (the frivolously named 'Tattycoram' for the Meagles' replacement daughter/plaything). As King notes, these naming practices are a form of subjugation through which the characters find 'only limitation'.[58]

In the context of the representation of animals, both of these theorisations—to name or not to name—hold particular potency. The decision not to name an animal can be seen as an act of devaluing the animal's specific identity. In the child's game of 'Animal, Vegetable, Mineral', nonhuman animals are most often referred to in generic terms. A human may be located as 'William Shakespeare' or 'Marie Curie', but nonhumans are usually 'an elephant' or 'a rhinoceros', rather than a particular mammal living on the plains of the Eastern Cape of South Africa. Rouben Cholakian calls this an 'absorption' of the singular into the collective, of the specific into the general.[59]

Part of my project has been to treat humans in the same way: to distance readers from the human subjects, perhaps even to encourage readers to regard the human characters as zoological specimens. A young man sitting in a granny flat

---

58   King 1990, 684.
59   Cholakian 1992, 217.

that seems like a cage; a grown man devising more discursive cages for himself. Conversely, on the rare occasions when I do name animals the act of naming serves to subjugate or control them. Charlotte is one of only two characters named in the novel. In the story, several names are considered for the budgerigar, each of them working to undermine her identity: from the infantilising 'Bunty' to the bizarrely reclassifying choices of 'Tiger' or 'Zebra'. Once Charlotte is chosen (an oblique reference to another fictional animal), this becomes a fixed term for the bird, overriding even her own corporeality: when one bird dies, the name simply transfers to another bird's body.

The other individual named in *The Flight of Birds* is Peter, the hapless worker in the story 'Magpies'. Like Charlotte, Peter's agency is continuously undermined: talked about rather than talked with. The narrator reflects: 'When he's out of earshot— or when we assume he's out of earshot—our conversation turns towards him.' The naming of Peter separates him from the collective camaraderie of the office workers; in Cholakian's words, 'collectivization serves a depersonalizing purpose: it defines a primordial lack and original hurt'.[60] In this way, 'Six Stories about Birds' begins a larger conversation about the stories we tell about all animals—human and nonhuman—and the damage our stories can cause.

---

60 Cholakian 1992, 218.

Call and Response

'Call and Response' returns to von Uexküll's idea of Umwelten, this time concentrating on the environments made by aural perception. In his essay 'Why Look at Animals?' John Berger presents a vision of the human–nonhuman confrontation in which two species look 'across a similar, but not identical, abyss of non-comprehension'.[61] But what happens if, rather than looking, we *listen* to nonhuman animals?

Here, I imagine two ways we could bridge the aural abyss. The first is to conceive a cross-species harmony: a song that incorporates all of 'nature'. In this, it resonates with the ornithologist F.S. Mathews' belief that 'birds with their music are the revelation of a greater world, one with just such a boundless horizon as that which we view from the mountain's summit marvelling that it is indeed the same narrow world we live in'.[62] The other is to assert a combative relationship between Umwelten, one which Frédéric Neyrat says 'humans tend to deny their precarious status as living beings intertwined with the becoming of the ecosphere'.[63] Neither of these is adequate: in the story the protagonist struggles to find an authentic way to perform what Alex Aisher and Vinita Damodaran call 'the multispecies assemblages that come together in place'.[64]

---

61 Berger 2009, 14.
62 Mathews 2004, xi.
63 Neyrat 2016, 36.
64 Aisher and Damodaran 2016, 36.

But how might we do this? In 'Call and Response', I highlight the inadequacies of our representations of nonhuman voices. The narrator makes a range of comparisons to try to describe the bird calls he hears. These analogies are deliberately clumsy, phrases that would make his 'literary mother roll over in her grave':

One call sounded like the release of a half-filled balloon, the spittly plastic ends flapping together as it zips around the room. One trebled like a baby giggling; another, a polite cough: short, tentative, as if it was asking permission to join in the fun. Another was a melodious metal detector: slow metronomic beeps and then, as it neared its target, increasing in tempo and delight. It was impossible to get the descriptions right. One was R2D2; another was Monkey from the TV show, whistling for his cloud. Another, an off-kilter Mr Whippy van: half a phrase of 'Für Elise' and then a sudden dissonant clang.

These analogies don't seem to affect the birds in the bush, but one bird in the story is harmed by symbolic representations. When the human is kept awake by the call of a koel the bird is subsumed into images that are just as clumsy as the comparisons of the birds in the bush, but these ones are also unsettling and violent: the call hurts 'like a migraine that was gripping my cheekbones', it 'gashes' and 'hacks' and 'lacerates'.

By imposing these images onto the bird's call the human is able to justify an actual assault against the bird: 'I grip the splintery handle and smash the broom into the trunk [of the koel's tree] … I hack the trunk again, and again, and then again.' The experiment I undertake here demonstrates the inadequacy of metaphor to create a meaningful space of encounter; we need other ways of depicting cross-species attentiveness. Perhaps we can return again to Grosz's speculative readings of nonhuman practices. Grosz conceives the songbird's call as 'the opening up of the world itself to the force of taste, appeal, the bodily, pleasure, desire—the very impulses behind all art'.[65] The narrator of 'Call and Response' is still trapped by his own linguistic snarls, but Grosz gives me another means of thinking about the way we might write stories about birds. In challenging the distinction we conventionally make between human and nonhuman art production, I might begin to change our way of thinking, from 'How can I write about birds?' to 'What might a bird's story look like?' or, in this case, 'What might a bird's song sound like?'

In the final moments perhaps the koel is able to free himself from the discursive control of the narrator. The narrator can't stop the koel from calling out and, defeated, the human stumbles back into his house. The koel is left alone 'crying into the void, waiting for a response'. It's only in the last sentence of the story that the word 'koel' is used to

---

65   Grosz 2008, 39.

describe the bird—although this is a human name it is better than having his song called a 'lacerating whoop'. The bird, on his own, and on his own terms, keeps calling. To build on Woodward's discussion of the meeting points between humans and other animals, moments like these are 'surely indicative not of the inscrutability of the animals themselves but of the humans' inability to respond to being addressed by a nonhuman animal'.[66]

Flocking

One of the focuses of the story 'Flocking' is the ways we use groups and communities to make us feel safe, but also the ways these collectives can trap us in confining systems of meaning. The story is enlivened by an observation made by Philip Armstrong and Laurence Simmons in their work *Knowing Animals*. They point out that the concept of collective terms or nouns of multitude first came into language through the practices of mediaeval European hunters who used collective terms to characterise and control their prey.[67] But what happens to the subjects once they've been collected? Berger famously asks us to read Van Gogh's *Wheatfield with Crows* through the lens of 'this is the last painting he completed before he died'.[68] In my mind, the painting has already been infected with

---

66 Woodward 2008, 165–166.
67 Armstrong and Simmons 2007, 7–8.
68 Berger 1972, 27–28.

death: above the thick waves of yellow wheat hover a murder of crows. Why a 'murder'? How better to control nonhuman animals than to describe them in abstract and often disparaging nouns: a pitying of turtledoves, a siege of herons, a weight of albatrosses? The nouns 'demonise' the birds, transforming them into a threatening 'contagious transport of impersonal affects'. Armstrong and Simmons conclude that the birds don't operate as individuals but 'as one'; they have been discursively 'herded'. Collective nouns, then, are another example of human stories about birds.

How might humans come to understand this discursive control? How might we experience this in our own bodies? In 'Flocking', the human boy, like the birds, is incorporated into a range of collective nouns: the birds of the subtitles in the story, and also 'a seminar of students, a shuffle of colleagues, a kinship of a new family'. Like the birds, he becomes part of a discourse, 'paper-thin', not real.

Do You Speak My Language?

On the surface, 'Do You Speak My Language?' appears to be the story in the novel least concerned with the lived experiences of birds. The apparent focal point of the story—the court case brought against Men at Work—is an entanglement of human devising. However, moving alongside this discussion is a continuing exploration of the question 'What might a bird's story look like?' The emphasis here is on challenging the dichotomy human–animal and reconfiguring it into Grosz's notion of 'the human within the animal'. Thus, the question generates another: 'What might a human's voice sound like if we thought of it through avian terms?' As in 'Six Stories' I begin with the flipside question: 'What might a bird's voice sound like if we thought of it through human terms?' Many of the scholarly and cultural texts I include in the story value humans over birds, constructing a human-centred vision that is as narrow as the law's tight grasp on creative collaboration. Sarvasy's notion of 'warblish' is less focused on bird calls than it is on human manipulation of the calls into stories; the scientific accounts of kookaburra kinship make a point of comparing the birds' behaviour to human social structures.[69]

However, the fictocritical context also creates a space for these accounts to be viewed from multiple angles and thus undermine a singular hegemonic control. In order to promote a multifaceted conversation, I concentrate on a communicative act common to both humans and birds: that of repetition. In some contexts a repetition of a phrase or an idea is part of creative and collaborative processes (as in the singing of a round or chorus songs or intertextual homage) or an indicator of a community (as in shared language or intergenerational activities). In other contexts, though, repetition is treated punitively (as in cases of copyright infringement or mimicry

---

69   Sarvasy 2016; Baker 2014; Dalziell et al. 2015; Benichov et al. 2016.

used to deceive rival birds) or as a pathology (the spiralling thoughts of depression or obsessive-compulsive disorders). By intermingling these different ways of thinking in a 'speculative exercise' the work sparks new ways of thinking about the creative act—for both humans and birds. In the end, building on Jonathan Lethem's reading of language as a 'commons', it emphasises the productive ways we might consider connections and commonalities across species lines.[70] The question might become: 'What might a bird–human story look like?'

Further to Fly

One of the significant theoretical frames for this story is Mary Louise Pratt's notion of the 'contact zone', which enters into discussions about human–nonhuman interaction via Donna Haraway.[71] Pratt defines contact zones as meeting places between cultures; specifically points of 'highly asymmetrical relations of power', as in the relationship between invader and first inhabitants or masters and slaves. The contact zone is usually viewed as a discursive site, in which one person's culture is suppressed, transmogrified or even destroyed by another's. The contact zone I've created in my story is, initially at least, more literal—but it becomes discursive. What was

---

70 Lethem 2007.
71 Haraway adapts Pratt's concept in *When Species Meet* to examine 'how [cross-species] subjects are constituted in and by their relations to each other'. Haraway 2008, 216.

central for me in the story was the way the human takes this moment of impact and refashions it to erase the bird from his life story. 'Such are the dynamics of language, writing, and representation in contact zones,' Pratt states.[72] The stories we tell about our moments of contact with animals affect real animals. Many of us are able to recall 'The time I hit a ... [bird, or other nonhuman animal]', but the stories we tell to structure these events don't often change our future actions. Researchers into the effect of human–animal road accidents have shown that there is little or no correlation between human awareness of the violence cars can cause animals and the adoption of mitigation strategies to reduce these impacts.[73] Rather, what happens is that drivers tend to reduce the trauma by creating narratives that mitigate culpability ('It just jumped out at me') or obfuscate the death of the animal with a concern for something else ('The damage to the car was negligible'). Daniel Lunney argues that this creates 'a culture of denial'. Like the protagonist of 'Further to Fly', we raise a discursive shield to protect ourselves from facing the injury or death of another living being.

The later sections of the story make textually manifest Melissa Boyde's discussion of 'vested and invested interests' in the stories we tell about animals: the animals we choose to represent and the ones whose traces we remove from

---

72 Pratt 1991, 34–35.
73 Ramp et al 2016, np.

our narratives.[74] I employ what Raymond Malewitz calls 'self-cancelling language' to erase the bird from the human's perception of the moment. I use negative descriptions to describe the contact between the man and the rosella, even before the moment of impact. The first appearance of the flock of rosellas is presented in a state of confusion. The man can't see them because he is 'momentarily mesmerised by the flecks of dust in the air'; when they do come into his ine of sight he can only decipher parts of the birds, not the whole: 'their wings were flapping too fast, they were a dazzle of red and blue'. Even when he does take control of his vision, he is unable—or, more accurately, unwilling—to articulate the particular interaction between himself and the bird:

He wondered what that thump had been.
He had a fairly good idea what the thump had been.

The final sequence of the story takes the negative depiction to the extreme, as the man considers a range of possible narratives he could spin around the event—all the things that 'didn't happen':

He didn't move closer to the grille, kneel down in the dust and look into the bird's cloudy eyes. He didn't reach his hand past the sharp plastic and, gently, scoop out

---

74   Boyde 2013, 127, 132.

the broken body. He didn't take the bird and wrap it in a towel he kept in the glove compartment and he didn't take the bird to the vet in the next suburb.

During this process the bird waits 'for what was [really] going to happen', which is of course that the man constructs a story that minimises the impact of the death of the bird on the human's psyche: the bird's corpse is locked away behind a roller door and then erased from the man's consciousness. The man uses his linguistic power over the moment to justify and even forgive his violent act: he creates a story which justifies his decision not to take any action to alleviate the bird's suffering. In this moment the rosella 'is both held and not held', literally and narratively.[75]

By making explicit the discursive operation of denial I raise questions to change our actual interactions with animals with whose habitats we intersect.[76] In *The Lives of Animals*, Elizabeth Costello declares to her audience: 'Anyone who says that life matters less to animals than it does to us has not held in his hands an animal fighting for its life.'[77] Rose and van Dooren argue that we don't even need to hold dying animals to feel compassion for them. They state: 'The lives and deaths of [animals] … are here with us, entangled with ours, and

---

75 Malewitz 2014, 558.
76 Lunney 2012, np.
77 Coetzee 2016, 65.

short of ecocide they will remain so. Their presence can be understood as an ethical call, and the call can be experienced as a responsibility.[78]

The Pecking Order

'The Pecking Order' is a direct response to Carol J. Adams' conceptualisation of factory-farmed animals as 'absent referents'. I also draw on a range of scholarly material on the meat industry and human suppression of its violence, as well as studies of chickens: most obviously Annie Potts' *Chicken*, but also Ralph Acampora's 'Epistemology of Ignorance and Human Privilege', Karen Davis' 'Anthropomorphic Visions of Chickens Bred for Human Consumption', Potts and Armstrong's 'Picturing Cruelty: Chicken Advocacy and Visual Culture' and Hayley Singer's 'Writing the Fleischgeist'.[79]

'Behind every meal of meat,' Adams declares, 'is an absence: the death of the nonhuman animal whose place the meat takes.'[80] She elucidates a discursive process during which certain nonhumans shift from subjects to objects, and through which human cognition of animal suffering—and our complicity in their suffering—is eliminated. The process happens in a range of ways, both literal and linguistic. Factory farms and abattoirs, even when in close proximity to human

---

78 van Dooren and Rose 2012, 19.
79 Potts 2012; Acampora 2016; Davis 2014; Potts and Armstrong 2013; Singer 2016.
80 Adams 2014, 19.

places of living, are disguised or made invisible; dead animals are also packaged in such a way as to occlude their original source.[81] As a writer, I am interested in the way language comes into play to erase the subjectivity of the killed animal: 'to keep some*thing* from being seen as having been *someone*'.[82] Adams traces the ways that humans translate the murder of animals into culinary language. The slaughtered cow is turned into 'beef', the dead pig becomes 'pork'. In the case of birds, sometimes the original name is kept ('duck', 'turkey'), but their bodies are dismembered and reconstituted, so that 'many chickens' wings become chicken wings' or, worse, 'chicken nuggets'.

In the story, reinstating the suppressed meaning in the word 'chicken' changes the perspectives of two characters: the daughter chooses to no longer eat animal products, and the man realises his complicity in cultural behaviours around eating meat. The daughter's transformation occurs when she

---

81   See, for instance, the discussion in Tiffin 2017, 251 or the work of the artist Yvette Watt (discussed in Potts 2017). One of Watt's photographic series depicts factory farms as 'haunted' places, a place where animals are present, but can't be seen. Even the sites of abattoirs are rendered invisible. Watt tells a story of her intention to return to a factory farm to rephotograph it, but 'I couldn't find it to begin with. I found a farm near where I thought this one had been located, but it looked wrong … It took two more visits for the confusion to clear and for me to realise that I was looking at it [but hadn't recognised it]'. Quoted in Potts 2017, 77.

82   Adams 2006, 595.

works out the linguistic game humans play: that 'there's a *chicken* in the farmyard … and there's *chicken* you eat'. Once the daughter identifies the presence of the real animal she is able to see the violence we inflict on them. The man's relation to the absent referent is not so transformative; rather, his response demonstrates the ways in which the dominant-discursive conception of meat is so insidious: it's 'easier' (for the human) to choose to ignore the referent behind the signifier. Linda Martín Alcoff explains:

One of the key features of oppressive societies is that they do not acknowledge themselves as oppressive. Therefore, in any given oppressive society, there is a dominant view about the general nature of society that represents its particular forms of inequality and exploitation as basically just and fair, or at least the best of all possible worlds.[83]

The communal sites of the supermarket and the family backyard are used in the story to show up the 'best of all possible worlds' modern Australian humans have created. These are places of plenty and, more importantly, places that present the illusion of inclusion—where all (white, affluent) humans know their place. The man has experienced exclusion from social groups and tries to protect his daughter from this pain:

---

83   Alcoff 2007, 48.

'There are two words,' I wanted to say. 'There's part: the word you use when you're included, when you're in on the conversation. 'I'm part of the whole,' you might want to say. And there's part: when you leave the room, when you're cut away from the rest of the group, when a quadrangle of children sneer at you, when you don't know what happened on *The Goodies* last night, when someone catches you picking the bacon bits out of the potato salad.

Previously, the man has feigned amnesia as to why he continues to eat meat ('I don't remember what made me start eating it.'), but of course the story as a whole is an account of his remembering. To support this, in an attempt to keep the memory of the dead (animal) alive, I have structured the narrative to demonstrate, as Adams puts it, that even in the act of erasure 'the absent referent is both there and not there'.[84] Unlike in other stories in the novel—'Nocturne' or 'Call and Response', for example—I do not use section breaks to distinguish between temporal moments. Instead, the text is written as one long stream so that the different moments in the man's life are constantly 'present'. For instance, late in the story, two moments of hostility are brought together in successive paragraphs:

---

84 Adams 2010, 67.

'Made you step on the crack,' the boy guffawed.

'Tap tap tap tap,' my almost-friend sneered behind him.

My father-in-law said, 'What's got her goat?'

This deviation from conventional ways of marking the passage of time 'rub against readerly habits', as Haas puts it, displaying in an embedded the way that language can be manipulated to occlude unwanted meanings.[85] Similarly, the spectre of the man's father looms over his relationship with his daughter:

I watched her from across the table, licking off the gluey marinade to reveal the chlorine-white meat underneath, forcing the stringy flesh into her mouth. Her eyes glinting blackly, looking at me murderously.

My father watched me from across the table, his nails tapping against the marble.

Through this formal yoking, the man is not able to forget the traumatic referent hidden by the signifiers 'It's what we do in our family'. Despite all this, though, the chicken is still eaten, and the man still avoids thinking about the millions of birds suffering and dying for human gratification. In this story, the man is not able to free his consciousness from his own concerns to accept the lives of other animals. As Cary Wolfe argues: 'As

---

85   Haas 2017, 87.

long as this humanist and speciesist *structure* of subjectivization remains intact, and as long as it is institutionally taken for granted that it is all right to systematically exploit and kill nonhuman animals simply because of their species ...' then strategies like the justification of killing animals through the manipulation of language 'will always be available.'[86]

Nocturne

Whereas in other stories I have accommodated spaces for potentially meaningful cross-species encounters, in 'Nocturne' I take a different, even contradictory, approach. Some critics in the field counsel against any act of 'speaking for' nonhuman animals: this is based on a line of argument in broader critical theory that sees representations of others as 'discursively dangerous': an act that strengthens the speaker at the expense of the spoken-for.[87] While I think that, as Plumwood and Alcoff note, a speaking position is not inevitably imbued with hegemonic power, the 'speculative exercise' I undertake here is to explore the following premise: if I should not 'speak for' birds, what happens if I avoid representing them

---

86 Wolfe 1999, 117–118.
87 See, for instance, Armstrong's claim that 'novelists ... can never actually access, let alone reproduce what other animals mean on their own terms. Humans can only represent animals'. Armstrong 2008, 2. 'Discursively dangerous' is a term I borrow from Alcoff 1991–1992, 7.

entirely?[88] Might this encourage, as Armstrong suggests, 'significances, intentions and effects quite beyond the designs of human beings'?[89] What might this kind of story look like?

'Nocturne' explores this idea through the writing of the poet Mark Tredinnick. In his essay 'Days in the Plateau', Tredinnick relates an anecdote about driving on a track at night in the Blue Mountains:

> my lights picked out a shape on the tarmac. A shape that said *lump of wood*. I pulled alongside it. Thinking cat or possum. But it was frogmouth …
>
> I wound my window down, and she turned her amber eyes upon me without moving her head. She'd heard the car and seen the lights, and made of herself a broken branch. This is how frogmouths disappear. They raise their beaks and petrify.[90]

The sentence 'This is how frogmouths disappear' is the frame for the story: I test out ways that birds might make themselves disappear from the textual nets we cast over them.

---

88 Plumwood argues that 'human epistemic locatedness is not the same as anthropocentrism'. Plumwood 2002, 132. Alcoff states that 'it is not always the case that when others unlike me speak for me I have ended up worse off, or that when we speak for others they end up worse off'. Alcoff 1991–1992, 29.
89 Armstrong 2008, 2–3.
90 Tredinnick 2007, 138.

'Nocturne' refers to several stories we write that could be identified as discursively dangerous: from news articles to poetry. In the opening section the human does not interact with a real bird, only representations: 'He's seen pictures on the internet. Grumpy, crumpled faces, staring at the camera, enduring the human gaze.' The images of the frogmouth are deliberately envisioned through anthropocentric analogies: 'downturned old-man eyebrows'; 'beaks … wide and flat, like a schoolboy's cap'; 'torsos … like Banksia Men or fluffy boom mikes'. The birds are transformed into human playthings: their 'heads hinge open like a hand puppet'. The most damaging is the tale of the bird of sorrow, the nightjar who stands in for human depression.

As a counter to these narratives I create an opportunity for the frogmouth to fly away from the stories being told about her. In the story the human and a real frogmouth do not in fact cross paths. The story begins: 'He's never seen a tawny frogmouth, not in real life.' More importantly, at the end of the story the text conceives a different kind of space for the frogmouth, one which might allow for the bird to determine her own subjectivity. As with the lyrebird in 'What He Heard', I use negative syntax to describe the bird's action: 'But this bird doesn't want to snatch you away; she has no desire to scratch at your face.' In this depiction, the bird might avoid inclusion in the human's vision: 'you won't recognise her lying there'; 'you'll pass by' without seeing her. I'm not sure if this grants more or less agency to the frogmouth—or if my strategies around the lyrebird endorse a stronger relationship with birds. As Richard Terdiman has shown us, sometimes a total refusal to engage with a discourse only reinforces the perceived superiority of dominant power.[91] However, I do believe that there is something valuable in keeping a respectful distance from others, both literally and literarily.

Magpies

The story 'Magpies' takes as its starting point the accounts presented by animal behaviourist Gisela Kaplan in her *Australian Magpie: Biology and Behaviour of an Unusual Songbird* and her attempts to move readers away from 'moments of friction' between humans and birds. Kaplan notes: 'We [humans] regard ourselves as "benign" and magpies as "aggressive" because we perceive these attacks to be unprovoked. Whether or not we deserve the title of "benign" intruders is a matter of opinion.'[92] In the work, I explore how the stories and metaphors we construct around magpies contribute to this friction. To translate the ideas into fiction I use Malewitz's tactic of 'code-switching': a textual operation to confound or undermine conventional modes of representation. Malewitz tenders that a textual animal:

---

91   Terdiman 1985, 280.
92   Kaplan 2004, 120, 116.

might gain a temporary agency and legibility at the moment when it has ceased to function according to its assumed use value … In other words, a literary animal's agency can come into being when its behavior within a narrative temporarily exhausts, confuses, or transforms the use to which it has been put.[93]

Malewitz's approach involves drawing attention to a particular 'anthropocentric rhetorical device' and imbuing it with 'conflicting' values: this process causes a 'changed relationship' between humans and animals, as well as a change to the kinds of stories humans might be able to tell about animals.[94] In the story, I shift 'magpie metaphors' across different characters and scenarios, complicating the discursive codes. I apply the different behaviours to different characters in the story to challenge the binaries of benign–aggressive or victim–aggressor. The office leader is most often the magpie: 'Her black wings open and [Peter is] assaulted by the flash of white shards.' At other times Peter, the victim of bullying, becomes the magpie. His safe haven in the stationery cupboard borrows its description from an account of a magpie's nest in areas close to human habitation:

the outer layer of the magpie's nest may also incorporate wire, clothes hangers, fabric from hessian bags, binder's

_____

93 Malewitz 2014, 547.
94 Malewitz 2014, 547–548.

twine, silver paper, strips of clear plastic, rope, and even small adornments such as clothes pegs. The inner layer is like a second nest ... and much finer in structure. Materials used are softer and more densely packed.[95]

At some points the characters are both magpies, relating to each other as what Kaplan calls dominant or marginal roles in the flock of the office: dominant magpies 'walk along an imaginary territorial borderline ... They pace up and down, like a border patrol'; marginal magpies, like Peter in his final meeting, 'standing ... for hours "hugging" and facing the tree, beaks often pointing at the bark or touching the tree and adopting crouching postures without feeding or drinking'.[96] By using these code-switching images I aim to undermine the fixed human understanding of magpies by offering up multiple stories—and multiple metaphors—about their behaviour. At the end of the story, the narrator concedes that it is possible to see his manager as not only a bully but also a comforter of her colleagues. In the same way, I propose that a multiplicity of visions of magpies might free them from the harm caused by a single authoritative version. Fiction will always include analogy; even if we try to write plainly, without metaphor, the reader can always read even the simplest action as symbolic. But if fiction presents a multifaceted representation of an

---

95 Kaplan 2004, 50.
96 Kaplan 2004, 80, 31.

animal, one which does not fit neatly into human comparison, perhaps we might see beyond the metaphor, to see textual animals *as* animals.[97] Thus, the story involves a 'changed relationship' between humans and animals as well as provoking a change to the kinds of stories humans might be able to tell about animals.

And No Birds Sing

'And No Birds Sing' is a creative rumination on the relationship between the particular and the planetary that was stirred by my almost-meeting with the black cockatoos on the bridge. Several scholarly texts inform its structure and content. In his essay, 'Extinction, Encountering and the Exigencies of Forgetting' Rick De Vos writes about his interactions with stories about the great auk—as well the moment he is faced with an actual (albeit stuffed) bird. De Vos's essay showed me the ways I had been seduced by narratives of extinction and offered me alternative ways to think about it. In a similar way, Probyn-Rapsey's 'Nothing to See—Something to See: White Animals and Exceptional Life/Death' gave me the colour palette. Thom van Dooren's *Flight Ways: Life and Loss at the Edge of Extinction* gave me the phrase the 'dull edge' of extinction and the idea that an individual (bird or human) is 'a single knot in an emergent lineage: a vital point of connection

---

97 For more detailed investigation into how we might be approach texts to read 'animals as animals', see McHugh 2009a, 25.

between generations': this provided me with a temporal shape for the work. Finally, Ursula K. Heise's *Imagining Extinction: the Cultural Meanings of Endangered Species* illuminated for me the anthropocentric value many human texts place on nonhuman species extinction.[98]

These critical works do not pose identical views of how we do—or, better yet, should—respond to the loss of a complex biodiversity. Part of Heise's project is to demonstrate the ways the stories we tell about extinction tell more about human cultural concerns than the loss of a particular species: the death of the final passenger pigeon 'stands in' for the disappearance of the American frontier; the extinction of the Hokkaido wolf comes to symbolise the shift from traditional to modernised Japan.[99] De Vos takes this further, proffering that the stories we tell about extinction are a discursive strategy to 'forget' our culpability in the real animals' deaths, a process of removing the connections between our forward-thinking 'actively and methodically separating the history of another species and its extinction from our own history, anticipating and denying any connection.'[100] The stories of the last great auk, the disappearance of the dodo, the final days of the passenger pigeon in Cincinnati Zoo, De Vos states, are not legitimate engagements with the overwhelming loss of a species. Rather, the stories are imbued with a kind of

---

98 De Vos, 2017; Probyn-Rapsey 2013; van Dooren, 2014a; Heise 2016, 48.
99 Heise 2016, 44, 38–39.
100 De Vos 2017, 2–3.

substitute grief: an aesthetically appealing performance the human can indulge in without being overwhelmed by the comprehension of the real deaths. They become merely a list of names, like the list that accompanies my story, separated from real lives—and real deaths.[101]

Counter to De Vos's views, van Dooren argues that the story of an individual animal's death—or, even, a direct contact with their dying moments—is an essential part of humans confronting the knowledge of extinction in a meaningful way. The power of grief, he argues, is when the focus is on the particular, the specific living being. When it comes to the final moments of extinction, there is only one animal, and we must accept that knowledge. He cites Glenn Klingler's description of the last Hawaiian Hoʻokena bird: 'after it lost its mate it cried out for weeks … a terribly high-pitched sound, like an inconsolable moaning … The Hoʻokena bird is so obviously looking for company, but there is none to be found—nowhere'.[102] And we too can grieve with the Hoʻokena, and the last great auk, and the last passenger pigeon. Van Dooren says: 'Mourning offers us a way into an alternative space, one of acknowledgement and respect for the dead.' As Thomas Attig puts it: 'As we grieve, we appropriate new understandings of the world and ourselves

---

101 Listing is of course another discursive structure: indeed, Leonard Lutwack points out that 'a favourite literary device from antiquity to the Renaissance was the catalog of birds, or the listing and brief description of as many different species as a writer could muster from his own observation'. Lutwack 1994, 231–232.
102 Klinger quoted in van Dooren 2014b, 275.

within it.'[103] It may even prevent further deaths of species. Van Dooren proposes that 'learning to mourn extinctions may also be essential to our and many other species' long-term survival'.[104]

These complex understandings of extinction weave in and out of 'And No Birds Sing'. I draw directly on De Vos's work in my descriptions of the human's use of the accounts of bird extinctions as 'a cover story … to paper over the real experience'. It's a way of discursively managing any grief he might feel for the birds, in the same way that his father eulogises his mother into a story that removes any sense of her as a real embodied being: 'something to say to people when there's an empty space in the conversation'. To overcome the potency of these structures (about the death of the human and the extinction of the birds), Attig says: 'We … become different in the light of the loss as we assume a new orientation to the world'.[105] This proves to be a difficult task for the character— and for me as a writer. In the end I yield to the human's need to mourn without shame: 'he wails. The wail washes over everything … the wail will always be there … he will never stop wailing'. He is grieving for his mother, but he is also grieving for others: for the rosella he killed, for the budgerigar he failed to protect, for the chickens he's eaten. He wails 'by the side of the

---

103 Attig quoted in Heise 2016, 139.
104 van Dooren 2014b, 275; van Dooren 2014a, 143.
105 Attig quoted in van Dooren 2014b, 283.

road, in the vestibule staring at an open doorway, at a barbecue over a plate of chicken wings ... Even the birds will hear it'. The wail returns us to Rose's lament, included at the beginning of these field notes. It also takes us towards Diamond's reading of Elizabeth Costello. Diamond sees Costello as 'wounded': overwhelmed by humanity's violence towards animals. She writes:

What wounds this woman, what haunts her mind, is what we do to animals. This, in all its horror, is there, in our world. How is it possible to live in the face of it? And in the face of the fact that, for nearly everyone, it is as nothing, as the mere background of life? ... [Costello's woundedness] lets us see one of the difficulties of reality, the difficulty of human life in its relation to that of animals, of the horror of blotting it out of consciousness.[106]

The stories I tell are about more than just one human's mourning for another, but about grieving for humans' violence towards nonhuman animals as well as towards our planet. To borrow a reflection from van Dooren: 'mourning ... is about more than any single species, or any number of individual species, but must instead be a process of relearning our place in a *shared world*'.[107]

---

106 Diamond 2008, 47, 55.
107 van Dooren 2014b, 285.

Aves Admittant

The story 'Aves Admittant' continues the exploration of extinction, extending it to think about potential futures of the planet. It contains echoes of two texts: Roy Scranton's *Learning to Die in the Anthropocene* and John Beck's 'The Call of the Anthropocene'. Discussing Edgar Allan Poe's 'MS. Found in a Bottle' Beck quotes the narrator who reflects that even though there may be 'little time' left 'to ponder upon my destiny', there is 'time enough to report the fact'.[108] Our 'report' may be a cry of anguish and fear (as in 'And No Birds Sing'), but it may also be a call of hope.

Most importantly, I am indebted to Nicholas Carlile, island ecologist, from the Office of Environment and Heritage, NSW, who showed some potential ways we might work towards the future in the present. His research and ideas are the foundation for this story.[109] Of course, I am aware of the ethical concerns raised in the field of animal studies towards interventions like the ones attempted by the characters in this story and the 'regimes of violent-care' that use the name of conservation to value one species over another.[110] It is important to note that the care of one animal can be paired with active hostility

---

108 Beck 2014, 406.
109 See Carlile et al 2003; Priddel 2006; Priddel and Carlile 2009; Priddel et al 2014.
110 For a detailed and nuanced exploration of the 'decision making about which animals are cared for, but also about those that can, or must, be "sacrificed" in the name of conservation', see van Dooren, 2015.

towards another, like the rabbits who become footnotes in the story of attempting to save the Gould's petrel. As van Dooren shows, often conservation focuses not so much on biodiversity, but on '*native* biodiversity': 'the right kinds of diversity in the right places'.[111] However, like van Dooren, I have chosen to include within my project 'a descriptive and situated account' of a particular human decision to work alongside a particular bird. The story offers one way to think through our complicity in the ecological crises we are faced with. I argue that humans are implicated in the depletion of biodiversity—on Cabbage Tree Island and in many other sites—and that we have a responsibility to take into account all potential ways of responding to the consequences of climate change.

In 'Aves Admittant' I play with these opposed views on the stylistic level. I place the events of the story in an explicitly imagined space: a temporal location which may or may not be 'real' within the narrative world. Central to the story's stylistic strategy is its use of future tense. The story begins: 'Years and years from now, *I'll be* working as an island ecologist undertaking research on Cabbage Tree Island and my dad will come along as a volunteer assistant. *It'll be* part of my postdoc.' (emphasis added) Gerald Prince gives a seemingly straightforward definition of the future tense as the narration of events 'that are yet to come or may never come'.[112] However,

---

111 van Dooren 2015, 7, 24.
112 Prince 1982, 183.

the second clause in Prince's description provokes a more complex way of thinking about its function. Future tense allows writers to play with what Nelson Rojas calls the 'connotative value' of stories.[113] The story presented is not yet mapped: the protagonist's daughter may or may not grow up to be an island ecologist and her father's narrative may or may not resolve on the cliffs of Cabbage Tree Island. Similarly, the interventions made by ecologists may or may not lead to the protection of a species or may or may not lead to the death of other animals. Ecologists, like the father and his daughter, are considering a potential future which may also lead to a reflection on their present actions. As Rojas writes: 'The use of the future [tense] serves to stress the importance of a "present" moment.'[114] The stylistic strategy I employ in 'Aves Admittant', then, is another way we might draw upon a speculative approach to representing animals.

The Flight of Birds

The final story, 'The Flight of Birds' is a retelling—and a reconfiguration—of a story contained in Katharine Briggs' *British Folk-Tales and Legends*.[115] It reflects on the way nonhuman animals are used in fiction as symbols of human psyche, but, more importantly, posits whether it may be

---

113 Rojas 1978, 681.
114 Rojas 1978, 681.
115 Briggs 2002, 29–32.

possible for animals in stories to move beyond symbolic value and be admitted as agents ungoverned by human interests. My starting point for the 'speculative exercise' here was to ask: Is it possible to move the fairy tale from a story 'about' birds to a story 'with' birds? What might the human story look like if it was reconfigured as a bird's story?

These questions cannot be answered simply. In the original fairy tale the birds are clearly not agents, but even in the more 'realist' retelling of the story the birds function as extensions of the character's emotional state. The human is still caught up in a vision of the birds as reflections of his own anxieties:

> To the young man, the seagulls' feathers look moth-eaten, tinged with dirty yellow. Their red beaks are faded, sun-bleached. One bird is missing an eye: the black jagged hole glares. Another is missing a foot: it's been severed by a net, or hacked off by schoolkids, the young man imagines.

Later, the symbolic value of the gulls changes, so that they become the human's salvation:

> Then they all glide skywards. For a moment the young man isn't certain if they levitated or if the rocks dropped from under him. They're all in the air above him, sharp against the blue sky. They form

a synchronised circle that wheels above the young man's head. Even the one with the missing foot flies smoothly, turning this way and that, letting the sun catch his wings at different angles. Even the one with the gaping eyehole can drift and swoop through the air. In fact, it's impossible to tell which bird is which: they are all perfect, all elegant, all miraculous.

Both sequences are held tightly by the character's perspective: the descriptions are located always in relation to the young man's vantage point. Moreover, the descriptions used in the text could only made by a human: later, the movement of the birds is compared to a 'concertina' and a 'lung'; the feathers 'glint', like a mirror or glass. But despite this control there also are brief points in this description where individual birds are given access to the narration: the seagull with the missing foot is given agency to 'let ... the sun catch his wings'; the seagull with the gaping eyehole is given permission to 'drift and swoop'. These are only fleeting moments—the birds are soon viewed from the human perspective so that it is 'impossible to tell which bird is which', and the birds will soon disappear into the horizon—but nevertheless these are the moments that offer a new way for the young man to perceive his world, one which may allow for birds to be accepted on their own terms. As Plumwood comments, 'our willingness and ability to recognise the other as a potentially intentional being tells us whether we are open to potentially rich forms of interaction and relationship which have an ethical dimension'.[116]

The final line of the story is an attempt to take Plumwood's ethical dimension further, to accede to 'due respect for difference'.[117] I had some difficulty with the last sentence. In an earlier version of the story I phrased the image of the flying birds in this way: 'He will remember unfathomable shapes disappearing into an open blue sky.' My use of the word 'unfathomable' was intended to indicate the depth of the seagulls' actions, a richness that was complicated and multifaceted. I was building upon Maurice Merleau-Ponty's analysis of da Vinci's symbolic use of birds in which he proposes da Vinci's birds are 'riddles' that may be impossible to decipher, but in the process of trying to comprehend we come closer to 'the meaning of the flight of birds'.[118] Of course, words have several meanings, and 'unfathomable' can be read as 'incomprehensible' which, as I have noted, might lead to connotations like 'unworthy' and 'not worth noticing'. Consequently, the line becomes: 'He will remember sparking strips of white against an open blue sky.' There are two key focuses in the rewritten sentence. The first is 'sparking' which I use with the intention for the image to inspire new ways of thinking about birds in flight.

---

116 Plumwood 2002, 181.
117 Plumwood 2002, 193.
118 Merleau-Ponty 1966, 22.

The second is the use of 'open blue sky' in the final moment, which shifts the perspective away from a human life and emphasises the space around the character. It puts into action Plumwood's call for what humans see as 'background' to become the foreground of our experience.[119] What might a bird's story look like? One which is not dependent on a human for its meaning.

Further Encounters

Nevertheless, as van Dooren notes: 'It is not enough for two such beings to have lived alongside each other, in proximity to one another; rather, they must also in some way have become at stake in each other, bound up with what matters to each other.'[120] One more thing needs to be said about my stories— and storytelling in general. Rowlands talks of a 'shadow' agenda that exists in all human writing, saying: 'Each story has what we might call a dark side; it casts a shadow. That shadow is to be found behind what the story says; here you will find what the story shows.' This is echoed by Garber's response to *The Lives of Animals*: 'What does the form of [a text] … displace, repress, or disavow?'[121] What has animated me the most in the writing of *The Flight of Birds* is the ways my continued reading of critical engagements with nonhuman animals has divulged

---

119 Plumwood 2002, 104.
120 van Dooren 2014b, 283.
121 Rowlands 2009, 3; Garber in Coetzee 2016, 74.

my own blindness to my asymmetrical power relations with animals and how this is made manifest in my writing. A telling point was brought to light in a correction made by one of the editors on an earlier version of the manuscript. In the story 'Do You Speak My Language?' I had written the sentence: 'Of course, I'm not thinking about *what* the bacon was before it sizzled into the frying pan ...' (emphasis added) The editor, in pale pencil, had crossed out the 'what' and replaced it with 'who'. Like many critics in the field, I'd tried to be careful with my pronouns.[122] In fact, the story 'What He Heard' gains greater power when the personal pronoun is used to refer to nonhuman animals as well as humans: the 'he' of the title gives equal reference to all three beings in the story. But the pig who was killed for eating was overlooked by me. As McHugh says: 'when language bites, it bites hard'.[123] And there are other animals who are overlooked in the stories: I've already mentioned the rabbits of Cabbage Tree Island, but it is also worth noting the dog who lives with the human family. The dog wanders in and out of the stories, a background character. My treatment of these animals reveals my dependence on the categories that sanctions our culture's endowment of some subjects as 'humanised animals' (animals permitted to have subjectivity) and others as 'animalised animals' (those denied

---

122 See, for instance, Woodward's statement: 'I refer to animals ... as "who" not "which" and by their genders rather than the pronoun 'it' which designates object or inanimate status'. Woodward 2008, 14.
123 McHugh 2017, 14.

any agency).[124] In my stories the 'humanised' dog would never be neglected by the human: despite the fact that his food is kept in the vestibule alongside Charlotte the budgerigar, the dog 'ambles in, hoping for a secret biscuit' even as Charlotte flies through the doorway. In contrast, the 'animalised' rabbits are barely worth mentioning, their deaths are not worth mourning (or so the characters believe).

Despite these 'shadows' in my text, through the writing of the stories—and through the many discoveries I made in the field of animal studies—my relationships with the birds in my surroundings has certainly been transformed. As Marco Caracciolo states:

Acknowledging the limits of our imaginative and linguistic resources is, in itself, a moral gesture that may make humans more respectful of nonhuman life … [it] paves the way for an empathetic relationship with animals that does not aim at complete understanding (which in turn raises suspicions about anthropocentric reduction) but at a more intimate sharing.[125]

The stories I tell here are still told by a human and are about humans, but as I have noted, telling human stories and asking

---

124 For more detailed discussion on 'humanised' and 'animalised' animals, see Wolfe 2014, 101.
125 Caracciolo 2014, 500–501.

the question 'What might a bird's story look like?' are not mutually exclusive activities. The human in the stories wants to have meaningful and conscientious encounters with the birds in his life: the budgerigar he keeps as a pet, the kookaburra who lives in his garden, the magpies outside his office window, the sparrows in his school quadrangle, the koel in the tree, the lyrebird singing in the ruined schoolhouse, the chickens pecking in the mud, the rosella in the bush, the seagulls soaring over the ocean. He wants to hold the Gould's petrel 'warm and alive' in his hands. He wants to turn towards what Woodward describes as 'a gaze, initiated by the animal, meditative in its quietness and stillness and which compels a response on the part of the human, as it contradicts any assumed superiority of the human over the nonhuman animal'.[126] He does this only once. In 'What He Heard', at the moment of contact between the two animals, the human and lyrebird look each other in the eye: 'The bird paused, a lidless eye staring at the intruder. He, the man, did not look away'.[127] The human wants to feel— as I wanted to feel as I watched the three black cockatoos

---

126 Woodward 2008, 1.

127 Even here, I don't get it quite right. After writing the story I read Plumwood's advice that 'you must never look a lyrebird too boldly in the eye as it steps past you at close quarters, or it may interpret your interest as evil intent and take fright; if you want to avoid alarming it, feign boredom and take an occasional sideways or casual glance from under your lashes'. As Plumwood puts it, 'it helps to know how the other will read one's actions, what the etiquette of an interspecies encounter is likely to be'. Plumwood 2002, 192.

flying—what van Dooren and Rose call 'attentive[ness] to another's presence, to their way of being in a place'.[128]

Running through Rose's writing is a call for an 'ethical relationship' between the human and the nonhuman animal: 'The heart of ethics,' she affirms, 'is the call from the other.'[129] Ethical relationships depend on a process of active reflection. Rose reminds us that 'ethical relationships ... hinge on taking responsibility for one's actions, and considering ramifications in both short and long terms'.[130] Writing fiction, I believe, is one of the strategies that will allow for ethical relationships to be rehearsed and represented, 'to make room ... in our activities in shared places'.[131] In many of the experiences with birds in the book I expose the violence and damage we inflict on birds through our actions and through our stories. But by moving away from the question 'How can I write about birds?' to 'What might a bird's story look like?', I also imagine processes through which we might be able to respect birds as agents of their own lives. Even in the contact zone there can be 'exhilarating moments of wonder and revelation ... and new wisdom'.[132] The stories that form my novel are speculations, prompts to think through in an immersive way the questions of how human lives intersect with the lives of birds. They are

---

128 van Dooren and Rose 2012, 17.
129 Rose 2013, 11.
130 Rose 2008, 56.
131 van Dooren and Rose 2012, 17.
132 Pratt 1991, 39.

glimpses into the worlds of birds and they embrace potential modes for telling bird stories: encounters that spark against an open blue sky.

Acknowledgements

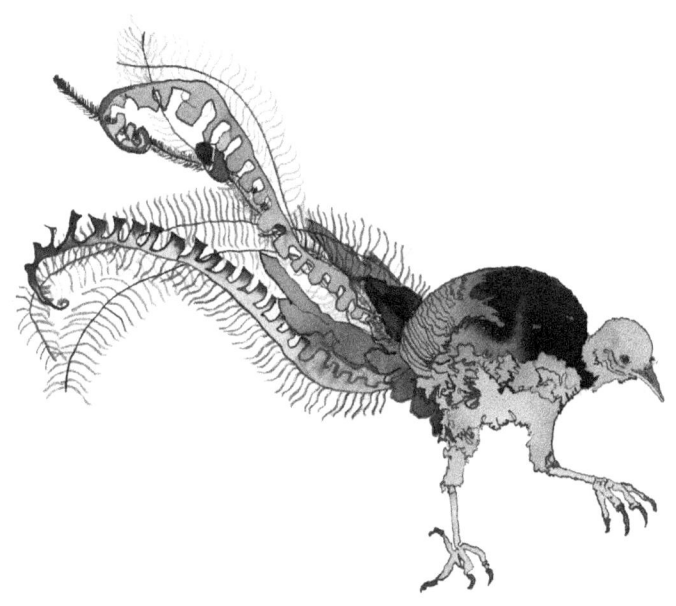

As the Field Notes indicate, the research undertaken for this novel has been multifarious, involving reading from scholarly and non-scholarly sources, as well as discussions with colleagues and friends. Both the tacit and the explicit material needs to be acknowledged more formally. I take the opportunity here to cite my research and to thank those people who shaped and challenged the writing.

The epigraphs for the novel are from William Blake's 'Jerusalem' (1961 [1820]) and Theodore Roethke's 'Meditations of an Old Woman: First Meditation' (1961[1958]). The latter is reprinted by permission from Faber and Faber Ltd and Penguin Random House, copyright © 1955 by Theodore Roethke; used by permission of Doubleday, an imprint of Knopf Doubleday Publishing Group, a division of Penguin Random House LLC. All rights reserved.

My capacity to engage with the ideas in this book is only possible because of my involvement in the Centre for Critical Creative Practice (C3P) at the University of Wollongong, and in particular its Material Ecologies (MECO) research strand. Many, many thanks to Sue Turnbull and Su Ballard, co-directors of the centre, and especially to the MECO practitioners and thinkers who have taught me so much about birds (as well as about trees, wombats, weather patterns, ghosts, plastic bags, drones and Alexa devices). The project really began as we walked and worked together at Bundanon. Thank you Su Ballard, Louise Boscacci, Brogan Bunt, Nicky Evans, Agnieszka Golda, Mike Griffiths, Eva Hampel, Lucas Ihlein, Madeleine Kelly, Jo Law, Cath McKinnon, Ted Mitew, Chris Moore, Jo Stirling and Kim Williams.

The project came alive when Melissa Boyde gave me her support and shared her insights with me. Melissa, thank you for your limitless enthusiasm and generous championing of the work. Without your interest I would not have pushed myself to think about *all* the implications of writing about human and nonhuman animals. As will be seen from my references below, the project has been informed, extended and cajoled by many essays in *Animal Studies Journal*, so I thank you for including my work in this space.

From Sydney University Press, thanks to Fiona Probyn-Rapsey and Melissa Boyde for rich and insightful editorial advice, and for pushing me to think beyond myself. Thanks to Agata Mrva-Montoya, Denise O'Dea and Alexandra Guzmán for patience and generosity. Thanks to Louise Thurtell for extraordinary copy editing.

The work flourished during my LitLink Residential Fellowship at Varuna in 2016. Thank you to Jansis O'Hanlon, Vera Costello and Sheila Atkinson for kindness and food!

Thank you to Denise Young, Michelle Haines Thomas, Diana Jarman and Hayley Lawrence for sharing wonderful nights reading and eating. Special thanks to Peter Bishop for talking about music and for calling this book a novel.

Thanks to Noel Broadhead from the University of Wollongong Library for his copyright advice and enthusiasm for the project (especially the kookaburra story).

Thanks to Anne Collett, who gave me the 'Birds' issue of *Kunapipi* at exactly the time I needed it. The collection of essays and poems in this issue informed and enriched all of the stories here, directly and indirectly.

Thank you to my Creative Writing and English Literatures colleagues at the University of Wollongong (staff and students) who work so hard and are always generous with their time and collegiality. Thanks to the following for listening to and reading drafts and knowing what I'm going through: A.J. Corradini, Shady Cosgrove, Daniel Fudge, Chloe Higgins, Chrissy Howe, Luke Johnson, Susie Lenehan, Cath McKinnon, Scott Tahvanainen, Alan Wearne and Ika Willis.

Thanks to Andrew Craig and the other swimmers at the Continental Pool for many, many conversations about birds. (Sorry I couldn't include the pelican story.)

Thanks to Tara Palajda, Jo Durtnell-Smydzuk, Alli Knaggs, Jacinta Landon and Jenny Gales for keeping me sane during the writing process. The work is dedicated to Jenny.

Special thanks to my trusted readers Kate O'Donnell,

Cathy Hunt and Dayne Kelly: I depend on you. Thank you, Kate, for the multiple conversations about every aspect of the work, and especially for workshopping of the last line with me.

Extraordinary thanks to Amy Kersey for her extraordinary birds in this book. They are truly the greatest things in the world. Thank you, Amy.

Thanks to Damien, Hershey and Honey for their patience when I'm away and their love when I come home.

What He Heard

The epigraph for the story is from David Mitchell's novel *Black Swan Green*. Copyright © 2007 by David Mitchell. Reprinted by permission from Hodder and Stoughton Limited (worldwide) and from Penguin Random House (USA).

A version of the story appeared in *Animal Studies Journal* in 2015. Thanks to Melissa Boyde. It was written on a retreat organised by the MECO network at UOW. Thanks especially to Su Ballard and Kim Williams.

I'm grateful to Shady Cosgrove, Scott Bazley and Seattle Brooks Bazley for their hospitality sharing their cabin at Wombeyan. I'm especially grateful to Sterling for telling the ghost story, and to Dai Fan for listening to it with me.

Six Stories about Birds, with Seven Questions

The epigraph for the story is from Freya Mathews' 'Living with Animals' (1997).

The statistics I cite at the end of the story are from Adrian Franklin's 2007 essay 'Relating to Birds in Postcolonial Australia'. I also cite Professor Mike Archer from the Australian Museum; this quotation is taken from Franklin's essay.

Other texts inform the stories within the story:

Cinderella

The main version I used was from Jakob and Wilhelm Grimm's *The Complete Fairy Tales* (2007).

I allude to the Grimm stories 'The Three Languages', 'The Seven Ravens', 'The Golden Bird' and 'Hansel and Gretel'.

I also refer to Shaena Lambert's 'Kublai Khan and the Sun Bird: A Fairy Tale' (2001) and Fernán Caballero's 'The Bird of Truth' (2002).

New Caledonian Crows

The two YouTube clips featuring David Attenborough are real and can be found at https://bit.ly/THXr6z and https://bit.ly/2Otk7c2. Thanks to Su for sending them to me.

I cite directly Alex Weir, Jackie Chappell and Alex Kacelnik's 2002 article 'Shaping of Hooks in New Caledonian Crows'.

Birds of Paradise

I cite directly Alfred Russel Wallace's *The Malay Archipelago: The Land of the Orang-Utan, and the Bird of Paradise. A Narrative of Travel, with Sketches of Man and Nature* (1869) and Oliver Goldsmith's *A History of the Earth, and Animated Nature* (1825).

The newspaper article the narrator refers to is a fiction.

Thanks to Yaron Lifschitz for giving me an internship at the Australian Museum all those years ago, and telling me the story of the legless birds.

St Kevin and the Blackbird

I cite two lines from Seamus Heaney's poem, 'St Kevin and the Blackbird' (1992). Reprinted by permission from Faber and Faber Ltd.

The Siege of Acre

I cite directly T.A. Archer's *The Crusade of Richard I, 1189–92* (1889) and Helen Macdonald's *Falcon* (2016 [2006]).

I also draw upon the discussion of the Crusades in Helen Macdonald's *H Is for Hawk* (2014). The documentary the narrator watches is fictitious.

Thanks to Louise D'Arcens for introducing me to *H is for Hawk* and to the story of Philip and Saladin.

The Swan and the Goose

Thanks to Pamela Mildenhall and the Con Voci Chamber Choir for introducing me to the story. I've drawn heavily on the bittersweet melody in Bob Chilcott's musical version of story, first performed in 2008.

Call and Response

The epigraph for the story is from Don Stap's *Birdsong: A Natural History* (2005).

'Call and Response' is based on walks into the Leura Valley taken during my stay at Varuna, the Writer's House. I've moved the sign from its location near the Ferber Steps and added a few words. Apologies to the lyrebirds who were taken out of the story.

Flocking

The epigraph for the story is from Shakespeare's *Hamlet* Act V, Scene ii.

In the story, I quote from Samuel Taylor Coleridge's 'The Rime of the Ancient Mariner', John Keats' 'Bright Star' and T. S. Eliot's 'The Love Song of J. Alfred Prufrock'. The last poem is reprinted by permission from Faber and Faber Ltd.

Thanks to State of Play for letting me watch them flock. This story is for Denise Young—not for the Drama, but for her kindness to me when I was a young man.

Do You Speak My Language?

The epigraph for the story is from David Wills' 'Meditations for the Birds' (2011).

Special thanks to John Littrich, School of Law, University of Wollongong for explaining legal processes to me and providing me with many resources for the story.

I have referenced several legal, critical and creative works directly in the story. I cite them here in order of appearance:

The episode of *Spicks and Specks* was broadcast on 26 September 2007. Part of the episode can be seen at https://bit.ly/2J670r6.

A summary of the judgement from the original case, *Larrikin Music Publishing Pty Ltd v EMI Songs Australia Pty Limited* (2010) FCA 29, can be found at https://bit.ly/2pU2i7k.

Michael Leunig is quoted in Nicolas Suzor and Rachel Choi's 'The Down Under Book and Film remind us our Copyright Laws are still Unfair for Artists' (2015).

The Facebook page I refer to does exist and is still accessible. I invented some of the postings.

Colin Hay's comment that the costs for the case were 'something like sixty grand' is cited in Justice James Edelman's 2016 paper 'The Nature and Function of Intellectual Property: Lessons from Down Under', presented at the Intellectual Property Society of Australia and New Zealand Inc.

The YouTube clip featuring Piedmont High warblers is real and can be found at https://bit.ly/2P05e0r.

The Girl Guides judges' comments and letter from the Executive Committee of the Girl Guides comes from the summary of the judgement from the case *Larrikin Music Publishing Pty Ltd v EMI Songs Australia Pty Limited* (2009) FCA 799. This can be found at https://bit.ly/2CQRKOy.

Marion Sinclair's statement that 'Kookaburra' is 'not

composed by me' is from P.A. Howell's 'Sinclair, Marion (1896–1988)' (2012).

A summary of the judgement from the appeal case *EMI Songs Australia Pty Limited v Larrikin Music Publishing Pty Limited* (2011) FCAFC 47 can be found at https://bit.ly/2PFGuHJ.

The story about the kookaburra and the lyrebird can be found in 'Aboriginal Legends: The Kookaburra', published in the *Argus* in 1952.

The statement made by the managing director of Larrikin Music is from Justice Edelman's presentation at the Intellectual Property Society of Australia and New Zealand Inc. (see above).

The study of mimicry as 'parasitic deception' is from Anastasia Dalziell, Justin Welbergen, Branislav Igic and Robert Magrath's 'Avian Vocal Mimicry: A Unified Conceptual Framework' (2015).

The notion of 'the commons' comes from Jonathan Lethem's 'The Ecstasy of Influence' (2007).

The discussion of kookaburra 'joint songs' comes from Myron C. Baker's 'The Chorus Song of Cooperatively Breeding Laughing Kookaburras (Coraciiformes, Halcyonidae: *Dacelo Novaeguineae*): Characterization and Comparison Among Groups' (2004).

The concept of 'warblish' comes from Hannah Sarvasy's 'Warblish: Verbal Mimicry of Birdsong' (2016). The warblish phrases I used are from Sarvasy's text (including *Shit a Brick!)*

and also taken from Abby P. Churchill's *Birds in Literature* (1911).

The Australian Law Reform Commission report *Copyright and the Digital Economy* is reprinted by permission ALRC.

Sandra Day O'Connor is cited by Jonathan Lethem (see above).

Lydia Goehr, Jim Samson and Jonathan Lethem are cited in Chris May's 'Jurisprudence V Musicology: Riffs from the Land Down Under' (2017).

The notion of 'entrainment to rhythms' is from Jonathan I. Benichov, Eitan Globerson and Ofer Tchernichovski's 'Finding the Beat: From Socially Coordinated Vocalizations in Songbirds to Rhythmic Entrainment in Humans' (2016).

Greg Ham's statement is quoted in 'Flute Riff Left a Sour Note for Ham' (2012).

Further to Fly

The title for the story is borrowed from Paul Simon's song 'Further to Fly' from his album *The Rhythm of the Saints*. The epigraph is from Euripides' *Phoenissae* (lines 1515–1525), translated by E.P. Coleridge.

A version of the story appeared in *Southerly* in 2017. Thanks to Melissa Boyde for championing my work, and also Elizabeth McMahon and Michelle Hamadache.

Apologies to Sarah Miller and my father for stealing their cars and using them in the story.

The Pecking Order

The epigraph for the story is from Carol J. Adams' 'The War on Compassion' (2014).

As discussed in my field notes, I am also indebted to the work of Ralph Acampora, Carol J. Adams, Karen Davis, Philip Armstrong, Hayley Singer and especially Annie Potts for their engagement with the lives and deaths of chickens and other nonhuman animals.

For the depiction of chickens' behaviour (especially 'tidbitting'), I have drawn upon Carolynn L. Smith's 'Referential Signalling in Birds: The Past, Present and Future' (2017).

Nocturne

The epigraph is from John Webster's *The Duchess of Malfi* (Act I, Scene i, 30).

The lines from the poet belong to Mark Tredinnick's 'Days in the Plateau' (2007). His story of the tawny frogmouth also made its way into his extraordinary *The Blue Plateau: A Landscape Memoir* (2009). Reprinted by kind permission from the author.

Again, I quote from Samuel Taylor Coleridge's 'The Rime of the Ancient Mariner', John Keats' 'Bright Star' and T.S. Eliot's 'The Love Song of J. Alfred Prufrock'. The last poem is reprinted by permission from Faber and Faber Ltd.

I was introduced to the story of the bird of sorrow through

Ignácz Kúnos's *Forty-Four Turkish Fairy Tales* (1913). I have adapted the story to serve my purposes.

Thanks to Olena Cullen for giving me her office and showing me the birds outside the window. These tawny frogmouths have saved my life on a number of occasions.

Magpies

The epigraph for the story is from Gisela Kaplan's *Australian Magpie: Biology and Behaviour of an Unusual Songbird* (2004). Reprinted by kind permission from the author.

I've taken the majority of the information about magpies from Kaplan's book and I've given Peter a few of her key phrases. Thanks to Gisela Kaplan for her observations on and insights into the story.

Thanks to Diana Jarman for telling me that magpies are 'much maligned' creatures.

And No Birds Sing

The title of the story is from John Keats' 'La Belle Dame San Merci'. The epigraph is from 'The Annunciation' by W.S. Merwin, collected in *The First Four Books of Poems*. Copyright © 1975 W.S. Merwin, used by permission of The Wylie Agency LLC.

As discussed in my field notes, I acknowledge the work of Rick De Vos, Ursula K. Heise, Fiona Probyn-Rapsey and Thom van Dooren for enriching this story.

There is no definitive list of extinct birds, but I am grateful to the following sources:

Avibase: The World Bird Database: https://bit.ly/2CQCmlk

The IUCN Red List of Threatened Species: www.iucnredlist.
org

Ornithology: The Science of Birds: https://bit.ly/2PFGNCn

Any errors in the list are my own.

Virginia Woolf's suicide note can be found in her obituary in the *New York Times* (3 April 1941) and at: https://nyti.ms/1lLVvWY.

I quote two lines from T.S. Eliot's *The Waste Land*. Reprinted by permission from Faber and Faber Ltd.

I am grateful to Richard, who drove me to Concord Hospital.

Aves Admittant

The epigraph is from John Berger's *Ways of Seeing* (1972).

Thanks to Jo Stirling for introducing me to the Gould's petrel and telling me stories about her trip to Cabbage Tree Island. Many thanks to Nicholas Carlile, island ecologist, from the New South Wales Office of Environment and Heritage, for his immense generosity in sharing his research and ideas with me. The supervisor in the story is definitely not Nicholas, but I have given many of Nicholas's stories to the character. Any mistranslations are my own. Special thanks for inviting me to Cabbage Tree Island: I have rearranged some places on the island, invented a few spaces and simplified a few of the practicalities. Thanks to the Faculty of Law, Humanities and the Arts, University of Wollongong, for funding my study leave.

The story was shaped by Nicholas's research on the Gould's petrel, especially:

Nicholas Carlile, David Priddel, Francis Zino, Cathleen Natividad and David Wingate's 'A Review of Four Successful Recovery Programmes for Threatened Sub-Tropical Petrels' (2003).

David Priddel, Nicholas Carlile and Robert Wheeler's 'Establishment of a New Breeding Colony of Gould's Petrel (*pterodroma leucoptera leucoptera*) through the Creation of Artificial Nesting Habitat and the Translocation of Nestlings' (2006).

David Priddel and Nicholas Carlile's 'Key Elements in Achieving a Successful Recovery Programme: a Discussion Illustrated by the Gould's Petrel Case Study' (2009).

David Priddel, Nicholas Carlile, Dean Portelli, Yuna Kim, Lisa O'Neill, Vincent Bretagnolle, Lisa Ballance, Richard Phillips, Robert Pitman and Matt Rayner's 'Pelagic Distribution of Gould's Petrel (*Pterodroma leucoptera*): Linking Shipboard and Onshore Observations with Remote-Tracking Data' (2014).

The Flight of Birds

The epigraph is from the song 'It Never Was You' from the musical *Knickerbocker Holiday*, music by Kurt Weill, lyrics by Maxwell Anderson.

I came across the original tale in Katharine Briggs' *British Folk-Tales and Legends* (1977).

As with the other fairy tales, I have adapted it to serve the young man's circumstances—but Briggs' ending is as ambiguous as mine.

Thanks to Su, for linking my vision to art history: in particular for directing me towards Merleau-Ponty.

A version of the story appeared in *Animal Studies Journal* in 2014. Thanks, again, to Melissa Boyde for her swift and overwhelmingly kind response to the story. Thanks also to Cathy Cole for suggesting I submit the story.

Thanks to Amy for buying crusty bread the night when I came home on the bus.

Works Cited

Aboriginal Legends: The Kookaburra (1952). *The Argus*, 3 October. https://bit.ly/2yp238T.

Acampora, Ralph (2016). [Provocations from the field] Epistemology of Ignorance and Human Privilege. *Animal Studies Journal* 5 (2): 1–20.

Adams, Carol J. (2014). The War on Compassion. In John Sorenson, ed. *Critical Animal Studies: Thinking the Unthinkable*, 18–29. Toronto: Canadian Scholars' Press.

Adams, Carol J. (2010). *The Sexual Politics of Meat: A Feminist-Vegetarian Critical Theory*. Twentieth Anniversary Edition. New York and London: Continuum.

Adams, Carol J. (2006). 'A very rare and difficult thing': Ecofeminism, Attention to Animal Suffering and the Disappearance of the Subject. In Waldau, Paul and Kimberley Patton *A Communion of Subjects: Animals in Religion, Science, and Ethics*. 591–604. New York: Columbia University Press.

Aisher, Alex and Vinita Damodaran (2016). Introduction: Human-Nature Interactions Through a Multispecies Lens. *Conservation and Society* 14 (4) October–December: 293–304.

Alcoff, Linda Martín (2007). Epistemologies of Ignorance: Three Types. In Sullivan, Shannon and Nancy Tuana, eds. *Race and Epistemologies of Ignorance*. 39–58. Albany: State University of New York Press.

Alcoff, Linda Martín (1991–1992). The Problem of Speaking for Others. *Cultural Critique* 20 Winter: 5–32.

Aloi, Giovanni and Rod Bennison (2011). Sue Coe: I Am an Animal Rights Activist Artist (interview). *Antennae* 19 Winter: 106–109.

Anker, Elizabeth Susan (2011). Elizabeth Costello, Embodiment, and the Limits of Rights. *New Literary History* 42 (1) Winter: 169–192.

Archer, T.A. (1889). *The Crusade of Richard I, 1189–92*. New York and London: G.P. Putnam's Sons.

Armstrong, Philip (2008). *What Animals Mean in the Fiction of Modernity*. Abingdon: Routledge.

Armstrong, Philip and Laurence Simmons (2007). Bestiary: An Introduction. In Simmons, Laurence and Philip Armstrong, eds. *Knowing Animals*. 1–24. Leiden and Boston: Brill.

Arnold, Matthew (1945 [1882]). *The Poetical Works of Matthew Arnold*. Oxford: Oxford University Press.

Australian Law Reform Commission (2014, Feb). *Copyright and the Digital Economy: Summary Report*. https://bit.ly/2pXsUEr

Baker, Myron C. (2004). The Chorus Song of Cooperatively Breeding Laughing Kookaburras (Coraciiformes, Halcyonidae: *Dacelo Novaeguineae*): Characterization and Comparison Among Groups. *Ethology* 110: 21–35.

Beck, John (2014). The Call of the Anthropocene *Cultural Politics* 10 (3): 404–414.

Benichov, Jonathan I., Eitan Globerson and Ofer Tchernichovski (2016). Finding the Beat: From Socially Coordinated Vocalizations in Songbirds to Rhythmic Entertainment in Humans. *Frontiers in Human Neuroscience* 10 (255) June: 1–7.

Berger, John (2009 [1977]). *Why Look at Animals?* London: Penguin.

Berger, John (1972). *Ways of Seeing*. London: BBC and Penguin.

Blake, William (1961 [1820]). Jerusalem. In *The Poetical Works of William Blake*, 380.

Boyde, Melissa (2013). Mining Animal Death for All It's Worth. In Johnston, Jay and Fiona Probyn-Rapsey, eds. *Animal Death*, 119–136. Sydney: Sydney University Press.

Briggs, Katharine (2002). *British Folk-Tales and Legends: A Sampler*. London: Routledge Classics.

Brower, Matthew (2013). The Bird Effect (Interview with Ceri Levy). *Antennae*. 27 Winter: 52–61.

Caballero, Fernán (2002). The Bird of Truth. *Marvels and Tales* 16 (1): 73–83.

Caballero, Krista and Frank Ekeberg (2014). Birding the Future. *Leonardo* 47 (5): 498–499.

Caracciolo, Marco (2014). 'Three Smells Exist in this World':
Literary Fiction and Animal Phenomenology in Italo Svevo's
'Argo and His Master' *MFS: Modern Fiction Studies* 60 (3):
484–505.

Carlile, Nicholas, David Priddel, Francis Zino, Cathleen
Natividad and David B. Wingate (2003). A Review of Four
Successful Recovery Programmes for Threatened Sub-
Tropical Petrels. *Marine Ornithology* 31: 185–192.

Cholakian, Rouben C. (1992). The (Un)naming Process in
Villon's *Grand Testament*. *The French Review* 66 (2): 216–228.

Churchill, Abby P. (1911). *Birds in Literature*. Worcester, MA: The
David Press.

Coetzee, J.M. (2016 [1999]). *The Lives of Animals*. Princeton:
Princeton University Press. Edited and with an introduction
by Amy Gutmann.

Coetzee, J.M. (2010 [1999]). *Disgrace*. London: Vintage Classic.

Copeland, Julie (2005). Elizabeth Grosz: The Creative
Impulse (Interview). *Sunday Morning* 14 August.
https://ab.co/2QVEo6M

Dalziell, Anastasia H., Justin A. Welbergen, Branislav Igic and
Robert D. Magrath (2015). Avian Vocal Mimicry: A Unified
Conceptual Framework. *Biological Reviews* 90: 643–668.

Davis, Karen (2014). Anthropomorphic Visions of Chickens Bred
for Human Consumption. In John Sorenson, ed. *Critical
Animal Studies: Thinking the Unthinkable*, 169–185. Toronto:
Canadian Scholars' Press Inc.

De Vos, Rick (2017). Provocations from the Field—Extinction, Encountering and the Exigencies of Forgetting. *Animal Studies Journal* 6 (1): 1–11.

Derrida, Jacques (2002). The Animal that Therefore I Am (More to Follow). David Wills, trans. *Critical Inquiry* 28 (2) Winter: 369–418.

Diamond, Cora (2008). The Difficulty of Reality and the Difficulty of Philosophy. In Cavell, Stanley, Cora Diamond, John McDowell, Ian Hacking and Cary Wolfe *Philosophy and Animal Life*. 43–90. New York: Columbia University Press.

Edelman, James (2016). The Nature and Function of Intellectual Property: Lessons from Down Under. *Federal Court of Australia*, 19 October. https://bit.ly/2Ouhk2d.

Emerson, Robert M., Rachel I. Fretz and Linda L. Shaw (2001). Participant Observation and Fieldnotes. In Atkinson, Paul, Amanda Coffey, Sarah Delamont, John Lofland and Lyn Lofland, ed. *Handbook of Ethnography*, 352–368. London: Sage Publications.

Flavell, Helen (2004). Writing-Between: Australian and Canadian Ficto-criticism. PhD thesis. Murdoch University, Perth, WA.

Flute Riff Left a Sour Note for Ham (2012). *Sydney Morning Herald*, 19 April. https://bit.ly/2yL4B0l.

Franklin, Adrian (2007). Relating to Birds in Postcolonial Australia. *Kunapipi* 29 (2): 102–125.

Gibbs, Anna (2003). Writing and the Flesh of Others. *Australian Feminist Studies* 18 (42): 309–319.

Goldsmith, Oliver (1825). *A History of the Earth and Animated Nature*. Philadelphia: Grigg and Elliot.

Grimm, Jakob and Wilhelm Grimm (2007). *The Complete Fairy Tales*. Jack Zipes, ed. London: Vintage.

Grosz, Elizabeth (2011). *Becoming Undone: Darwinian Reflections on Life, Politics, and Art*. Durham and London: Duke University Press.

Grosz, Elizabeth (2008). *Chaos, Territory, Art: Deleuze and the Framing of the Earth*. New York: Columbia University Press.

Haas, Gerrit (2017). *Ficto/critical Strategies: Subverting Textual Practices of Meaning, Other, and Self-Formation*. Bielefeld: Transcript.

Haraway, Donna (2008). *When Species Meet*. Minneapolis and London: University of Minnesota Press.

Heaney, Seamus (1992). St Kevin and the Blackbird. In *The Spirit Level*, 20–21. London: Faber and Faber.

Heise, Ursula K. (2016). *Imagining Extinction: The Cultural Meanings of Endangered Species*. Chicago and London: University of Chicago Press.

Herman, David (2014). Animal Worlds in Modern Fiction: An Introduction. *MFS: Modern Fiction Studies* 60 (3) Fall: 421–443.

Hinchliffe, Steve (2010). Where Species Meet. *Environment and Planning D: Society and Space* 28 (1): 34–35.

Howell, P.A. (2012). Sinclaire, Marion (1896–1988). *Australian Dictionary of Biography*, National Centre of Biography,

Australian National University. adb.anu.edu.au/biography/ sinclair-marion-15924

Kaplan, Gisela (2004). *Australian Magpie: Biology and Behaviour of an Unusual Songbird*. Clayton: CSIRO Publishing.

King, Sigrid (1990). Naming and Power in Zora Neale Hurston's *Their Eyes Were Watching God*. *Black American Literature Forum* 24 (4) Winter: 683–696.

Kúnos, Ignácz (1913). *Forty-Four Turkish Fairy Tales*. London: George C. Harrap and Co.

Lambert, Shaena (2001). Kublai Khan and the Sun Bird: A Fairy Tale. *Marvels and Tales* 15 (2): 224–228.

Lethem, Jonathan (2007). The Ecstasy of Influence. *Harper's Magazine*. February: 59–71.

Lingis, Alphonso (2003). Animal Body, Inhuman Face. In Wolfe, Cary, ed. *Zoontologies: The Question of the Animal*. 165–182. Minneapolis and London: University of Minnesota Press.

Lunney, Daniel (2012). Roadkill: An Ecologist's View of an Unresolved Issue in Wildlife Management. Abstract. In Animal Death Conference Program. University of Sydney.

Lutwack, Leonard (1994). *Birds in Literature*. Gainesville: University Press of Florida.

Macdonald, Helen (2016 [2006]). *Falcon*. London: Reaktion Books.

Malewitz, Raymond (2014). Narrative Disruption as Animal Agency in Cormac McCarthy's *The Crossing*. *Modern Fiction Studies* 60 (3) Fall: 544–561.

Marvin, Garry and Susan McHugh (2014). In It Together: An
    Introduction to Human–Animal Studies. In Marvin, Garry
    and Susan McHugh, eds. *Routledge Handbook of Human–
    Animal Studies.* London and New York: Routledge.

Mathews, F. Schuyler (2004 [1904]). *Field Book of Wild Birds and
    Their Music.* Honolulu: University Press of the Pacific.

Mathews, Freya (1997). Living with Animals. *Animal Issues*
    1 (1): 4–16.

May, Chris (2017). Jurisprudence v Musicology: Riffs from the
    Land Down Under. *Music and Letters* 97 (4): 622–646.

McCance, Dawne (2013). *Critical Animal Studies: An
    Introduction.* Albany: State University of New York Press.

McHugh, Susan (2017). Interview with Garry Marvin. *Antennae*
    39 Spring: 7–20.

McHugh, Susan (2011). *Animal Stories. Narrating across Species
    Lines.* Minneapolis and London: University of Minnesota
    Press.

McHugh, Susan (2010). Real Artificial: Tissue-Cultured
    Meat, Genetically Modified Farm Animals, and Fictions.
    Configurations. 18 (1–2): 181–197.

McHugh, Susan (2009a). *Animal Farm*'s Lessons for Literary
    (and) Animal Studies. *Humanimalia: A Journal of Human/
    Animal Interface Studies* 1 (1) September: 24–39.

McHugh, Susan (2009b). Literary Animal Agents. *PMLA*
    124 (2): 487–495.

McHugh, Susan (2006). One or Several Literary Animal Studies? Ruminations 3. H-Animal Discussion Network, 17 July. https://bit.ly/2AhZN4N

Merleau-Ponty, Maurice (1964). *Sense and Non-Sense.* Dreyfus, Hubert L. and Patricia Allen Dreyfus, trans. Evanston: Northwestern University Press.

Miller, D. A. (1981). *Narrative and Its Discontents: Problems of Closure in the Traditional Novel.* Princeton: Princeton University Press.

Mitchell, David (2006). *Black Swan Green.* London: Hodder and Stoughton.

Muecke, Stephen (2008). *Joe in the Andamans and Other Fictocritical Stories.* Sydney: Local Consumption Publications.

Neyrat, Frédéric (2016). Planetary Antigones: The Environmental Situation and the Wandering Condition. *Qui Parle* 25 (1/2) Fall: 35–64.

Ortiz-Robles, Mario (2016). *Literature and Animal Studies.* New York and London: Routledge.

Plumwood, Val (2002). *Environmental Culture: The Ecological Crisis of Reason.* London and New York: Routledge.

Pratt, Mary Louise (1991). Arts of the Contact Zone. *Profession.* 33–40.

Potts, Annie (2017). Interview with Yvette Watt. *Antennae* 39 Spring: 69–83.

Potts, Annie (2012). *Chicken*. London: Reaktion Books.

Potts, Annie and Philip Armstrong (2013). Picturing Cruelty: Chicken Advocacy and Visual Culture. In Johnston, Jay and Fiona Probyn-Rapsey, eds. *Animal Death*. 151–168. Sydney: Sydney University Press.

Priddel, David, Nicholas Carlile, Dean Portelli, Yuna Kim, Lisa O'Neill, Vincent Bretagnolle, Lisa T. Ballance, Richard A. Phillips, Robert L. Pitman and Matt J. Rayner (2014). Pelagic Distribution of Gould's Petrel (*Pterodroma leucoptera*): Linking Shipboard and Onshore Observations with Remote-Tracking Data. *Emu* 114 (4): 360–370.

Priddel, David and Nicholas Carlile (2009). Key Elements in Achieving a Successful Recovery Programme: A Discussion Illustrated by the Gould's Petrel Case Study. *Ecological Management and Restoration* 10 (1) May: 97–102.

Priddel, David, Nicholas Carlile and Robert Wheeler (2006). Establishment of a New Breeding Colony of Gould's Petrel (*Pterodroma leucoptera leucoptera*) through the Creation of Artificial Nesting Habitat and the Translocation of Nestlings. *Biological Conservation* 128 (4): 553–563.

Prince, Gerald (1982). Narrative Analysis and Narratology. *New Literary History* 13 (2) Winter: 179–188.

Probyn-Rapsey, Fiona (2014). Review Article: Multispecies Mourning: Thom van Dooren's *Flight Ways: Life and Loss at the Edge of Extinction*. *Animal Studies Journal*. 3 (2): 4–16.

Probyn-Rapsey, Fiona (2013). Nothing to See—Something to See: White Animals and Exceptional Life/Death. In Johnston, Jay and Fiona Probyn-Rapsey, eds. *Animal Death*, 239–252. Sydney: Sydney University Press.

Raghuram M.A., Nikhil R. Chavan, Ravikiran Belur and Shashidhar G. Koolagudi (2016). Bird Classification based on their Sound Patterns. *International Journal of Speech Technology* 19 (4):791–804.

Ramp, Daniel, Vanessa K. Wilson and David B. Croft (2016). Contradiction and Complacency Shape Attitudes towards the Toll of Roads on Wildlife. *Animals* 6 (6).

Roethke, Theodore (1961 [1958]). Meditations of an Old Woman: First Meditiation. In *The Collected Poems of Theodore Roethke*, 160. London: Faber and Faber Ltd.

Rojas, Nelson (1978). Time and Tense in Carlos Fuentes' 'Aura'. *Hispania*, 61 (4): 859–864.

Rose, Deborah Bird (2013). In the Shadow of All This Death. In Johnston, Jay and Fiona Probyn-Rapsey, eds. *Animal Death*. 1–20. Sydney: Sydney University Press.

Rose, Deborah Bird (2008). Judas Work: Four Modes of Sorrow. *Environmental Philosophy* 5 (2): 51–66.

Rowlands, Mark (2009). *The Philosopher and the Wolf: Lessons from the Wild on Love, Death and Happiness.* London: Granta.

Sacks, Sam (2015). The Rise of the Nameless Narrator. *The New Yorker*, 3 March. https://bit.ly/17OfteC

Sarvasy, Hannah (2016). Warblish: Verbal Mimicry of Birdsong. *Journal of Ethnobiology* 36 (4) December: 765–782.

Scranton, Roy (2015). *Learning to Die in the Anthropocene: Reflections on the End of a Civilization.* San Francisco: City Lights Books.

Singer, Hayley (2016). Writing the Fleischgeist. *Animal Studies Journal* 5 (2): 183–201.

Smith, Hazel (2005). *The Writing Experiment: Strategies for Innovative Creative Writing.* Crows Nest: Allen and Unwin.

Smith, Hazel and Roger Dean (2009). *Practice-Led Research, Research-Led Practice in the Creative Arts.* Edinburgh: Edinburgh University Press.

Sorenson, John (2014). Introduction: Thinking the Unthinkable. In Sorenson, John ed. *Critical Animal Studies: Thinking the Unthinkable.* xi-xxxiv. Toronto: Canadian Scholars' Press Inc.

Stap, Don (2005). *Birdsong: A Natural History.* New York: Scribner.

Stengers, Isabelle (2015). *In Catastrophic Times: Resisting the Coming Barbarism.* Andrew Goffey, trans. Open Humanities Press.

Suzor, Nicholas, and Rachel Choi (2015). The Down Under Book and Film Remind Us Our Copyright Laws Are Still Unfair for Artists. *The Conversation,* 29 July. https://bit.ly/2AfYR0I.

Terdiman, Richard (1985). *Discourse/Counter-Discourse: The Theory and Practice of Symbolic Resistance in Nineteenth-century France.* Ithaca: Cornell University Press.

Tiffin, Helen (2007). Pigs, People and Pigoons. In Simmons, Laurence and Philip Armstrong, eds. *Knowing Animals.* 244–265. Leiden and Boston: Brill.

Tredinnick, Mark (2009). *The Blue Plateau: A Landscape Memoir.* St Lucia: University of Queensland Press.

Tredinnick, Mark (2007). Days in the Plateau. *Kunapipi* 29 (2): 135–141.

Trexler, Adam (2015). *Anthropocene Fictions: The Novel in a Time of Climate Change.* Charlottesville: University of Virginia Press.

van Dooren, Thom (2015). A Day with Crows: Rarity, Nativity and the Violent-Care of Conservation. *Animal Studies Journal* 4 (2): 1–28.

van Dooren, Thom (2014a). *Flight Ways: Life and Loss at the Edge of Extinction.* New York: Columbia University Press.

van Dooren, Thom (2014b). Mourning Crows: Grief and Extinction in a Shared World. In McHugh, Susan and Garry Marvin, eds. *The Handbook of Human–Animal Studies.* London and New York: Routledge. 275–289.

van Dooren, Thom and Deborah Bird Rose (2012). Storied-places in a Multispecies City. *Humanimalia: A Journal of Human/Animal Interface Studies* 3 (2) Spring: 1–27.

Vollstädt, Maximilian G.R., Stefan W. Ferger, Andreas Hemp, Kim M. Howell, Till Töpfer, Katrin Böhning-Gaese and Matthias Schleuning (2017). Direct and Indirect Effects of Climate,

Human Disturbance and Plant Traits on Avian Functional Diversity. *Global Ecology and Biogeography* 26 (8): 963–972.

von Uexküll, Jakob (1957 [1934]). A Stroll through the Worlds of Animals and Men: A Picture Book of Invisible Worlds. In C.H. Schiller, ed. *Instinctive Behavior; the Development of a Modern Concept.* 5–80. New York: International Universities Press.

Wallace, Alfred Russel (1869). *The Malay Archipelago: The Land of the Orang-Utan and the Bird of Paradise. A Narrative of Travel, with Sketches of Man and Nature.* Adelaide: University of Adelaide. https://bit.ly/2AfUkLw.

Wedde, Ian (2007). Walking the Dog. In Simmons, Laurence and Philip Armstrong, eds. *Knowing Animals.* 266–288. Leiden and Boston: Brill.

Weir, Alex A.S., Jackie Chappell and Alex Kacelnik (2002). Shaping of Hooks in New Caledonian Crows. *Science* 297 (5583): 981.

Wills, David (2011). Meditations for the Birds. In Berger, Anne-Emmanuelle, and Martha Segarra, eds. *Demenageries: Thinking (of) Animals after Derrida,* 245–263. Amsterdam and New York: Rodopi.

Wolfe, Cary (2014). *Animal Rites: American Culture, the Discourse of Species, and Posthumanist Theory.* Chicago and London: University of Chicago Press.

Wolfe, Cary (2008). Introduction: Exposures. In Cavell, Stanley, Cora Diamond, John McDowell, Ian Hacking and

Cary Wolfe *Philosophy and Animal Life*. 1–42. New York: Columbia University Press.

Wolfe, Cary (1999). Faux Post-Humanism, or Animal Rights, Neocolonialism, and Michael Crichton's *Congo*. *Arizona Quarterly* 55 (2) Summer: 115–153.

Woodward, Wendy (2008). *The Animal Gaze: Animal Subjectivities in Southern African Narratives*. Johannesburg: Wits University Press.

Woolf, Virginia (2001 [1929]). *A Room of One's Own*. Ormskirk: Broadview Press.